KILLER IN A WINTER WONDERLAND

KILLER IN A WINTER WONDERLAND

A Rosalie Hart Mystery

Wendy Sand Eckel

First published by Level Best Books 2023

Author Photo Credit: Wendy Sand Eckel

First edition

ISBN: 978-1-68512-536-3

Cover art by Level Best Designs

This book was professionally typeset on Reedsy.
Find out more at reedsy.com

For Charles and Calvin

Praise for Killer in A Winter Wonderland

"*Killer in a Winter Wonderland,* the 4th Rosalie Hart mystery shows readers a Rosalie we would love to meet over a signature holiday coffee. But rest assured she would soon have us telling her our personal story. One of the great pleasures in this compelling novel is Rosalie's passion for coaxing stories from friends, suspects, and bystanders alike. In fact her astute listening skills prove critical to solving the mystery as characters endearingly and terrifyingly reveal themselves. Wendy Sand Eckel is a wonderful writer who delivers a suspenseful plot brought to vivid life by well-rounded characters who satisfyingly change and grow as the novel unfolds."—Susan Moger, award-winning author of *Of Better Blood*

"In *Killer in a Winter Wonderland,* the 4th Rosalie Hart mystery, Wendy Sand Eckel delivers a coolly crafted plot, compelling characters, satisfying suspense, and fabulous food. In this book, Rosalie's passion for coaxing stories from friends, suspects, and bystanders (like her chef's arrogant lover) is on full display. The setting, Cardigan, a fictional town on the Eastern Shore of Maryland, is brilliantly brought to life in this book as in the previous three. This time it is winter and the murder of a man on a bicycle, at first seen as an accidental hit-and-run, is delightfully devious. Wendy Sand Eckel's characters are fully realized in every book. Rosalie and her family and close friends learn and grow and change in each succeeding book."—Advanced Copy Review

Chapter One

Holidays are fickle things, Christmas most of all.

Christmas can fill us with joy and anticipation of the wonders that are about to unfold. It can tease us with the faintest pang of hope that peace will blanket the earth at last. Twinkling lights pierce the shortest, darkest days of the year, and our senses are indulged with nutmeg and mulling spices, peppermint bark, and iced cookies. And who can't feel optimistic in front of a crackling fire?

But Christmas can be tricky. Through all the grandeur, the traditions, the celebrations, the choirs resounding through the rafters, memories of Christmas past nudge the grief we manage to store away during the rest of the year—memories that become bolder, achier and a little harder to bear.

For me, Rosalie Hart, Thanksgiving was recent history. A glass container of mashed potatoes, which I would most likely reconstitute into fried potato cakes for lunch, was all that remained. The tablecloth had been dropped at the cleaners, and the pumpkins fed to the chickens and goats. My Annie had returned to Duke to take her final exams.

All of which meant that my Christmas season was upon me. And I already knew this one was going to be a challenge in many ways.

On Monday morning, I sat at my kitchen table at my home in Cardigan, a small, historic town on the Eastern Shore of Maryland, chin in hand, slowly spinning my phone with the tip of my finger.

The click of Dickens' nails on the wood floors announced Tyler Wells would not be far behind. Despite his age, Dickens hadn't lost his Labrador sense that every day was a new adventure with endless possibilities, at least for a minute or two. I gave his ears a good scratch, and he slumped onto his bed.

Tyler, the man who leased my farmlands and the man I was very much in love with, stood in the doorway.

"Morning," he said as the scent of fresh cool air breezed into the room. His crooked smile stirred up a series of flips through my stomach. He stopped and took me in. "You okay?"

"First of all, good morning to you." I stood and wrapped my arms around his neck. It was an effort as I was at least a head shorter, but it was my favorite place to be, my cheek on his chest, the scent of sandalwood soap, my fingers threading through his sandy-blond hair.

He stepped back. "Let me guess. This melancholy I'm detecting has to do with Annie's departure."

"Damn, you're good." I tucked my unruly dark hair behind my ear. "And I just learned Annie is going to Dubai with her father for Christmas. No, correction—for her entire winter break."

Tyler's lips curled into a wry smile. "*Dubai*? Could he come up with a more un-Christmas-like destination?"

"I hadn't thought about that, but yes, a legitimate question. It's puzzling, to say the least."

"Command performance?"

I shrugged. "She seemed to be a little excited, but who can tell with a text."

"This guy knows no bounds. Did he even run this by you?"

"Radio silence."

Tyler headed over to Mr. Miele. "Are you going to be okay with this new development?"

I followed him over to the coffee maker. "You mean having a Christmas without Annie? It's unimaginable. Even if we aren't together on Christmas Day, I at least expect to fill her stocking."

He stirred several spoonfuls of sugar into his coffee and faced me. "Isn't Oliver supposed to come down from New York?"

"My brother said that a couple of months ago. I sure hope he does, but we are a family—Oliver, Annie, and me. It only works if all three of us are here."

"I'm submitting a request to be adopted into this family."

"Adoption accepted." I laughed. "You know I want to be with you every minute I can."

"Well, I'm sorry, Rosalie. Ed should have worked you into Annie's Christmas."

"It's all going to be very strange. I mean, why put presents under the tree if there's no one to open them? And, for that matter, why put up a tree at all?"

He draped his arm around my shoulder. "Should be an interesting holiday."

"Um, Tyler? I've been thinking."

"Uh oh."

"Maybe we should tell Bini about our relationship. You know that we're a thing. I don't like having to hide it. It doesn't feel right. Or necessary."

Bini Katz, a long-time family friend of Tyler's, was our only farm employee, and Tyler and I had kept our relationship a secret so that things wouldn't be, as he put it, 'weird.'

"You mean tell her we are in love?"

"Yes, that."

He shrugged. "Okay."

"She won't be upset, will she? Has she ever hinted she was in love with you?"

"Bini? Good lord, no. Our families have been on the shore so long there's a good possibility we are related. Not to mention, I'm twelve years older than her."

"You two work so well together."

"Yes, we do. I don't know what I would do without her."

"Okay, so—"

Bini, whose timing was reliably uncanny, shut the front door with a thud. Tyler's arm dropped from my shoulder as she entered the kitchen in a thick thermal hoodie and Wrangler jeans. Pushing her hood from her head, she started for the Miele but stopped and looked at us. "What's wrong with you guys?"

"Bini," I said, twisting my fingers together. "Tyler and I want you to know that, well, we, um, we are in love." I gave my head a sharp nod. "With one another. We're in a relationship."

"Hah," Bini said. "Are you serious?"

I glanced at Tyler. He was frowning, most likely thinking my idea was a big mistake.

She filled a stainless steel mug with coffee. I rolled my lips in, waiting for her to speak.

"Do you think this is breaking news?"

"I'm sorry?" I said. "You knew?"

"Like from the first time I met you. We were sitting on the front stoop drinking beer, remember? You guys were so smitten I wasn't sure if I was gonna take the job." She snapped on the lid. "And that's the last I want to hear about any of this. Got it?" The arc of her eyebrows made it clear her question was rhetorical. "Now I am going to feed the goats something other than pumpkins."

The door slammed.

I stole a glance at Tyler. There was that crooked smile again. I covered my mouth and tried to stifle a laugh. Tyler's guffaw made it impossible not to let out my own, and by the time we stopped laughing, tears streamed from my eyes, and my stomach felt as if I'd just done fifty crunches.

Chapter Two

After I was dressed and showered, my mother's pearls around my neck, I said goodbye to Dickens, who didn't seem to notice, and headed for my car. The chickens clucked and flapped, hoping I had breakfast scraps. "Sorry, ladies," I sang, "I only ate a banana."

A cool breeze restyled my hair, and a hint of wood smoke met my nose as I walked. A stubborn brown leaf, finally forced to let go, pirouetted to the ground in front of me.

I was almost to my car when a gunshot pierced my serenity. White-tail deer hunting season was upon us. I hunched my shoulders at another rapid round of "pop—pop—pop," and picked up the pace.

Although it was just a few miles into town, I always enjoyed the transition from life at Barclay Meadow, my home and farm, to managing my café. I noticed a blue heron waving its heavy wings low over the Cardigan River as I drove. The Eastern Shore of Maryland is a flat and lush stretch of land between the Chesapeake Bay and the Atlantic. 'The Shore' was a unique, quirky part of the world, and over time, I had grown to love living here. In Cardigan, one was never less than a mile from a sprawling farm or a tidal waterway. The weather was clement, the atmosphere friendly, the stores locally owned.

My restaurant, The Day Lily Café, located in an historic building on Main Street, had grown chilly overnight. I turned up the thermostat and dropped my things on the bar. Although our grand opening was a year and a half ago, I still held my breath every time I walked through the door, pinching myself to confirm it was all really mine. The ochre walls, the color of a Tuscan hillside at sunset, glowed in the early morning light.

I started the hot pot to make a cup of tea for Glenn Breckinridge, my best friend and head waiter, who had asked me to meet him here this morning. The text arrived at 6:00 AM, and I had no idea why he wanted to get together at the café on our day off.

At seventy-three, Glenn Breckinridge was an intelligent, elegant man. We got to know one another when we both arrived in this close-knit community feeling friendless and a little lost, realizing not long after that between us we shared an enormous amount of curiosity and a passion for getting to the bottom of things. Our inquisitiveness had gotten us into some sticky situations, but in the end, we had teamed up to right a few wrongs.

With the promptness of a bullet train, Glenn pushed through the door separating the kitchen from the restaurant just as the digital clock on the coffee makers glowed 9:00. He draped his coat over the back of a bar chair and kept his plaid Burberry scarf around his neck. Nudging his wire-rimmed glasses up his nose, he said, "Thank you for meeting me, dear."

I set the tea with a side of lemon on the marble counter as he sat down. "Is everything all right?"

He frowned. "I'm not really certain."

I sat next to him. "I'm listening."

"And you're very good at that." He gave me a warm smile and took a sip. "So here's my concern. You see, my neighbor, Bill Rutherford, and I have an arrangement. We are both widowers and live alone, so one night over a martini, we agreed to turn our outside lights off every morning to signal to one another we were alive and well. You never know what can go bump in the night."

"That's actually pretty smart."

"We thought so. You think of these things when you live alone."

"And Bill's light was still on this morning?"

"Yes, and his bike isn't in the rack by the sidewalk. I knocked on his door twice, and I've texted him so many times my thumbs hurt. But no response. Not even an emoji."

"Maybe he has a lady friend."

"Oh, believe me, I thought of that. He's quite popular with the women in our community. But it's not like him to ignore a text."

"Is it time to call Sheriff Wilgus?"

"What do you think?"

I picked up my phone. "What could possibly go wrong?"

Chapter Three

The café had warmed, and Glenn and I brought out the last of the cinnamon muffins from yesterday's champagne Sunday brunch. The sheriff was on his way and hopefully would have good news about Bill Rutherford.

I licked the cinnamon topping from my fingers. "I guess I need to start decorating here."

"Don't do it on my account," Glenn said as he brushed crumbs from the counter into a napkin.

"You don't like Christmas? Did I know this about you?"

"I've done my best to ignore it since Molly passed."

I studied him. Glenn was one of the most optimistic people I knew. It was unusual to see him so introspective and sullen.

"I get that," I said. "The first Christmas after Ed and I split, I bought a Charlie Brown Christmas tree on the 24th and promptly took what was left of it down on the 26th. I did it for Annie, but I knew Christmas would never be the same for me."

"I pretty much white-knuckle my way through December." He checked his phone. "I believe I'm correct in thinking the Sheriff's office is only a block away. What could possibly be taking him so long?"

"Tell me about Christmas with your Molly, Glenn. What was it like?"

"Oh, Rosalie, I don't know that I can."

I placed my hand over his. "Tell your story. I think it will help."

"Where do I begin? It's hard to capture Molly in words. It wasn't that she was extravagant over the holidays." He stared out the window.

"You're doing great." I sat back in my chair.

His eyes met mine. "The rooms would be filled with the scent of fresh pine. She placed candles in the windows, and the house would glow like a warmed heart. On Christmas Eve, we would open our home and encourage everyone we knew to stop in for a holiday toast. Oh, the food she would make. Her whiskey balls were enough to get you tipsy in one bite. Spiced wine simmered on the stove while Teddy, my oldest, played carols on the piano. Teddy is a very good musician." He paused at the memory, and I wondered how his sons felt about the current omission of Christmas from Glenn's life.

"Oh, Rosalie, the house was so full of love and hope and joy. We would all gather around as Teddy played, and my soul would swell at my good fortune." Glenn stopped. His head fell forward. "I'm not capturing it."

"Oh, but you are." I leaned in. "What was your favorite carol?"

"God Rest Ye Merry Gentlemen, for certain."

"And what would you give her for Christmas?"

"Molly was beautiful, inside and out, and in no need of adornment, but I bought her jewelry just the same. Her birthstone was sapphire."

"How lovely."

"And all I did was drag in the tree and start the fires. She did everything else. I wonder if I knew how fortunate I was at the time." He crossed his arms. "Did I take it all for granted?"

"It doesn't sound like it. I wish I could have met Molly."

"You two would have been as thick as thieves." He gazed over at me. "You are very much alike. I think that's why I'm so comfortable with you." He smiled. "I never thought about it that way before, but I believe it's true."

"Hart?"

And just like that, the mood evaporated in a 'poof' with the arrival of Sheriff Wilgus. "In here," I called.

Joe Wilgus pushed through the doors from the kitchen and sauntered into the restaurant.

"Thanks for coming, Joe," I said and waited for his reaction. Although we'd known each other for three years, it was only a few months ago that he finally allowed me to call him by his first name.

He frowned but said nothing.

"Thank you for coming, Sheriff Wilgus," Glenn said. "Have you heard anything about Bill Rutherford?"

The sheriff glanced over at the array of professional-grade Miele coffee machines, and I hopped up to make him a cup.

"Unfortunately, I have bad news, Mr. Breckinridge."

"I knew it," Glenn said. "I just knew it. What happened?"

He tucked his thumbs in his belt. "A river keeper spotted him and his bike along the side of the Cardigan River early this morning."

"He's dead?" Glenn said, his voice cracking.

"I'm afraid so."

Chapter Four

The next morning, I was up early, ready to begin my day. I had errands to run and a restaurant to prep. But I couldn't stop thinking about Bill Rutherford. My curiosity had often gotten the better of me, and how and when Bill died occupied my thoughts throughout the night. As I waited in my kitchen for an espresso, I wondered if Glenn was on the same wavelength. Despite grieving his friend, I was pretty sure he, too, would be riddled with questions as to how Bill Rutherford's body ended up next to a river on an innocent Sunday evening.

I walked down the front steps, espresso in hand, appreciating the honks of the Canada Geese flying safely overhead now that the goose hunting season had passed. Despite a rocky beginning, Tyler and I had spent the last few years working in harmony to get the house and farm of Barclay Meadow up and running again. Now the farm was producing organic fare again, the chickens and goats were fat and happy, and the house seemed content to be lived in again.

When my Aunt Charlotte died quite suddenly from a stroke five years ago, I was summoned to her will reading by a lawyer who practiced in Cardigan. Within eight years, I had lost my father to a heart attack, my mother to a short but deadly bout with breast cancer, and Charlotte, who had been a loving presence my entire life.

I had been living in Chevy Chase at the time, married and busy guiding Annie through high school. A few days after I learned of her death, I drove out to the law office of David Bestman. David invited me in and motioned to an easy chair. He talked for several minutes about how much he liked my aunt, how charitable she had been. His remarks felt genuine. It appeared he adored Aunt Charlotte. And who didn't?

When he flipped open a manila folder and announced she had left her entire estate to me, I blinked a few times and said, "I'm sorry?"

"Everything, Rosalie, the farm, all three hundred acres, the house, and its contents. She wanted you to have it." He flashed me a warm smile. "You seem surprised." He turned the folder around for me to see.

I was so shocked I felt short of breath. I hesitated, "Yes, it's incredible. But what if I don't want it?"

David sounded perplexed. "You had no idea?"

"No, of course not."

"You can do what you want. And I understand this may be overwhelming, but I suggest you don't make a decision hastily. Barclay Meadow has been in your family for generations." Elbows on his desk, David pressed the tips of his fingers together. "Yes, it's a big responsibility to take on, but it's a beautiful farm. One of the prettiest in Devon County. And Miss Charlotte put it entirely in your hands." He studied me. "Rosalie, doesn't that say a lot about how much she trusted you? Especially knowing Barclay Meadow meant the world to her."

I stood, unsure what to do next. He really was a nice man. "Thank you, David. Those are wise words, but I just don't know what to say. Now, if you'll excuse me, I need some air."

I clenched my teeth the entire drive back to Chevy Chase. I didn't even notice the Chesapeake Bay Bridge, a span so high and long on a normal day it would have made my palms sweaty, my head light. Instead, I breezed right over it, my brain flooded with more urgent thoughts.

Barclay Meadow had been built by my mother's ancestors in the mid-eighteen hundreds, right before the Civil War. Eventually, it became a summer home, Baltimore offering more business opportunities for the Barclay family. But when Charlotte lost her husband and the hope of ever having children to the Vietnam War, she returned to Cardigan and brought the house and farm back to life. She updated the kitchen and leased the farmland to a young man who had an interest in organic farming. Tyler

Wells and Charlotte Barclay became fast friends and loyal business partners until the day she died. Barclay Meadow was her life.

When I arrived home that night and explained everything to my husband, he immediately said, "Sell it."

"But, Ed, it's been in my family for over one hundred and fifty years."

"You hated growing up on a farm in rural Virginia. You're a city gal now. What would you do with that dump of a house and all those acres?" He flipped to the next page of the *Washington Post*. "Maybe we could subdivide it. Make some cash."

Ed wasn't totally wrong. I didn't *hate* growing up on a farm. I had some happy memories, but the thought of maintaining Barclay Meadow was daunting. And maybe unnecessary. I had a full life. I may have loved my summers catching fireflies and baking bread with the best aunt in the world, but I wouldn't lose those memories by selling the farm.

And so I did nothing. When I received letters and countless emails from a Tyler Wells asking if he could continue leasing the land, I ignored them. I paid the taxes, which annoyed Ed, but nothing else. It wasn't until one sunny fall morning after we had delivered Annie to her freshman year at Duke that I felt my first pang of gratitude Charlotte had made Barclay Meadow mine.

Ed announced on that pristine September day he was in love with another woman. A much younger and thinner one whom he confessed he'd been seeing for over a year.

Four hours later, I was sitting in the kitchen at Barclay Meadow wondering what sort of coffee pot I could FedEx overnight.

Chapter Five

Later that morning, I decided to pay a visit to Joe Wilgus. The sheriff's office was in the old train depot at the end of Main Street. Lila, his red-headed watchdog, fluffed her curls as I stepped into the foyer. She was past retirement age but loved her job because she always had the inside scoop on the latest gossip in town.

"Good morning," I said. "Is Joe in his office?"

She scowled. "I don't like you calling him Joe when he's on duty."

I peeked in his door. He was frowning at his phone.

"What do you call him?" I said.

"I call him Joey. I have his whole life. But that don't mean you should."

"Okay. I won't call him Joey. Can I go in?"

"Well—" She crossed her arms.

I dropped a white bag on her desk. "Double chocolate chip cookies."

She snatched up the bag as I strolled into his office. I set a coffee cup and another white bag on his desk and sat in the chair opposite his. He reached for the coffee without looking up.

After a moment, he said, "I'm stuck on Wordle. You play?"

"Every morning with my first coffee. Annie and I compare results."

He looked at me over his thick black glasses. "What's your starter word?"

"Slate. And you?"

"Bacon."

I crossed my legs. "I got it in three today."

"I don't believe you."

"Want a hint?"

"No. Wait, I think it's got a 'y'. Don't tell me it's antsy?"

"Bingo."

He tapped in the letters. "That's just a dumb word." He dropped his phone face down on his desk. "I know why you're here."

"How did he die?"

"Blunt force trauma."

I thought for a moment. "Did he hit a tree?"

"The blunt force was from behind."

"Behind? Did he get hit by a car?"

"It's a possibility, and that's all I'm saying."

"Do you know why he was riding his bike?"

He leaned forward and popped the lid from his cup. "Bill was an athletic guy. He played eighteen holes with his three buddies every Sunday afternoon, rain or shine, winter or summer. Then they sat at the Country Club bar and had a few drinks. Bill liked to ride his bike on those days to keep fit. And it's only a couple of miles. He's got all kinds of lights on that thing. Or, he had. Everyone knew to look out for him at 5:30 on a Sunday. Or maybe you didn't. Did *you* hit him?"

"And no one's come forward?"

"Coulda been anyone."

"You know my next question," I said, gazing directly into his eyes.

"Yes, I'm going to look into it."

"Joe, I wonder if you could give a heads up to all the body shops in town. Ask them to let you know if anyone comes in with front bumper damage, that sort of thing."

"You know, Hart, this was most likely an accident."

"I honestly hope that's true." I picked up my purse and stood. "I'll let you know if I hear anything at the café."

I waited. He was staring into his cup. At last, he looked up. "Sounds good."

I gasped. "It does?"

"Don't push it, Hart."

"Oh, one more thing. What's a river keeper?"

"They protect the waterways around here. Keep an eye on things. This young woman gets in a kayak as much as she can and paddles around the Cardigan River. She's good. Uncovered all kinds of stuff. First time finding a dead body, though. She's pretty shook up."

"Oh, I know all too well about that."

He chuckled. "That's right. Ha! You did, too. Only as far as I know, she didn't throw up on the crime scene."

Chapter Six

On that Wednesday, like most days we were open for business, I was the first to arrive at the restaurant. Being alone in the café was my zen. I took in the quiet, the stillness, knowing it would all change very soon, and started up the coffee makers. The Day Lily had recently undergone an expansion, and we were now open for lunch and dinner Wednesday through Saturday, with a champagne Sunday brunch to top off the week.

We offered a relatively small farm-to-table menu accented with a daily special. And with the renovation, I now had a bigger bar and a freshly-framed liquor license. It hadn't taken long for us to acquire some regular customers who had already developed favorites. It was a balance, keeping the menu fresh and seasonal while serving people what they loved to eat. But I was grateful to be earning a living doing what I loved most — nurturing people with delicious, healthy-*ish* food.

Crystal Sterling, the waitress who worked alongside Glenn, was the second to arrive. In her mid-twenties, she had an ethereal way of floating through a room. Tall and thin, she kept her hair in a long blond braid that ended at her hips. A bit clairvoyant, or maybe a lot clairvoyant, Crystal had a Celtic tattoo that curved behind her ear. Her sky-blue eyes were always opened wide, and she seemed to have access to an overwhelming amount of incoming data, data that most of us weren't attuned to.

She tucked her hobo bag under the counter and tied a small black apron around her hips. She stood next to me but said nothing.

"Morning, sweetie," I said. "Tea?"

"I'll make some in a bit." Crystal crossed her arms, and we both gazed out the front window at the shop across the street. "'A Well-Loved Home' has quite a window display this year," she said. "Mary went all out."

"There are a lot of moving parts."

"It looks good. Festive." Crystal cleared her throat. "As if this were a holiday season."

"Um, sweetie, are you getting some sort of vibe?"

"That's the problem, Miss Rosalie. There's no vibe in here at all. At least not a Christmas vibe."

"Oh, that. Annie is going to Dubai for her entire break, and Glenn's neighbor died suddenly Sunday night." I looked at Crystal, but she continued to stare out the window.

"I'm sorry for you both, but you've got to get your butt in gear. Mary might have some decorations for sale. You can keep it simple but do something." She walked over to the hot pot. "Our customers will expect it. And," she reached for a mug, "be disappointed without it."

"Message received."

She dunked a tea bag up and down and turned to face me. "Have you thought about some sort of peppermint latte coffee special?"

"That's actually a good idea. Why didn't I think of that?"

"I'll just say one more thing, and then I'll mind my business."

"What?" I truly wanted to know.

"Christmas is about generosity. All the holiday traditions this time of year are about light and giving."

"You're right. I don't mean to make it so much about me."

"Okay." She dropped her tea bag in the trash. "And Miss Rosalie? I'm sorry about Annie, but you will be with her before the holidays are over. I know this."

"Really?" I uncrossed my arms. "How? When?"

She shrugged. "I just know. It's a feeling."

My mouth fell open just as the sound of our cook's motorcycle grew louder, overpowering our conversation. It popped and barked and fell silent.

"Master Chef is here," Crystal said, rolling her eyes.

CHAPTER SIX

I pushed through the doors to the kitchen and watched as Custer Wells stubbed out a cigarette butt in the gravel with his sneaker. When I was in search of a cook, Tyler Wells, cue the man I'm in love with, asked me for his one and only favor to date: give his nephew a job. According to Tyler, Custer had a good sense in the kitchen and was in need of work as per his parole.

Custer closed the door, helmet in hand. "Hey, boss," he said as he dropped the butt in the trash, his trademark black bandana wrapped around his forehead.

He was Tyler's nephew through and through—the gemstone green eyes, the smile, messy sandy blond hair, and an irreverence for most things. When my Annie first met him, the word infatuated was an understatement. They had a fling that ended abruptly when Custer attended culinary school in D.C. during our renovations.

He was now in a hot affair with Monique Dujardin, the head chef at Bistro Dujardin, a Michelin-Star-rated restaurant in Washington. In her early forties, Monique was twenty years his senior. When Custer wasn't cooking, he was glued to his phone, texting, or more likely sexting, with Monique.

"Did you get the tuna for the special?" he asked.

"The *Ginny Way* brought in a fresh catch. It looks pretty good. How are you going to prepare it?"

"How does anyone prepare Ahi tuna?"

"Please just tell me, Custer."

"Of course, I'll tell you, but you gotta loosen the reins, boss. I know stuff now. Let me take it out for a ride."

"I'm trying. And I know you are very talented. But this café is my livelihood." I clenched my fists, trying not to overreact. "I think the key to a successful chef is one who has mastered the art of cooking, but who also keeps a tab on what her patrons like to eat."

"Seared with a soy, garlic, and ginger dipping sauce, arugula salad on the side."

"It sounds delicious."

Custer peeled off his jean jacket and hung it on a hook. He was slightly shorter than his uncle, but they both had the same defined muscles. The biggest difference was Custer's were always a little more tensed, as if he lived his life believing he had something to prove.

"You okay?" he said.

"Absolutely. I'm just thinking. Oh, we need to put the grilled cheese back on the menu. Several of our regulars were disappointed last week when it was gone."

"Can I switch out the cheddar?"

"No, I don't think so."

"How about cheddar and pepper jack?"

"Fine."

"I have another idea how to elevate it. I'll experiment."

I picked up a stack of folded napkins fresh from the cleaners. "Did you have a nice few days off?"

"Just got back from D.C. this morning, so, yes. It was, as you say, nice."

I brushed my hair from my face, realizing today had already triggered quite a few unexpected emotions, especially about Annie. She seemed to handle the breakup with Custer pretty well. And they led different lives. But I still didn't know how much it affected her. She really was taken with this guy.

Custer approached. "Ready to rock it?"

"You bet."

I set the napkins on the counter, and we bumped our fists together, followed by a double high five. "Let's do this."

Chapter Seven

Welcome to the Day Lily Café
A gathering place offering simplicity,
freshness, with a focus on locally sourced ingredients

Plant-based Wednesday Specials:
Lunch: Hungarian Mushroom Soup with coconut milk, paprika croutons, and Sweet Potato Fries
Dinner: Winter vegetable lasagna and balsamic vinegar salad

D*o your little bit of good where you are; it is those little bits of good put together that overwhelm the world.*
– Archbishop Desmond Tutu

* * *

And we were rolling. Crystal had the dining room in tip-top shape, and Custer and I had everything prepped and ready to go. Glenn was in charge of our budget and printing the menus, which he did at home, so there was no need for him to arrive before ten, and, being Glenn, that's exactly when he entered the restaurant.

"Hey," I said. "You okay?"

"Is it summer yet?" He reached for his apron under the counter. "Bill's funeral is tomorrow afternoon. I'd like to slip out."

"I'll go with you. If we need to shut down for a few hours, I think our customers will understand."

"I'm not sure why I'm taking this so hard. We were acquaintances, each other's neighborhood watch, but I really don't know much about him. Just that he seemed like a good enough man." Glenn exhaled a long sigh. "It's just, one minute he was my neighbor, the next he's dead."

"Are you curious about what happened?"

"I'm assuming he hit a tree; maybe a car got too close, and he had to swerve." His brows dipped. "Do you know something I don't, my dear?"

"I stopped to see the sheriff yesterday."

A spark appeared in Glenn's eye. "And?"

"Blunt force trauma." I paused. "From behind."

Glenn's forehead creased. "No. Someone—"

"That's all I know."

"Good lord, Rosalie." A lock of hair fell onto his forehead. "Good lord."

Chapter Eight

In addition to being in charge of beverages, I was responsible for serving the customers seated at the bar, who were usually either overflow or regulars. Janice Tilghman wiped her mouth, having just finished the tuna special.

Still one of my favorite friends, Janice, and I had been playmates as children. She grew up on a beautiful farm next to my Aunt Charlotte's, where I spent six weeks every summer. Our first encounter was in the summer I was six. I was sitting on the tree swing in the backyard, comforting my favorite doll who had just been punted like a football by my older brother, Oliver. As I picked leaves out of Edith's hair, I noticed Janice peering through the trees.

"Who the heck are you?" she said.

"Rosalie Charlotte Finnegan. And who might you be?"

"Janice. I'm seven, and you look too little to play with me."

"I'll be seven soon."

"How soon?"

"Soon enough. This is my doll, Edith. She's not feeling well. She took a bad tumble."

Janice stepped out of the trees. "I only have brothers."

I perked up. "Me too!"

The screen porch door slammed, and Oliver walked over to me. "I'm sorry about Edith. It's just, I forgot my football, and Aunt Charlotte doesn't have one."

I motioned my head toward Janice. She stood wide-eyed, mouth open as she stared at Oliver.

"Who's she?" He slid his hands in the back pockets of his pants.

Janice wore denim shorts and an Elvis tee. Her blond hair hadn't been combed in a while, but she stepped proudly into the middle of the yard and rolled her shoulders back. "I'm Snow White, and this is my new best friend, Rose Red."

Delighted at her words, I hopped off the swing and joined her.

She gave Oliver a once over. "And you can be Prince Charming when we need you to be."

* * *

"How was the tuna?" I asked Janice.

Glenn approached and looked down at her empty plate. "I think she liked it."

"Oh, it was plenty good." She frowned. "But I'm still hungry."

"We are going to sell out of desserts," Glenn said. "Everyone who orders the tuna wants something else to eat."

I filled a dish rack with coffee mugs. "Dessert, Snow White? It's on the house."

"I'll have a grilled cheese with fries."

"Custer has been adding kimchi and Thousand Island dressing to the grilled cheeses," Glenn said.

"He what?" My mouth dropped open.

"What is that?" Janice scowled. "Sounds nasty."

"He's also doing something unusual with the bread."

"What is he doing to the bread?" I said, wondering if Custer's lofty ideas about fine dining weren't going to fly on the Eastern Shore of Maryland.

"Instead of butter, he coats the outside with mayonnaise. He said it adds flavor and allows the cheese to melt longer."

"Mayonnaise?"

"I'll have one of those," Janice said. "But without the Kimbucktwo gunk. What is it, anyway?"

"Pretty much-pickled cabbage and some other veggies." I dried my hands on my apron.

"Yeah, um, definite no to that. Oh, hey, you guys, I'm having a party on December twenty-second. Be there or be square."

Glenn and I exchanged a knowing glance. He had decided to ignore Christmas, and I was tempted to join him. "I might be busy," we said in unison.

Janice's head reared back. "What's going on with you two? Did the zombies get you?"

My shoulders fell. "I'm sorry, Snow White. I'll put it on my calendar. I love your parties. I'm just a slow starter this season."

"That's more like it."

"Table six is ready for their check, Mr. Glenn," Crystal said.

"Thank you, dear. Are you holding up okay?"

"Always."

"I'll put in your order," I said to Janice. "Regular fries or Old Bay?"

She drummed her thumbs on the bar. "Old Bay, no question. Just make sure Custer doesn't add something funky to 'em."

Chapter Nine

When things had slowed after lunch, I decided to head over to 'A Well-Loved Home' as Crystal had suggested. Mary Pickens, the proprietor of the popular home decorating store, was behind the counter.

"I need holiday decorations for the café," I said. "Tasteful but minimal."

She peered over her readers. "Those trees have been very popular."

A forest of metal trees whose limbs were coated with tiny white lights glowed in the corner of the store. "What do you think? Maybe five in my front windows?"

"Yes, an odd number is always best. Let me think—okay, you'll want three of the smaller ones and two large."

I waited while she stacked the boxes on the counter. "Mary, you're divorced. How do you celebrate Christmas?"

She waved a dismissive hand. "I've got it down to a science. I make a chocolate pecan pie and go to my daughter's house on Christmas morning. I give everyone gift cards, including the children, because that's all they want these days. And on the twenty-sixth, I shut down the store for two weeks and go on a Caribbean cruise with my girlfriends. Piece-o-cake!"

"No stress?"

"Not a smidge.

"Gift cards?" I said. "That's what they want?"

"Oh, yeah. You can never get the clothes right these days. And they have everything else. Toys just clutter up my daughter's house, and she doesn't need any more of that. Can you carry these boxes yourself?"

"I think so."

Mary tied my boxes together with twine and patted the top. "I'm telling you, Rosalie. Gift cards and then the cruise."

Chapter Ten

As I drove down the long lane lined with gnarly Cypress Trees leading to Barclay Meadow that night, I allowed the fatigue I'd been fighting to wash through me. I wasn't a leisurely bath type of gal, but for some reason, the iron-claw-footed tub tucked under a window in my bathroom called to me like a friendly siren. Epsom salts would be nice. Maybe a glass of wine.

Once I rounded the ancient boxwoods in the center of the drive, I was surprised to see Tyler's pickup next to the vegetable gardens. It was after 8:00. I rarely saw him on Wednesday nights.

I climbed the front steps and stopped. The porch light illuminated a large pine wreath on the door spiked with holly and magnolia branches. A glistening gold bow with trailing satin ribbons had been fastened to the top. At least someone was in a holiday mood.

"Tyler?" I called as I made my way to the kitchen. The room was empty. Looking over my shoulder, I noticed a warm glow emanating from the living room. I slipped out of my coat and looped it on a hook. I was still in my café uniform: white blouse, above-the-knee black skirt, and black tights, and I wondered briefly if I smelled of grilled cheese and kimchi. Fluffing my hair, I followed the light.

"'Bout time," he said.

Not only was the fire blazing, several candles had been placed in strategic places around the room. Their flames flickered and danced, causing the shadows on the ceiling to look like a chorus line. Two glasses with deep bellies sat next to a decanted bottle of wine on the coffee table. Wishing I'd remembered a touch of lipstick, I walked over to Tyler. "Seems a Christmas elf put a wreath on the front door."

He patted the sofa next to him. "Merry Christmas. Thought I'd give you a little nudge into the holiday spirit."

"You and a few other people."

He filled the glasses. Red bubbles foamed as he poured. "This is a rouge champagne," he said and held out a glass. "The guy at the wine and cheese shop said it's perfect for a cold winter night."

We clinked our glasses, and I took a delicate sip. "Mm. This is delish." I eyed a plate of melted brie garnished with rosemary sprigs. "You've outdone yourself, Mr. Wells. Where did you find the wreath?"

He slathered a toasted baguette with cheese and held it out for me. "Actually, I made it."

"You what?"

"You're welcome. You know, I've never put much thought into Christmas, but this is my first one *officially*," he winked, "in love with you. And I'm starting to think it could be fun."

I sat back and bit into the brie. "I feel all warm and cozy. And here I was just going to take a hot bath."

"Warm and cozy is good." He took a long swig of wine.

"You really made the wreath?"

"Bini showed me how to wire the branches together. Then I went into town and stopped at Kevin's flower shop. He picked out the bow, saying it had to be gold and very large. He's a big fan of yours, by the way."

I smiled. "I love that guy."

"How was your day?"

"Busy. Glenn and I are going to Bill Rutherford's funeral tomorrow. I think Glenn's having a hard time grappling with the fact his neighbor is dead and may have been murdered."

Tyler tensed. I eyed him warily, wondering how he was going to react.

"Who said he was murdered?"

"He was riding home on his bike. It looks like he was hit from behind."

He shook his head. "Rosalie, Rosalie." His smile enabled me to start breathing again. "Let's hope it was an accident."

"And if it wasn't?"

He thought for a moment. "I told you that afternoon two months ago I love every part of you. Including the fact you're as curious as a cat." He set his glass down. "I just hope you have nine lives."

"Thank you, Tyler. That means everything to me."

"And Joe Wilgus?"

"I'm just keeping my eyes and ears open. He's going to look into it."

He refilled our glasses and leaned back into the sofa cushions. I took a long sip as he drew circles on my knee with his thumb.

"Are we going to get a tree?" he said.

"Yes." His touch sent heat waves through my core. "I like the idea of reinventing Christmas. Maybe start some traditions of our own. Oh, I almost forgot to tell you, Crystal said I will see Annie over the holidays. She doesn't know when or where, but I will."

He gazed at me with those green eyes, his lids at half-mast. "That's wonderful." His thumb inched up my leg. More circles. "Mind if I stay the night?"

Chapter Eleven

Once everyone had arrived at the café the next morning, I served mocha lattes topped with a dollop of whipped cream, crushed candy cane, and shaved white and dark chocolate. I distributed the mugs and waited for their reactions. After waking up feeling very happy and a little more Christmasy, I'd been experimenting all morning.

"Wow," Crystal said, a spot of whipped cream on her upper lip. "It's perfect. And you put tree lights in the front window. It feels more festive in here already."

Custer tasted the coffee concoction and frowned. "It's pretty good. But I think you need something to balance the sweetness. Grated nutmeg, maybe cinnamon?"

Crystal set her empty mug on the bar. "It's perfect as it is." She eyed Custer. "You know, master chef, everyone was still hungry after they ate the tuna yesterday."

"Yes, you mentioned that," Custer said. "And the omelet on Sunday didn't have enough cheese. Is that correct.?"

"I'm just giving you customer feedback. Don't shoot the messenger." She tucked her hands in her apron pockets. "And what's special today? Pea shoots and a cracker?"

"Glad you asked." He ducked into the kitchen.

Glenn set his mug on the counter. "That latte was illegally delicious."

"Thanks. Do you think we'll be selling very many today?"

"I'll suggest it as a dessert."

The kitchen door pushed open, hard, jostling Glenn. He caught his glasses in midair.

Custer set a large plate on the bar. "This ought to fill people up. Seems my job is more about feeding the hungry than cooking high-end cuisine. So, here's your special, boss."

I narrowed my eyes. It was the largest burger I'd ever seen. "Are those French fries in there?"

"Yes. Before you is the Day Lily," he made air quotation marks, "Café monster burger special. Here we have a one-pound wagyu beef burger with bacon, Thousand Island dressing, crushed potato chips, cheddar *and* mozzarella cheese, French fries, mayo, sweet pickle relish, and for those looking to make it seem healthy, lettuce, and a tomato."

He stepped away, hands behind his back.

The front door opened, and Sheriff Wilgus strolled into the room. "You got coffee yet, Hart?" He stopped and took in the burger. "Whoa. Is that on the lunch menu? It's about time you started serving real food."

"I say no more." Custer bowed his head and returned to the kitchen.

* * *

"Good morning, Joe," I said.

Glenn's mouth twitched as if debating to say what was on his mind. Unable to resist, he said, "Hello, sheriff, are you here for your morning joe?"

"Hah," Crystal spat out a laugh.

"Once, Mr. Breckinridge," he said and held up his index finger. "You get to say that once in your lifetime." He eyed Glenn under heavy brows.

"I apologize, Sheriff. Rosalie has made mocha lattes this morning, and I think the sugar and caffeine kicked in simultaneously."

"I'll have one of those." The sheriff sat in a bar chair and set his hat next to him.

I fired up the Miele. "Any news?"

"Jeremy at 'crash and go' said someone brought in his car with front end damage yesterday. Guy said he hit a deer."

"You don't say," Glenn said. "Who was it?"

"Jimmy Nevins. A local."

"Did you speak to him?" I said.

"One of my deputies gave him a call. Jimmy has an alibi. Said he was watching the Ravens game at the Cardigan Tavern at the time Bill was hit. He's got a room full of alibis."

I picked up my phone and typed. "Well, that could be. The Ravens played the Steelers at 4:00 last Sunday."

The sheriff secured his hat on his head and grabbed his to-go cup. "I'll have one of those burgers for lunch today. Medium rare. Shoot me a text when it's ready." He stopped and faced us. "There's something else you two ought to know."

"What's that?" Glenn said.

"Coroner found a bullet in Bill's back. Whoever hit him must a shot him to make sure he was dead."

Glenn looked at me and blinked a few times. "He *was* murdered."

"We know that for certain now," the sheriff said. "Stay alert."

Chapter Twelve

Although we didn't have much time before opening, I called a meeting for the four employees of the Day Lily Café. "Custer," I said, "I hope you know that I appreciate your talent very much. Please don't stifle your creativity. We all know the burger is over the top, but it's a fabulous idea. We have your curried carrot soup as a special today, and it is, as you say, elevated. I love how we are serving the bowls with just the crispy prosciutto in the bottom and having Crystal and Glenn fill them table-side with the small pitchers you picked out."

"I'm thinking maybe chopped pistachios croutons, too," he said, gripping his coffee mug with both hands.

"People seem surprised when I just set the bowl in front of them with no soup in it," Crystal said. "I agree. It's like a ritual or something, pouring the soup over the prosciutto. It makes it seem more special."

"And the crisped prosciutto doesn't get soggy," Custer added.

"What about the burger?" Glenn said.

"Let's see, were those frozen French fries, Custer?"

"Yes, boss."

"Do we have any Yukon golds?"

He nodded.

"Okay, let's do the burger, shoe string Yukon gold fries, maybe an aioli instead of the Thousand Island?"

"Blue cheese aioli," Custer said.

"Great idea. Can we toss up a lettuce salad instead of just a lettuce leaf and tomato? Maybe a touch of balsamic? Oh, and yes to the bacon. Or maybe bacon jam? Not enough time?"

"I can handle it."

"Excellent. What do you think about a brioche bun? I could call the bakery and get a special delivery."

"We need to start a half hour ago," Custer said.

"But you're okay with the changes?"

"You make the salad?"

"Yes, of course. Grab your chalk, Crystal. I will dictate."

"That burger would be good with a nice craft IPA," Glenn said.

Custer shook his head. "I'm not really sure what just happened here."

"Teamwork," I said. "Let's take it out for a ride."

* * *

Welcome to the Day Lily Café
A gathering place offering simplicity,
freshness, with a focus on locally sourced ingredients

Today's specials:
Roasted Carrot Soup
with cumin, crispy prosciutto,
and pistachio croutons

Candy Cane Mocha Latté
Freshly roasted espresso and cream
topped with crushed candy canes and
shaved white and dark chocolate

Today's debut dish:
Day Lily Gourmet Burger
Wagyu beef topped with
crispy shoestring fries, blue cheese aioli,
bacon jam, and

a fresh chopped salad
served on a toasted brioche roll

The best burgers are simple, juicy, and messy.
— Bobby Flay

Chapter Thirteen

By one-thirty, the lunch crowd had thinned, and Crystal and Custer gave us the okay to leave for Bill Rutherford's funeral. We headed to my red Mercedes convertible parked in the alley behind the café.

On my fortieth birthday, Ed had tied a scarf over my eyes and led me out to our driveway in Chevy Chase. Feeling certain what was about to happen, I felt as if I was in one of those commercials aired during the Christmas season when a spouse surprises their partner with a brand new pickup truck, sometimes with a puppy inside. Why is that ever a good idea? Who wouldn't want to choose their own vehicle? Let alone a pet. But Ed was giddy as he guided me down the front steps.

He removed the blindfold, and there it was. A red Mercedes six-cylinder convertible wrapped in a massive silver bow. "To keep you young," he had said.

I stared at the ostentatious red paint. "Where's my Prius?"

"I traded it in. Got a great deal. Everyone wants a hybrid these days." He rubbed his hands together. "So what do you think? I special-ordered it from Europe. They don't make standards in the US anymore."

I was speechless for many reasons, among them being it was a standard transmission. Ed said he would teach me how to drive it. It would be fun. It wasn't.

I had resented the impracticality of the car for the past four years. But two months ago, I was followed by an enormous black SUV with tinted windows. No, scratch that, chased. And that's when I decided I liked the car. Maybe even loved it. And maybe it saved my life. Now, I found zipping around a corner and accelerating into a curve with the top down to be a lovely way to get around town.

Glenn ducked his head and climbed into the front seat. My bracelets jingled as I put the car into reverse.

"I'm happy you have finally decided to embrace this car," Glenn said. "It suits you more than you ever realized."

"I never thought of it that way. Sometimes, I wonder if what happened with Ed jaded this gift. That he was probably already in the market for a younger model. But maybe in his own way, Ed was trying to jazz up my life. I mean, I was driving a beige Prius. Happily, albeit, but it was beige."

"I didn't know there was such a thing as a beige car."

"Taupe?"

"So why don't you let 'er rip."

I giggled. "The church is less than a mile away."

Glenn buzzed his seat back. "We now know Bill was murdered."

I glanced at him. "Are you interested in looking into this a bit?"

Glenn lowered the visor and folded his hands together. "Are you?"

"He was your neighbor. And, did you know this? He's Santa."

He frowned. "I'm sorry?"

"Bill dressed up as Santa and rode in the firetruck in the Christmas Eve parade."

"The man wasn't a pound over 170."

I shrugged. "Must be a good costume."

"Indeed."

"So the answer to my question is yes," I said. "The sheriff asked us to keep our eyes and ears open. I mean, it's practically an invitation to begin an investigation. Right?" I glanced over at Glenn.

A small smile appeared on his face. "I believe it's our civic duty, my dear. Perhaps we should start today."

Chapter Fourteen

After the boiler-plate service, Glenn and I headed down the basement steps to the church's reception room. The space was beyond uninviting, with cinder block walls painted a pale green and overhead fluorescent lights that cast a dim gray pall over everything in their swath. One long table hosted a buffet of ham sandwiches and coleslaw with room-temperature bottles of water. Glenn and I found a spot along the far wall and took in the scene, watching and listening, wondering if the killer had risked attending Bill Rutherford's funeral.

This wasn't our first investigative visit to a funeral. Glenn and I had looked for clues at another service a year ago and discovered our first suspect sitting in the front pew. I clutched the strap of my purse and leaned back against the wall. Scanning the small gathering, I looked to see if anyone seemed nervous or uneasy. Was anyone genuinely grieving? The answer to that, so far, was no one. Not a single teardrop.

"Notice anything?" I said to Glenn.

"I'm looking for Bill's son. He must be here somewhere."

"Oh, Glenn. That woman who just came down the steps. She's dabbing her eyes. Our first mourner. Do you know her?"

Glenn narrowed his eyes. The woman was in a skin-tight black wrap dress and heels. She clutched another woman's arm and shook her head.

"She lives in my community," Glenn said. "Abby the Fitness Angel."

"Wait, is that really what she calls herself?"

"Apparently. She speed-walks the neighborhood every morning. And I've heard she has some sort of fitness podcast or TikTok or Instagram or all of the above. She calls herself an influencer. I've never really paid attention."

"She seems to be at least a little upset."

"I have no idea why. I guess I need to go to one of our community's happy hours. They really aren't my thing. But maybe I could learn more about who is doing what to whom." Glenn crossed his arms. "You know, Rosalie, I like my house just fine. But I had no idea living in an over fifty-five community was so demanding. I live a quiet life. I'm content with the café and Gretchen. But somehow, I feel I'm letting people down by keeping to myself."

"Peer pressure," I said. "It never goes away no matter how old we get." I frowned. "Speaking of age, she doesn't look very old. But she has to be at least fifty-five, right?"

"That's correct."

Abby, the Fitness Angel, moved on to the ham sandwiches.

"Look, I spy a coffee urn. Want a cup?"

He looked at me, his brow furrowed. "You aren't serious."

"Well, no, not really. I just need something to do with my hands."

A man who seemed to be in his late forties approached. "Are you Mr. Breckinridge?"

"Why, yes, I am. And you?"

"I'm Neil. You were my dad's neighbor, is that correct?"

Glenn straightened his posture and shook Neil's hand. "Yes, that's right. I'm very sorry for your loss."

"Thank you. I'm still in shock that my father got hit by a car." He took a long sip from a water bottle, the plastic collapsing with a crackle as he drank. "And even more that it killed him."

Glenn and I exchanged a quick glance. My guess was we were both wondering if Neil knew yet that his father had been shot in the back.

He frowned. "I just don't get it. I mean, my dad was a triathlete. He had that ride timed. He could get from the country club to his house in seven minutes and seventeen seconds."

"Hopefully, we will have some answers soon," Glenn said.

"You and my dad had a system, right? And that's how you knew he was missing. Thank you for that."

"Well, as widowers, it seemed like a good way to check in on one another."

"You're a widower?" he said. "Then I'm sorry for *your* loss."

"Wait," I said, "Wasn't your father?"

"No way. My mother is alive and well in Boca Raton. My father often said she was 'dead to him,' but no, he divorced her thirty years ago."

Glenn's head reared back. "I had no idea."

I gave Glenn's hand a small squeeze. He was honest to a fault and prided himself on it. Learning Bill had lied to him would be hard for him to take in.

"I'm Rosalie, by the way. I'm very sorry this happened. Do you live nearby?"

"D.C. area. It's where I grew up."

"So, is your mother here?" I scanned the room, wondering what the ex-Mrs. Rutherford might look like.

"That wasn't going to happen. Let's just say it wasn't an amicable divorce. Did either of you really know my father?"

"Not well," Glenn said. "But he seemed to be very popular. Look at all the people here."

"It's thinning out pretty quickly," Neil said. "I specifically said no booze to keep it short. You see, that's the thing. My father was a lot of fun at parties. He drank a lot and turned the music up, and loved to be the center of attention. Been like that his whole life. Was he well-liked? That's hard to believe. Did he get a party started? Oh, yeah. Was he a good father? Husband? Let's just say he was a good provider. Guy knew how to make a bunch of dough." Neil closed his eyes for a moment, then opened them. "Woo. You got me talking. His dying so suddenly has really churned up a lot." He removed a handkerchief from his back pocket and blotted his forehead. "Sorry to overshare."

"Please, don't worry." I smiled. "Glenn and I have both been through it. Losing a loved one stirs up so many memories and emotions."

A young woman approached with coal-black hair highlighted in purple and a nose piercing. Heavy liner rimmed her eyes. She was about my height, which means she was short, and wore low-waisted black denim jeans with several carefully placed rips and tears.

"Are you Neil Rutherford?" she said.

"Who's asking?" Neil said.

She crossed her arms tight against her chest. "Your sister."

Chapter Fifteen

Neil blinked a few times, as if taking in the fact this young woman could actually be related to him. He certainly didn't deny it outright. I looked back at her, searching for similarities in their appearance, and there it was, underneath the heavy makeup, her round gray eyes were identical to Neil's.

"What's your name?" I asked.

"Summer. My birthday is in October, and my mother named me Summer." She looked back at Neil. "I don't want anything from you. I just want you to finally know I exist."

"I have no idea what to say." He shook his head and said to Glenn, "Why did I say no booze?"

"How old are you, dear?" Glenn said.

"I'm sixteen. I drove myself here. My mother is at work. Don't you want to know who she is?"

"I'm pretty sure you'll tell us anyway," Neil said.

"Her name is Michelle. She worked at the country club marina where your dad kept his boat. Sixteen years ago, he gave her permission to board."

Neil's lips curved into a small smile. "I'll bet he did."

I studied him. He didn't seem particularly surprised. "So, Neil, your father never mentioned Summer?"

She rolled her eyes. "I didn't even know my father was alive until a month ago. My mother told me he was killed by a sniper in Iraq."

I rolled my lips in. There's a story here. Glenn gave my arm the slightest little nudge.

"Um, Summer, I'm sorry to be rude," Neil said, "but I need some time to take all of this in. It's been a hell of a week." He tightened the cap of his water bottle. "Maybe you could give me your number?"

She handed him a business card. "I don't have any other siblings, Neil."

"Neither do I. But right now, I'm going to exit this scene." He took a deep breath and held it in. Exhaling, he looked up at the ceiling and said, "Nicely done, Dad."

Summer watched him go. She faced us, eyes filling with tears. "I really don't want anything from him." Her arms fell to her sides. She made her way to the buffet, stuffed a ham sandwich in her sweatshirt pocket, grabbed another, and took the cement stairs two at a time.

Chapter Sixteen

When I trotted down the steps and into the kitchen Friday morning, Bini was seated at the table, gripping her phone. She was smiling, a rarity for certain. She typed and smiled again. I waited for her to realize I was in the room.

More texting and a small laugh.

I cleared my throat. "Morning, Bini."

She looked up. "Hey. FYI, I ran your dishwasher. You must have forgotten last night."

"It wasn't quite—" I stopped. "Thank you, Bini."

The sky was heavy with clouds. Another gray day. I poured a coffee and turned around, studying her behavior. Not only was it rare to see her smile, it was even odder to see her on her phone. Most days, she left it on the kitchen counter so it wouldn't get damaged while she worked. From what I had witnessed, it seemed a phone was simply a necessity for Bini. She literally used it only as an actual telephone. At least until this morning. "Coffee, Bin?"

"No, thank you." She stood, pushing the chair back from the table, and popped the hood of her sweatshirt on her head. After tucking her phone in the back pocket of her jeans, she said, "You need eggs?"

"No brunch until Sunday, so we're good."

"Oh, right. I keep forgetting you don't serve breakfast anymore." She smiled. "I sure do miss those muffins."

My mouth dropped open.

Her hip bumped a chair as she walked over to the demilune by the front door. "I can't seem to remember anything these days." She shook her head. "Sorry, I gotta switch gears." Snatching up her work gloves, she headed outside.

Chapter Seventeen

Menu Insert

Fettuccine Alfredo
In 1909, Italian restaurateur, Alfredo Di Lelio,
made his first batch of Fettuccine Alfredo
for his wife who had been weakened
after giving birth to their first son.
When she regained her appetite, she announced
Fettuccine Alfredo
must be added to the menu
in their restaurant, Il Vero Alfredo.
Still thriving in Rome, Il Vero Alfredo
continues the practice of
tossing the three simple ingredients:
Pasta, butter, and parmigiano, table-side
to the delight of its eager patrons

* * *

After hosting a five-day Italian cooking class with Chef Marco Giovanelli in October, I declared Fridays at the Day Lily: *Notte Italiana*. During the first, much-anticipated cooking class with Marco, I failed miserably at making fresh pasta dough and was directed by our very dashing chef to toss it in the trash. It landed with a thud. Now, after weeks of practicing, I could knock out a batch of fresh pasta in under five minutes.

Once we had cleaned up after lunch and everyone took their much-needed break Friday afternoon, I got to work. By the time Custer showed up for the dinner shift, ribbons of fettuccine dangled over wooden racks in every corner of the kitchen. "You want me to come up with a sauce?" he said as he pulled a coffee mug out of the dishwasher.

"We are serving Fettuccine Alfredo tonight."

"How very Olive Garden of you." He shook his head as he headed into the restaurant. I washed my hands and followed him.

I tossed a dish towel on the bar. "Fettuccine Alfredo was invented in 1909 by Alfredo di Lelio. There's a story here. I'm putting it in a menu insert."

"So? It's just pasta with a bunch of butter and heavy cream, maybe a little parmesan." He sipped his coffee. "Heart attack on a plate."

"Not the way di Lelio made it. Only butter and parmesan. His secret was in how he tossed the pasta. Can I show you?"

Once Custer cooked up a batch of my pasta, I made the sauce. "We need just a small amount of pasta water." It simmered on the stove as I added a sizable amount of melted butter. *"Triplo burro,"* I said. "Triple the butter, according to Alfredo." I whisked the butter and water vigorously. "Now we add the parmesan and continue whisking." When the mixture had emulsified, I poured it over the pasta. "This is the important part. It's all about the tossing. Alfredo would do this step at the patrons' table. Apparently, he was quite theatrical." The more I mixed, the creamier the pasta became. *"Sale e pepe,* and there you have it."

Custer popped a forkful into his mouth. "Whoa," he said while he chewed.

"I want you to make this table-side tonight. What do you say?"

"We can't add anything to this? Maybe some shrimp?"

"No shrimp. At least not tonight."

"It will take me out of the kitchen a lot."

"I'll have your back. And you can wear your bandana, we won't make it a big deal. Just a little fun." I handed him the spoon and fork. "You try tossing. Maybe you can ham it up a bit?"

"That cooking school made you a little nuts, you know that?"

"So did yours, if you must know." I smiled. "Just makes everything more interesting."

Custer's phone buzzed. He reached for it and swiped up.

I watched as he continued to read. "Um, Custer? I do believe you're blushing."

Chapter Eighteen

Crystal arrived not long after. "Hanukkah starts at sundown. I think we should celebrate all the holidays, so I brought a menorah. Maybe we could put it in the window?" She tied an apron fresh from the cleaners around her waist. "I wrote down the prayer you're supposed to say. We don't open for dinner until five. There shouldn't be too many customers in here. Is that okay?"

"I'm looking forward to it."

She set her phone on the bar. "Did you know Bocelli has a Christmas album? Perfect for *Notte Italiana*. I'll connect my phone to the speakers if that's okay. I'll keep the volume down."

Custer entered the room with an empty coffee cup. "Boss will give you the special today, Crys. It seems we have a suggested five-course dinner." He walked over to the coffee machines.

"That actually sounds like a good idea. You should be happy. You're all about upgrading the menu." She stared at his back. "You aren't going to change out anything, are you, master chef?"

"I'll let you know." He slurped his coffee and returned to the kitchen.

Her shoulders fell.

"What's going on with you two?"

"It's just, well, he thinks he's better than me now that he went to that culinary school. He barely talks to me, and he keeps changing things, which makes me look stupid in front of the customers."

"Should we call a meeting?"

"No, no, no, no, no. This is my issue as much as it is his." She clutched the crystal pendant she wore on a thin black cord around her neck. "You see, Miss Rosalie, I work hard to be the way I am. To be spiritual, kind, open to the universe for all it has to offer. But that's not how I was raised. And sometimes, I slip back into the ways of my family growing up. You know, all the worst qualities: jealousy, mistrust, anger. It's hard. But I can't stop trying to be the person I want to be. So, no meeting. I will figure out how to work with Custer in a positive way." She huffed out a sigh. "But right now, I think he's being an arrogant narcissist." She laughed. "Like I said, I still have a little work to do."

"You got this. And I will help in any way I can." Andrea Bocelli crooned "Oh, Holy Night." "Oh, that sounds perfect. Thank you, sweetie."

"See, that's why I think the holidays are so important to me. I absorb so much of the joy and hope. But for some reason, this year, it's like Christmas has a rough edge. It's harder. Everyone seems so depressed. I don't know if it's always like that, and I'm just now noticing, or if we're in some bad vortex."

"Blame it on the moon?"

"Blame it on Pluto. Pluto is a little minx, always wreaking havoc."

Chapter Nineteen

"Rosalie," Glenn said while adding the menu inserts. "I received a text from Neil Rutherford this morning. Seems he is tied up at work but is worried about his father's house. He asked that I check up on things. You know, food going bad, pipes bursting, faucets dripping." He snapped a menu shut and picked up the next. "He told me where the key is hidden." Closing the next menu, he said, "It's actually a pretty clever place."

"Do tell," I said as I wiped down the counter.

"His grill. It's a perfect spot for me because I never open mine."

I dropped the sponge into the stainless steel sink. "I don't suppose I could join you? Tomorrow morning?"

"I was hoping you'd say that. Be at my place at eight. Shall I have some coffee at the ready?"

"I'm pretty sure I'll be fully caffeinated by then, but thank you."

Glenn carried the menus over to the hostess stand. "What are you thinking, my dear?"

"We will need to be thorough. Just to ensure everything is in order."

"My thoughts exactly."

* * *

Welcome to the Day Lily Café

A gathering place offering simplicity,
freshness, with a focus on locally sourced ingredients

CHAPTER NINETEEN

Friday's Notte Italiana

Antipasti: Bruschetta with tomato jam and fresh mozzarella

Pasta: Fettuccine Alfredo

Prepared table-side by Master Chef Custer Wells

Secondi: Clams simmered in garlic broth

Contorni: Greens with parmesan crisps

Dolci: Ice cream topped with rosé balsamic vinegar

In Italy, food is an expression of love.
*— **Joe Bastianich**, restaurateur*

* * *

We gathered around the window ledge where Crystal had placed the menorah. She held a matchbook in her hand. "Ready?"

"Yes," Glenn said, "Please."

"Praised be thou, O Lord our God, ruler of the universe, who has ordained that we kindle the lights of Hanukkah. Amen."

"Amen," Glenn, Custer, and I said in unison.

Crystal scratched the match alive. The candle flickered and glowed, and I felt as if my holiday meter nudged up another notch.

"Flip the sign, Crys," Custer said. He turned to walk back to the kitchen but stopped. He eyed the chalkboard. Hands on his hips, he said, "Crystal? What's with the master chef?"

"Isn't that what you call yourself?" she said tentatively.

"Absolutely not."

Crystal flipped the door sign to 'open' and said softly, "It's only a matter of time."

"Would you like me to erase it, son?" Glenn said.

"Yes. Thank you."

Chapter Twenty

Our only new addition to the staff after the expansion was Nathan McFeeley, a bartender from a nearby restaurant who had been looking for better hours and bigger tips. Nathan was an easy-going, fresh-faced graduate from college who was struggling to pay off his student loans. His Negronis had become very popular with the regulars, and he was always willing to pitch in when the rest of us got overwhelmed. Of Irish descent, he had been blessed with a head of thick red hair that he could never quite tame.

"Sorry I'm late," Nathan said as he entered the restaurant carrying a large bag of ice. "Anything I need to know?"

"I found those ice cube trays you wanted, you know, the ones that make the big square cubes?"

"Terrific. See, now I'm like Custer, elevating my cocktails."

I tossed him an apron. "Is he getting under your skin too?"

"Nah." He dumped the ice into the freezer under the bar. "Not really. I mean, just between you and me, he's got enough ego for all five of us, but he's a good guy. We're cool."

Which will make tonight all the more interesting, I thought to myself.

* * *

Glenn escorted a family of four to a table. I noticed several other groups of people reading the menu posted in the window. I quickly placed a reserved sign in front of the chair at the end. Tyler had been making a habit of spending his Friday dinners with me at the café. Once the animals were tucked in and the chores done for the day at the farm, he would shower at home and arrive at the café close to opening. Although we didn't take reservations, this was my one exception. I wanted him to be as close to me as possible, so the seat at the end was officially Tyler's on Friday nights.

Glenn approached, his iPad in hand.

"Any orders for the fettuccine yet?" I said.

"You bet. I hope Custer is up for this."

Custer was at the stove adding butter and parmesan to a pot of pasta water. He whisked vigorously. I noticed his signature bandana was history, and he had combed his hair. The cuffs of his chef's jacket were perfectly folded, not a stain on the cloth.

"Did you see we already have an order for the pasta?"

"Yes, boss." He tasted the sauce and dropped the spoon in the sink. "So how does this work again? I put the pasta in a big bowl, pour in the sauce, and toss it?"

"Dramatically," I reminded. "*Con Gusto*!"

Chapter Twenty-One

Now that the bar had been expanded, Nathan and I shared the space behind it. I made the nonalcoholic drinks, and he did the rest. So far, we had learned each other's habits and stepped out of one another's way as if it were choreographed.

Glenn placed a few dishes in the bin. "Gretchen just texted she's coming for dinner."

"Wonderful. I'll reserve the seat next to Tyler. He loves Gretchen."

I looked up to see Tyler by the door, chatting with Crystal. She laughed and handed him a menu. He looked up, and our eyes met. More butterflies.

Settled on the bar chair, he combed his hands through his hair and picked up the menu. "What am I eating tonight, Rosalie?"

"I suggest the five-course Italian dinner."

"Well, that was easy." He set the menu down and rested his elbows on the bar.

"Have you noticed anything different about Bini lately?" I said.

"You mean, why is she texting and not cleaning out the chicken coop?"

"Maybe there's a guy." I smiled.

"I signed her up for a cheese-making class on Wednesday nights. Did all of this start up yesterday?"

"Oh, my goodness. Maybe she met someone in the class. This is so exciting."

"For Bini. Not the farm."

"She's in the infatuation phase. Let her enjoy it. Red wine?"

"Affirmative."

"Nathan? We need a bottle of Alessa's pinot noir." My phone flashed. Custer was ready for the cart. I noticed Gretchen at the door. Born and raised in England, she was a petite woman who had married an American and moved to the States at a young age. Much like Glenn, she had a long and happy run at marriage. A perpetual smile on her face; it was as if she cherished every moment of life, always up for the next adventure.

Her historic inn on the edge of town was almost always fully booked, but she never once complained about the workload. I know people who practiced gratitude, but Gretchen was a pro. After having both lost their spouses of over forty years, Glenn and Gretchen were slow to enter another relationship. Once Glenn finally agreed to an evening at her inn, the deal was sealed when Glenn admired photos of Gretchen and her husband. Gretchen poured wine, and they sat for hours talking about the happy lives and loves they once had. All awkwardness was eliminated, and it was no longer about betraying their previous loves, but about celebrating they each had wonderful lives.

"Life is for living," Gretchen had said at the end of the night, and they had been doing just that ever since.

I motioned her to the chair next to Tyler and set another place mat and two wine glasses on the bar. "Be right back."

Custer held the door while I wheeled in the cart. "How many?" I said.

"Entire table of four ordered the fettuccine."

We pushed the cart through the door, and Glenn said, "Table seven."

I returned to the bar as Custer made his way to the patrons. Glenn joined me. As Gretchen slipped out of her coat, she said, "What's going on?"

Tyler watched as his nephew put the brake on the cart. "I have no idea."

"Read your menu insert," I said.

Two young couples smiled as Custer approached. One of the men dressed in a thick sweater rubbed his hands together. "This is going to be great."

Custer looked around the room. All eyes were on him. He seemed nervous, fidgety. He didn't greet the couple and kept rolling his shoulders back and moving his head side to side as if trying to crack his neck. At last, he poured the butter and cheese onto the pasta and tossed. I could see he was trying to be dramatic, but at one point, he flung the noodles too high, and a large dollop landed on the floor. After that, he treated it more like a salad. He served the couple, shaved some extra parmesan on the pasta, and returned to the kitchen.

I took a deep breath, feeling I never should have pushed Custer to perform. He did his magic in the kitchen with no audience, alone with his muse to inspire him. He was a lot like a writer, spending endless hours perfecting their craft, but rarely face-to-face with the consumers of their art.

"He'll do better next time," Crystal said.

"I'm sure it will still taste amazing." I rubbed my arms.

Nathan stood next to me, a dish towel on his shoulder. "That wasn't supposed to happen, was it?

"No." I looked at Tyler. "I'm sorry. I humiliated your nephew."

"No, you didn't."

"It's a restaurant," Gretchen said. "Things get messy." She sipped her wine. "Oh," she said, "this wine is hunky dory."

"I'll second that," Tyler said. "Hunky dory."

"I'm going to check on Custer."

* * *

Custer's palms were flat on the counter, his head low.

"Hey," I said to his back. "Would you like me to serve the pasta? I don't mind. Or maybe we should just plate it. No drama."

Without moving a muscle, he said through clenched teeth, "Do you think I would be standing here if I gave up every time I failed?"

I swallowed. "No, of course not. I'm just thinking it may have been a silly idea of mine."

Raised in a dysfunctional home, Custer had often turned to philosophers, such as Lao Tzu, to guide him. It wasn't always his first response, but once he could find his center, he allowed the feelings to wash over him and regained his composure.

I waited, hoping he would find his way this time.

"I will continue to serve the pasta." His back heaved in a deep sigh. "A man is not finished when he is defeated. He is defeated when he quits." He turned around.

"Custer, I don't know if you've realized what I've been trying to do lately, but I believe each meal has its own narrative. I want that to be our focus with our menus—give everything another layer of depth." I closed my eyes for a moment, trying to form my words the right way. "Does that make sense to you?"

"Of course. It's one of the reasons I came back here. I may not say it, but I learn from you, Rosalie. Sometimes, I have to remember to let it in. That I don't know everything."

"You're a talent," I said. "And I'm thrilled you came back. We are creating something special. We've both studied with masters of our craft these past few months. And we are trying to give our customers a meal that is both nourishing and satisfying to their hearts and souls."

Custer closed his eyes and nodded. "Agreed," he said softly.

Glenn opened the door partway. "We have an adorable family waiting for some pasta—eager parents with two fresh-faced daughters." He caught my eye. "I hope I haven't interrupted anything."

Custer rolled his shoulders back. "Your timing is perfect, Mr. Glenn. How do you do that?"

"I'm not sure what I've done." He chuckled. "But I'm glad I did."

"You are always the perfect segue." Custer gazed over at me. "Thanks, boss. You want to whip up a couple of salads?"

Chapter Twenty-Two

Custer re-emerged from the kitchen, and I followed.

"Hey, Crys," he said. Can you cut the Bocelli for a sec?"

"Um, Okay?"

Custer looked down at his phone and punched it a few times with his thumb. *Bella Notte,* the song from *Lady and Tramp,* resounded through the restaurant.

Tyler caught my eye and mouthed, "Now what?"

The two young girls seated at the table grinned up at Custer as he approached. Hands tucked in their laps, their eyes grew wide as he added the butter and cheese sauce to the pasta.

"*Buonasera,* ladies," he said with flair.

They giggled.

Custer pushed up his sleeves and picked up a large wooden spoon and fork. He paused for a moment—I was pretty sure he was finding his zen—and began to blend the ingredients.

"Ladies? This is the *speciale* of the evening. Only the best for you," he said in a respectable Italian accent. He lifted the noodles high into the air, twisted his wrist, and they dropped perfectly into the bowl.

And they call it bella notte

He moved to the music, shifting from foot to foot, grinding his hips now and then. The family was transfixed.

"Crystal," he called.

"Now what?" she crossed her arms.

"It is time to taste the pasta. Come hither."

"Do you know about this?" she said to me.

"Not a clue."

Crystal sauntered over to the table, arms still crossed. The violins crescendoed.

"Ladies," Custer said. "We must taste it to ensure it is *perfetto*." He picked up a fettuccine noodle and put one end in his mouth. He motioned Crystal closer and put the other end between her lips. He began to pull the noodle into his mouth, eating as he went. With what appeared to be instinct, Crystal did the same from the other end. Their recent competitiveness kicked into full gear as they raced to get to the middle. When their lips met, Custer took the last bite and backed up.

The entire restaurant burst into applause. Gretchen was on her feet. Custer bowed dramatically, and Crystal curtsied, holding the sides of her small apron.

Bella Notte, indeed, I thought. Chef Alfredo would have approved.

Chapter Twenty-Three

Glenn and I agreed to meet at his house Saturday morning. Neil's request for Glenn to check up on things in his father's house was a perfect opportunity for us to do a little sleuthing.

Waterside Village, Glenn's development, was relatively new, located on what was once farmland on the outskirts of town. The homes were modest but tasteful, all of a similar design, with a variety of subdued color schemes.

When Glenn was nearing retirement, he and Molly, who had resided in Philly their entire marriage, had decided to take a leisurely drive to Cardigan, Maryland, one weekend. They fell instantly in love with this quaint, historic community. So much so that Molly suggested they make it their retirement destination. According to Glenn, she had always wanted a small sailboat and dreamed of joining the yacht club and having a sunset cocktail cruise every chance they could. They put a down payment on the house in Waterside Village the next day. Molly died from breast cancer before the closing.

After having lost his rudder when his wife passed so suddenly, Glenn did the only thing he could think to do and moved to the house in Cardigan. There were no sailboats or cocktail cruises on the river, but Glenn was doing his best to reinvent his life.

"Good morning, my dear," he said. "How are you feeling after last night?"

"Tired but ecstatic. What a night."

"Please, come in. I was just cleaning up in the kitchen."

Despite the small size of Glenn's home, it felt spacious and open. Not many furnishings other than a dining room table and a modest set of living room furniture, it was clear the majority of Glenn's time was spent in a recliner facing a mounted television, a remote, and a large stack of books on the side table topped with a spare set of spectacles.

On my way into the kitchen, I passed a credenza in the dining room that sported pictures of Glenn's children, grandchildren, and Molly. I stopped and inspected one from their wedding day. Glenn was gazing at Molly as if he couldn't believe his good fortune.

"Glenn?" I said. "What are your sons doing for Christmas?"

He stood in the archway between the two rooms, a sponge in his hand. "It's my off year. Theodore and Bennet are spending Christmas with their wives' families."

"So, will you host them here next year?"

He shook his head. "I always go to them. I arrive on Christmas day and leave early the next morning."

"Mary from A Well-loved Home said, when it comes to the holidays, gift cards and cruises are the only way to go."

"It's cash and chianti for me." He paused. "They get the cash, and I drink the chianti."

* * *

I hugged myself against the cold while Glenn searched for Bill's house key. The icy wind flapped the grill cover, and Glenn had to snatch it before it blew away.

"Let me hold that while you look," I said.

Glenn lifted the lid. "If you were a key, where would you hide?"

Another gust of wind fluttered the navy and white striped awning over Bill's patio. "Maybe it's in one of those magnetic boxes."

He passed his hands underneath the metal shelf. "Ah. I've always said you were a genius."

"Back door?"

"That's my guess. You know, Rosalie, Neil didn't seem to know many details about his father's home. He barely remembered where the key was located."

"I wonder how close they were." I clutched the cover.

"My guess is there was a distance between them." Opening the screen door, Glenn said, "I'd never met Neil before Thursday. He certainly didn't seem to visit very often." He pushed the door open. "If at all."

Glenn stepped into the house while I fought the wind to cover the grill. I was losing. "Oh," I said when the corner smacked my nose.

"Are you coming inside—" Glenn peered out. "Oh, my dear," he said and hurried to my aid.

"There," I said once we secured it in place. I exhaled. "Shall we?"

Bill's kitchen was spotless. Not a dish, crumb, or dirty spoon to be seen.

"There's a moldy lemon somewhere," I said.

"Maybe we should look around a bit before we clean up."

"I like that idea. Can I turn up the heat?"

"And I like that idea."

Bill's house was a mirror image of Glenn's but with higher-end furnishings. What looked to be original artwork adorned the walls. His television was massive, with speakers in all four corners of the room.

"You have an office, don't you, Glenn?"

"My second bedroom is my office, yes."

I passed a powder room and entered a small hallway. "I'm going to check in there. Do you think that's okay?"

Glenn stood behind me. "Neil asked us to look in on things. I'm sure he meant the bedrooms as well. Could be a leaky pipe for all we know."

"And if something happens to fall open, like a drawer or file, I'm just helping out, right?"

"Of course. I'll inspect the master bedroom." He stepped around me. "This place is immaculate. I wonder if he has a housekeeper. And, I wonder if he or she has any openings."

"Not to be maudlin, but they do now."

"Mm. Yes. I hadn't thought of it that way." He adjusted his glasses. "Too soon?"

"Perhaps."

The second bedroom was indeed Bill's office. A large antique desk spread along one wall, a leather chair in each corner with a shared ottoman. Sitting in his desk chair, I sat back and folded my hands in my lap, wondering what sort of secrets this man may have harbored. And more importantly, if any of them would lead us to the killer.

Tilting my head, I read the labels of the files in a leather sorting rack: paid bills, bills to be paid, banking, taxes, Morgan Stanley. The slot for bills to pay was empty. Not surprising. It seemed this man was careful to dot his i's and cross all of his t's and probably always had backup toilet paper. I thought for a moment and removed the stack of banking papers, surprised to see he hadn't gone paperless. Scanning the most recent statement, I noted Bill Rutherford had several automatic payments: mortgage, car payment, utilities, insurance, and a five thousand dollar payment to Michelle Belle. I checked the month before, and there it was again. Five thousand dollars to Michelle Belle.

I found Glenn in the bedroom, opening and closing drawers. A large Peloton towered in the corner of the room.

"Find anything?" I said.

He pointed to a wall behind the door. "Take a look at this."

I stepped into the room. The entire surface was covered with framed photos of Bill with medals around his neck, running through finish line tape, awards, diplomas, newspaper articles.

"In the business world, we call this a 'love me' wall, " Glenn said.

"Looks like he ran a couple of marathons. Have you found anything else?"

"Medicine cabinet contained Viagra, steroids, melatonin, a statin, and hair dye."

"No condoms?" I said.

"Those are usually kept in a nightstand."

"Glenn, I think he knew about Summer. I found—"

He placed his hand on my forearm. "Did you hear something?"

I listened. A floorboard creak. My eyes widened. "Should we hide?" I whispered. "What if it's the killer?"

I hovered behind Glenn and followed him into the hallway. A very tan and thin woman stood in the middle of the living room.

"Oh!" she screamed. "I didn't know anyone was in here." She placed her hand over her heart. "You scared me half to death."

"Abigail, what are you doing?"

"Well, the door was open and—"

"And how exactly did you know it was unlocked?"

She shrugged. "I turned the knob. Anyway, I just thought I'd check on things." She took a deep breath and flashed Glenn a twitchy smile. "And you can call me Abby. I thought you knew that." She adjusted her spandex jacket. "And what exactly are you doing here?"

"Bill's son has asked us to check on things. Which is why I really don't think you should be here, Abigail. I'll escort you to the door."

She tried to step past him. "I just need to go in the office for a moment. I think I left something in there."

Glenn and I exchanged an interested glance. He blocked her way. "I can't let you do that. I'll tell Neil you have something here, but that's it."

Her eyes darted around the room. "I won't be but a minute."

I stood next to Glenn, hands on my hips. "Sorry, Abigail."

She narrowed her eyes at me, then turned to Glenn. "I understand you are helping a friend. That's very kind of you. If you would ask his son if I could come in for my things sometime, that would be lovely. Where do you keep the key?"

I noticed her false eyelashes as she batted her eyes at Glenn.

"In my pocket."

She sighed dramatically. "So hard to get, aren't you? Maybe I'll stop in and see you at the café. Butter you up. Oh, and please, call me Abby. You know, Abby the Fitness Angel?" She turned and walked toward the door, slowing at times to look around. Once in the kitchen, she ducked out of sight. I heard a drawer open and close. Glenn started after her, but she was already at the door.

"Toodles," she called. "Follow me on Instagram."

Glenn flipped the deadbolt. "What was that about?" he said, sounding disgusted.

"I don't know, but we need to find out."

"Did you see anything in the office that might belong to her?"

"No."

Glenn checked his watch. "I know we need to get to work. Let's do a quick clean-up and discuss our next move." He started for the kitchen but stopped. "You said something about Bill knowing he had a daughter. What did you find?"

"Do you know a Michelle Belle?"

"No. Why?"

"Remember Summer said her mother's name was Michelle? Bill Rutherford deposited five thousand dollars in a Michelle Belle's bank account every month. I think she might be Summer's mother."

"But Summer didn't know who her father was until a month ago."

"Glenn, is it possible her mother didn't want Summer to know about the money? And that maybe she kept it for herself?"

Chapter Twenty-Four

Glenn and I emptied the refrigerator and turned down the heat. While he was ensuring the outside water had been shut off, I carried the last trash bag out to the garage. Bill drove a charcoal gray Tesla. The plug was still in the charging station. I walked over to unplug it but wondered if that was a good idea. Deciding to leave it plugged in, I turned and noticed a stack of Pro-V 1 golf balls on a shelf. The sheriff had said Bill played with the same three partners every Sunday. He was riding his bike home from the country club when he was murdered, most likely after a round of golf.

I found Glenn in the kitchen. "I'll roll the trash out on Thursday." He looked over at me. "What's gotten into you?"

"Do you belong to the country club?"

"No, I've considered it, but now that the café is up and running again, we seem to be plenty busy." He scratched his nose. "Let's hear it."

"We have to find a way to get into the country club Sunday afternoon. I want to meet his golfing friends. I would imagine they will still play Sunday, even though Bill is gone. We need to find someone to get us in there." I combed my hands through my hair. "Gretchen?"

"I don't believe she's a member."

Rubbing my forehead, I said, "I've got it!"

"Who, my dear?

"Janice. Of course! I'll call her on my way to the café. Oh, are you free tomorrow afternoon?"

"Gretchen and I have plans to spend some time together. Her inn is on the candlelight historic house tour this season, and she finally has a moment to spare tomorrow."

"That's wonderful. You two deserve it. I'll take notes."

"Rosalie?"

"Yes?"

"Do you think the sheriff has told Neil his father was murdered? So far, the paper is calling it a hit-and-run. But shouldn't Neil know how his father died?"

"Could the sheriff be keeping it quiet for some reason?"

Glenn pulled on his jacket. "If he is truly conducting an investigation, shouldn't Neil at least be ruled out? Alibi, that kind of thing? Murders are often committed by the people closest to the victim. He or she would know Bill's habits well enough to find him on his bike at 5:30 on a Sunday evening."

"Maybe if Neil is a suspect, the sheriff doesn't want him to know just yet. That maybe he'll slip up somehow." I put my hands on my hips. "So much to think about. Let's meet up Monday or Tuesday morning. Hopefully, Janice will be free to take me to the club, and I'll have news. And I'll also invite," I paused, still uncomfortable with our new phraseology, "*Joe*, to have coffee with us." I buttoned my coat. "Oh, and Glenn?"

"Yes?"

"Perhaps you shouldn't keep the key under the grill."

"Not a chance."

Chapter Twenty-Five

On Sunday afternoon, I pulled my car into a slot in the Cardigan Yacht and Country Club parking lot. The horizon glowed a pinkish yellow as the Earth turned away from the sun. A pin flag whipped back and forth on a nearby green. I pulled my coat tighter around me.

There weren't many cars. Who would be playing golf on a day like today? Which dashed my hopes a bit that I was going to learn something. I started for the door but stopped. If Bill's golfing partners were here, maybe I might find some bumper damage.

I walked through the grass, inspecting the front of each car. I found a few crooked license plates and scratched fenders, but nothing indicating a collision with a man on his bike. I wondered how much damage that would cause to a hefty vehicle? Would there even be a dent? Maybe just a black smudge from the tire?

"What in the heck are you doing?" Janice called from the front door of the club. "It's freezing out there."

When I reached Janice and hurried in the door, she said, "You got to know the rules around here."

"No sneakers or jeans?"

Janice pointed to her legs and feet. She wore denim pants and high-top sneakers. "That ain't it." We stepped into a large lobby with a crystal chandelier overhead. "Number three," she said softly, "be nice to Fi, the bartender, or she won't wait on you. Two, don't use the bathroom in the pool house; there's a weird security camera in there. And three? Don't mess with a Langford."

"What's a Langford?"

"One of the oldest families in Devon County. And they rule this place."

I nodded. "Don't mess with a Langford. Got it."

* * *

Janice escorted me to a room overlooking the Cardigan River. A large, U-shaped bar made of a rich, glossy wood dominated the space. "You want to sit at the bar or a table?" she said.

I scanned the room. A few of the tables were occupied with people watching football. Several men were scattered around the bar, all in seasonal golf attire. "Let's sit at the bar." I looked back at Janice. "You're really allowed to wear jeans in here?"

She rolled her eyes. "It's a 'country' country club. You don't have to have buckets of dough to belong, and they will do anything to keep people coming during the winter months. So, the dress code is shoes and shirts. Oh, and no hats." She watched as I slipped out of my coat. "You look like you work here."

"I didn't have time to change after brunch. Do I smell like cinnamon muffins?"

She scrunched up her nose. "Bacon. It's making me hungry."

I draped my coat over the back of the chair and sat down. "This place is nice. I like a big bar."

She plopped down on the tall chair next to mine. "What are we doing here anyway? You looking to join?"

"Curious is all."

Janice frowned. "Not your best trait."

"Sometimes it actually is." I clasped my hands. "Besides, I'm too old to change."

"Getting old isn't what will make you change your ways. Getting yourself in a pickle will do it. Just don't do it here. My family has belonged to this club for two generations. Don't screw it up."

"I would never do that, Snow White. You at least know me better than that."

She exhaled. "I do. I definitely do." She rubbed her hands together. "Okay, then, let's have some fun. You and me out on the town. No husbands, boyfriends, cops, losers, just us."

A woman who looked to be in her early thirties approached. She had a nice smile and short, strawberry-blond hair. "Hey, Miss Janice. Vodka tonic?"

"What are we having, Rose Red?"

"Do you have a nice champagne?"

"Of course. You guys want to split a bottle? If you don't finish it, you can always take it home."

Janice slapped her hand on the bar. "Done. Thanks, Fi."

Fi looked at me. "Are you new?"

"A friend. I'm Rosalie."

"Hi, Rosalie. Welcome." She placed two square napkins on the bar and walked away.

A man dressed in what appeared to be the country club uniform, Black shirt and pants walked up to us. "Welcome to the Cardigan River Yacht and Country Club." He placed a manila envelope in front of me.

"What the heck are you doing, Mason?" Janice said. "Rosalie is my guest."

"I'm giving her a membership application. Our numbers are down."

My mouth dropped open. Down by one as of only a week ago.

He wedged himself between us and removed the application from the folder. "Right now, there's no initiation fee. And if Janice recommends you, that's all you need. You can ignore all the other requirements." He peered at me over his glasses.

"Thank you," I said.

"So? Are you going to apply for a membership?"

"I'm just now delivering their first drink," Fi said. "Cool your jets, Mason. You gotta quota or something?"

"No. It's just our numbers are down."

"You mentioned that," Janice said. "Instead of forcing that down her throat, why don't you focus on being hospitable? You know, sell the place."

"I'll just take this home for now," I said and moved the envelope to the side.

The cork popped. "It would actually be cool if you joined, Rose Red. Maybe we could take up golf."

While Fi expertly filled our glasses, I looked around at the other members seated at the bar. Two men were hunched over martinis. "Do you know those guys?" I said to Janice.

"Of course. It's Cardigan." Janice lifted her glass. "Cheers to Rose Red. My first bestie."

I clinked my glass against hers. "Rose Red and Snow White. They loved each other dearly and agreed that they would never separate."

She slugged some champagne and set her glass on the bar. "I think you should join. And no initiation fee is rare. We could have a girls' night out every week."

"I wonder if Tyler would come here with me."

"That man would follow you anywhere."

"I'll consider it. Let's toast to that." After another sip, I said, "Janice, do you know Michelle Belle? I think she works at the Marina."

"Michelle Belle?" Her lips twitched to one side. "Oh, you mean Micky B.?"

"That could be her."

"That's all I've ever known her as. She used to work at the marina here, but now she's out at Bayside. They have a restaurant, so she's got a full-time job." Janice took another sip. "You ever been out to Bayside? It's right on the Chesapeake. Great views. In the summer, boaters anchor out, and apparently, Micky wades through the water and delivers the drinks. She wears a bikini top and short shorts and lets the big tippers slide the money in her top. You don't want to know how many women despise her."

"Do you know her daughter?"

"Goth girl? Yeah, she's actually a pretty good kid. She keeps a low profile. No dad in her life. Crazy thing is, Micky has a really nice house next to the college. Nobody can figure out how she can afford it. Why do you want to know about the Belles? Wait," Janice narrowed her eyes, "are you and Glenn trying to figure something out again?"

"Did you hear about Bill Rutherford?"

"Oh, yeah. That was pretty awful. Did they ever figure out what happened?"

"He was hit by a car. No one has come forward."

"So I'm helping you, right? Am I on the team?"

"You are definitely on the team."

"Oh, I know something about Goth girl. I heard she's working at Birdie's now."

"Birdie's Shoe Store? I had no idea."

"That's just what I heard." Janice looked over her shoulder. "Oh, hey, Jen Sommers is in the dining room. She's taking my Tanner to the Baltimore Aquarium next weekend, and he wants to stay overnight at their house." Janice wiped her mouth with the back of her hand. "Jen has like five billion cats, and Tanner is allergic."

"How do you know he's allergic if you don't have cats?"

"He held a kitten once. Put it up to his face, you know, on his cheek? Within a minute, his eye had swollen shut, and his cheek was beet red. I said, Tanner, why'd you put that kitten on your face? And he said it's just so cute. I couldn't help it.

"Which is why I need to warn Jen. He's going to pick up one of her cats. I know it. He can't help himself. She's going to need a stock of Benadryl. I'll be back."

I sipped my champagne and stole a glance at the two men. The closest one was staring at me.

"You new?" He wore a navy V-neck windbreaker with the Cardigan Yacht and Country Club logo embroidered in red and white thread.

"I'm a friend of Janice's." I set my glass down. "Did you play a round of golf today?"

The man, whose face was red, most likely from the cold, had a large, shiny forehead and a friendly smile. He glanced at the guy beside him. "Every Sunday we can."

"It's a little windy."

He finished his martini and nudged his empty glass toward Fi. She seemed to know he was ready for another. "Sometimes the wind works with you, and sometimes it doesn't. Name's Patrick, by the way. Patrick Delaney."

"I'm Rosalie." I centered my glass on my napkin. "Can I ask you something? When you play golf at least once a week, do you get better? Does your game keep improving?"

"Ha!" said the guy next to him.

"This is Gunther Langford. He's laughing because the game of golf is a curse and a gift, all at the same time."

Langford? Rule number one: don't mess with a Langford. I cleared my throat. "How so?"

"You see," Patrick said, "when your drive is soaring 300 yards in a line so straight it feels as if it's taking your heart right along with it, that most certainly means you are going to four-putt. It's just how it is. And then the next time out, you spend twenty minutes on the putting green, and you are hitting two putts at the most. But your drive?"

"Not so straight?"

"Shanking every time as if it has a mind of its own."

"He speaks the truth," Gunther said.

"So why do you play?"

"Here's the irony," Patrick said, pushing up the sleeves of his windbreaker, "to get better, like you said. Sometimes, I want to throw my clubs in a water hazard because I just seem to be getting worse. But then you hit one of those drives I was talking about? And you know you'll be back next time for sure. You come back for that feeling. There's nothing better."

Gunther leaned in. "My wife walks the course with her friends three times a week. She says it's because of the three F's."

"I'm listening."

"Fun, fitness, and fashion."

I smiled. "Now I'm beginning to understand." I crossed my legs. "A friend of mine's neighbor played here every Sunday. He got hit by a car last week. Did you know him?"

"You mean Bill?" Gunther said with a grunt. Tall and fit with a thick head of dark hair streaked with silver, Gunther had an intensity about him that was unnerving. Don't mess with a Langford. Duly noted.

"Yes, that's his name," I said. "Bill Rutherford. My friend had noticed he didn't come home that night."

"He was our fourth," Patrick said. "It felt pretty weird today without him. We toasted to him a bit ago. It's all sort of surreal that the guy's really gone."

"Where's your third?" I said.

"Jonesy had to take care of some things," Patrick said, and I appreciated his friendly, talkative manner. Meanwhile, Gunther simply glared at me. "Jonesy said something about hitting a deer and getting his SUV in the shop."

Jonesy, I made a mental note: SUV in the shop. "So you played with Bill every Sunday? You must have liked him very much."

"Bah," Gunther said. "Guy cheated. I don't miss him one bit."

I took a small sip. "What do you mean he cheated?"

"He fluffed his ball," Patrick said. "You know, bettered his lie? That's cheating."

"We bet on every game we played," Gunther barked. "You don't fluff your ball when there's money on the line." He slid his glass toward Fi. "I saw him kick his ball out of the trap once. He didn't think I saw him, but I did." He looked over at me, eyes tensed. "I never understood why he rode that damn bike every Sunday. I know he was an athlete and all, but River Road is treacherous. There's no shoulder. It was just sheer stupidity." Gunther shook his head. "He had this arrogance about him, assuming drivers would make way. I saw him riding down the white line one time, and there was another car coming." Fi picked up his glass. "But that's how he was. In your face, you know? Like everyone had to yield to his force."

"Bad round, Gunther?" Janice had returned to her seat.

"We've been talking about Bill Rutherford," I said. "This is their first time playing without him."

Patrick shook his head. "I'm not saying I miss him. Gunther's right; he was a cheater. And a boaster, for that matter. It's just, well, he didn't have to die that way."

"Oh," Gunther said, "remember how every time he walked into the bar, he'd say, 'I'm only having one drink.' He'd make this big announcement like anybody cared what he did. He thought it was funny."

"And? Did he only have one drink?" I said, hands on the base of my glass.

The men exchanged a glance and rolled their eyes.

"Hey, this is a great party," Janice said. "This is my friend's first time at the club, and you guys are talking about a guy who got hit by a car. Straighten up. Show the girl a good time."

"Janice," I said. "It's okay. We've also been talking about golf. And I'm learning some things."

"Also about how Bill cheated," Gunther added. "He fluffed his ball."

"You got any snacks, Fi? Maybe some of that party mix?" Janice refilled our glasses. "So why did you guys play with him every week if he was such a pain in the butt?"

"Because we always won the annual tournament," Patrick said.

"And he never hesitated to buy a round," Gunther added. "But that was only because he wanted people to," he made air quotation marks, "*like* him."

"Well, there's a redeeming quality." Janice looked at me. "For the record, you two, I was hoping Rosalie would join. You'd like that, right?"

Patrick mumbled a yes, of course, nodding his head, eyes averted from Janice's scolding gaze. Gunther said nothing.

Fi set a wooden bowl filled with pretzels and small cheese crackers in front of us. Janice scooped up a palmful. She lowered her voice, "You get what you came for?"

"I believe I did."

Chapter Twenty-Six

As I sat at the kitchen table the next morning, Sweeney Todd, my adopted Maine Coon cat, leapt upon it, bunching up the tablecloth, barely able to stop himself from sliding off the other side. "Whoa there, tiger," I said and scratched under his chin. I unfolded yesterday's *Post*, and Sweeney immediately settled himself on the headlines.

Tyler arrived soon after. I still hadn't read a word, but I was enjoying watching the morning sun struggle to reveal itself through a heavy veil of clouds.

"Hey," he said and kissed the top of my head. "What's on tap for you today?" He walked over to the sink, wearing a thick fleece-lined denim jacket, his boots heavy on the floor.

"Annie is in Chevy Chase. She drove up last night."

He opened the sugar canister. "When do they leave for Dubai?"

"Tomorrow." Sweeney's swishing tail tickled my arm. We were both intently focused on Tyler's back.

When he finally turned around, he said, "You two look like you're about to snatch up a defenseless songbird."

"I'm thinking, is all. And Sweeney is waiting for you to acknowledge him."

He gripped his mug. "Do I want to know what you're thinking?"

"I might drive over to see Annie before she goes. Maybe take her out to dinner."

"What's stopping you? That's a terrific idea. I'd go with you, but the water heater in the goat barn isn't working right. With these temps, they can't go without water."

"You would go with me?" I smiled, feeling touched by his offer. "Have you ever even met Ed?"

"Nope." He downed his coffee and set the mug in the sink. "But I know for sure he's a fool." He winked and strode out of the room.

Chapter Twenty-Seven

For some reason, I still agonized over my appearance whenever I was about to see my ex-husband. And I didn't understand why. There were no more flutters or pangs of longing when I saw him, like there were those first few months after we separated. Why did I always want to look my best when we had an encounter?

The first time my parents met Ed, we were both students at the University of Virginia. Ed, a senior, had been busy deciding his future. He had applied to several MBA programs and interviewed on campus with high-end corporations as backup. In my sophomore year, I was blissfully happy living away from home, but had recently been addled with worry about what would happen to Ed and me once he graduated. I helped him with his applications, ironed his shirts for interviews, but he never once mentioned what part I would play in his life when he left UVA.

The kitchen of my family's farmhouse smelled of simmering onions. My mother greeted us warmly. After introductions, Ed, in his Beta Theta Pi polo shirt and khakis, me in a shift dress, put his arm around my shoulder and said, "I sure like your daughter, Emily." He smiled at me, his blue eyes twinkling, "and she sure is pretty." He gave my shoulder a small squeeze.

My mother bristled. "While I agree with you, there is a lot more to my daughter than being pretty."

I immediately tensed, filled with worry the day was going to be a complete disaster.

"Well, let's just say the first time I approached her wasn't because of, how do you say it...her substance?" He grinned. "Just sayin'."

CHAPTER TWENTY-SEVEN

The rest of the visit was more of the same. My father continued working on the farm until after sundown, leaving most of the afternoon with just Ed, my mother, and me. After the first thirty minutes, Ed had asked for a vodka tonic, and my mother, who wasn't much of a drinker, matched him drink for drink. I wasn't quite twenty-one, but was permitted one glass of red wine. At least, at first. As Ed continued singing his own praises, his hand possessively on my leg, my mother slid the whole bottle over to me.

By the time my father joined us, he eyed my mother. "Everything alright, Em?"

"Yes, of course."

"We having onions for dinner?"

"Oh, my. Well, they will certainly be caramelized." She stood. "Why don't you sit, and I'll make you a drink. Rosalie? Help me get dinner together?"

"Yes." I jumped up. "We should do that."

Ed had been perplexed on the drive back to Charlottesville. "I don't think that went so well. I'm not sure why. All I wanted to do was show them I'm a good match for you."

I eyed him, not quite sure how to respond. I clasped my hands in my lap and said, "My parents raised Oliver and me to believe the best kind of person has equal parts confidence and humility. We were raised to have both but to only *talk* about one."

"Ah, I see. Not enough humility? I wanted them to know I would be a good provider. Just in case, well—" He pushed on his flashers and pulled over along the highway. His eyes glowed in the dim light of the dashboard. He turned to face me. "In case you would marry me."

In his defense, Ed came from a family who valued accomplishments over cozy dinners and had spent his life endeavoring to make his parents proud. Seeing that my family wasn't a bit curious about his GPA, he began to view me differently, in a good way. That maybe I would round him out a little, soften his rough, competitive edges. When Ed was accepted into the Wharton School of Business, we set the wedding date for June twenty-first, in two years, the month after we both graduated.

Once she accepted I was going to marry Ed, my mother, who felt it her job to find at least one good quality in everyone, was on a mission to discover things she and Ed could bond over. When she learned he loved puzzles, she saved the morning crossword for him and often had a jigsaw puzzle with the pieces sorted on the dining room table. During baseball season, she made sure to have the Phillies game on and learned everything she could about the team, catchers, pitchers, division standings. She even read *A Wealth of Nations,* and they discussed economics into the wee hours of the morning, a fire crackling nearby. Ed began to feel at home, and just as I predicted, the contentious side of him softened. Ed and my mother grew to love one another very much.

Chapter Twenty-Eight

I tugged an above-the-knee, black sweater dress over my head and smoothed my hair. I added a pale red gloss and mushed my lips together. A pair of heeled ankle boots and my mother's pearls were the finishing touches. After walking through a spritz of my go-to perfume, I made my way downstairs.

Tyler frowned when I walked into the kitchen. "You look…nice."

"Thank you." I rolled my shoulders back, a wee bit unsteady in the boots.

He sized me up, his brow furrowed. "Is all this," he gestured toward my outfit, "for Ed?"

"Honestly? I'm not sure. I've been asking myself the same question." I stepped closer to Tyler. "I promise, it's not what you think. You're the only man who gives me butterflies."

Hands on his hips, he said, "Then why?"

"Maybe because I don't want to give him any reason to say to himself, 'boy, did I do the right thing leaving her.'" I swallowed. "And it may not be logical or rational or what I should be thinking, but it just is." I looked up at him. "I make no claims on sanity."

"Thank you for the explanation." His eyes wandered down to my legs and back up my dress. "Just make sure you wear that dress the next time we have a date."

Once the front door clicked shut, I took a deep breath. Now there's the flutter and then some—an entire kaleidoscope of butterflies. And it had zero to do with Ed.

* * *

I pulled up to the curb in front of the white colonial house in Chevy Chase that had once been mine. I paused on the sidewalk to process the flood of memories washing through me. Annie at all different stages of life: learning to walk, ride a bike, and drive a car. The parties and picnics and candlelit dinners, my mother and Annie foraging for nature treasures in the backyard. But all that screeched to a halt when the most prevalent and miserable memory took center stage: the day Ed's phone bleeped, and I picked it up.

When he entered the room, I told him he had a text from someone named Rebecca and asked if she was the new lawyer his company had recently hired.

I flinched when he snatched his phone from me. "Did you read it?"

"Of course not. Ed?"

And then the confession: "I can't do this anymore."

I suppressed a shiver. It wasn't even five o'clock. But dusk had already settled over this quiet neighborhood, one of the things I liked least about December. I started toward the house and noticed what had to have been Ed's BMW 7 series in the drive. As I climbed the stairs, I remembered something my father always said when confronted with extravagance: 'We are our acquisitions.'

Annie opened the door and wrapped me in a bear hug. "Mom! It's so cool you came over."

"I had to see you before you flew halfway around the world." I noticed she was in sweatpants, her hair in a messy ponytail. "Am I overdressed?"

She closed the door behind me. "Is it okay if we eat here? I have so much packing left to do. And I hate all my bathing suits."

"Who doesn't hate all of their bathing suits?"

Although Annie shared many qualities with her father, including a drive to succeed and one of those GPAs, she was often called my mini-me. We had the same thick dark hair, brown eyes, and a tendency to giggle when we were together. She was an empath, just like her mother: feeling deep, loving hard, listening to learn whenever she could.

"Can I help you pack?"

"No, I want to hang out with you. Dad ordered Thai food. I hope that's okay. He said you liked green curry chicken."

"Thai food is definitely okay. And, yes, that's still my favorite."

I looked around the living room. Not much had changed. You would never know it was December. There wasn't a Christmas card or decoration in sight. Jazz music riffed in the background.

"This feels weird to say, Mom, but can I take your coat?"

"Um, yes, you can, and yes, that feels very weird. Why don't I just drape it over the sofa."

"Better idea."

"Oh, I have something for you." I held out a box tied with a red and green bow."

She opened it and picked up a small gold charm.

When Annie turned seven, I gave her a gold-linked bracelet on her birthday. I had been gifting her carefully chosen charms ever since—souvenirs, milestone birthdays, graduation, pets, even a round glass container filled with gold flakes after our cruise to Alaska.

"It's a Christmas tree," she said.

"I wanted you to take Christmas to Dubai."

"Are those little diamond chips?"

"Focus on the word chips, but, yes. You probably won't be able to get it on your bracelet in time. I'm not sure where you can keep it."

"Yeah, there aren't a whole lot of tools around here. But I love it." She kissed me on the cheek. "I guess this is as close as I'll get to spending Christmas with you." Annie brushed a tear away.

A lump formed in my throat.

"Hello, Rose."

I looked up to see Ed in the archway between the living room and kitchen. I wondered how long he'd been standing there.

"Hey," I said.

"You look nice. I do believe you are getting younger."

"We both know that's not true." There it was. The reason I dressed up.

His first comment was reliably about my appearance. I met his gaze. "I hope I'm not keeping you from getting ready for your trip."

"Of course not. I'm very glad you're here." He smiled. Ed had always been elegantly handsome. In his late forties, his hair had begun to gray in all the right places, enhancing his blue eyes. A starched white shirt collar peeked out of a navy cashmere sweater. He was in stylish jeans and worn Italian loafers.

I jumped when a loud knock rapped on the front door.

"Door dash, Dad."

Ed crossed the room. "Nice alliteration, kiddo."

We sat at the dining room table for our take-out dinner. The lights had been dimmed and candles lit. I wondered by whom. Instead of my usual place in the chair opposite Ed, I sat across from Annie. Ed dished out our dinners and distributed the plates. He ducked back into the kitchen and returned with a bottle of champagne.

"I thought we could celebrate Annie's twenty-first birthday. I know it was in September, but it's nice to all be together." He filled our glasses.

"That's what this trip is," Annie said. "My birthday gift."

I held up my glass. "To the best daughter in the entire universe."

"I'll drink to that," Ed said.

Annie blushed. "Thanks, guys."

I straightened my posture, feeling grateful and ridiculously uncomfortable at the same time. A guest in my own home, eating from the dishes I had selected years ago. It was all so familiar and yet foreign at the same time.

"You okay, Mom?"

"Yes," I said and had some more champagne.

"How is the café?" Ed said. "I still want to eat there one day."

I swallowed. "Busy, thank goodness."

"How is Custer doing now that he's been to culinary school?" Annie munched on a won ton chip.

"You okay talking about him?" I said.

"I guess. I mean, things were cooling before he went just because of the physical distance between us, but I still thought we were in a relationship. I definitely wasn't seeing anyone else."

"What happened?" Ed said, sounding genuinely interested. The last time we discussed Custer, he wanted Annie to break up with him immediately, for one, because he wasn't a student at Duke, and two, because he was my cook.

"When he first started the classes, he was texting me all the time, the dishes he was learning to make, all the cool techniques, that kind of thing. I was excited for him." Annie smoothed the napkin in her lap. "But then he started talking about Monique, the chef, how amazing she was. And I knew pretty early on that she wasn't just his teacher."

"He had an affair with the chef?" Ed said. "How old is she?"

"Do you know, Mom?"

"I'm pretty sure mid-forties."

"Like you," Ed said. "Annie's *mother*."

"Exactly," Annie said. "So, Mom, how's his cooking? Has he improved?"

"Well," I set my fork on the plate. "I would definitely say yes. He's very set on elevating the menu. Like topping the salmon with lobster. And his Ahi tuna sells out every time it's on the menu."

"Interesting," Ed said. "Are you having to charge more?"

"Soon, but the portions are so small, I don't know if that will fly in Cardigan. Don't get me wrong, his food is delicious, and the plating is gorgeous, like a piece of art, but I'm having to do a lot of reining in."

"I'll bet it all looks amazing," Annie said as she pushed some fried rice around her plate. "He's always been a very visual guy. Does he do swirls?"

"And dollops. But he did add kimchi to the grilled cheeses."

Annie looked up. "Um...ew?"

"I'm sorry he's done this, Annie," I said. "He could have been more straight with you. And, honestly, I don't know how much longer he'll stay at the Day Lily."

Ed picked up his glass. "Bigger fish to fry?"

I looked at Ed. "That was pretty good."

Annie giggled. "That was really good, Dad." And the three of us shared a heartwarming laugh.

Chapter Twenty-Nine

I didn't stay long, knowing I had a drive and they were most likely leaving early. Annie walked me to the door and stood in front of me, arms by her sides. "What do you think?"

I noticed a gold chain around her neck. "The charm. You found a necklace?"

"I think it's perfect. You?"

"A definite yes. It will be by your heart." We hugged, and there was no way to stop the tears from forming in my eyes. I stepped back and placed my hand on her cheek. "You be careful."

"I will." She sniffled. "It will be weird being so far away from you. Especially during the holidays."

I brushed a tear from her cheek. "Tell me something I don't already know."

"Mom, what will you do?"

"Tyler said something about a tree. And there's a chance Oliver will come down from New York."

"Uncle Oliver? Are you kidding me?" She stomped her foot. "I'm going to miss seeing him *again*?"

Ed cleared his throat. I looked up. He seemed pensive, his brow furrowed, hands behind his back.

"Thank you, Ed. I had fun."

"Can I have your car keys for a sec?"

"Um, okay." I fished them from my purse.

He went into the kitchen and returned with a fairly large cardboard box. "I went through the Christmas decorations in the attic. I'm pretty sure I found all of your family ornaments. I thought you might want them."

"I absolutely do. Thank you."

Annie said our last goodbye, and I followed Ed to my car.

He beeped open the lock. "How's she driving?"

"Better than ever," I said. "It's a good car."

He set the box on the front seat and shut the door. "Rose?"

I braced myself, worried that what had been a nice evening was about to go south. I had been conditioned that way, to always be on guard that perhaps my read of an experience had been one hundred and eighty degrees different from Ed's.

"Rose, I want to explain why I've asked Annie to join me in Dubai." He paused, as if trying to get his words exactly right. "Yes, it's because of her milestone birthday. But it's more than that. I'm really trying to change our narrative, Annie's and mine. You know, from me being a self-involved, unavailable father to us having a genuine relationship."

"It's an awfully long way to travel to achieve that. Couldn't you do it in, I don't know, maybe the state of Maryland?"

"I wanted her all to myself for an extended period of time so she could see I'm for real. Not a fly-by, oh, hi, kind of thing. I'm nearing fifty. I'm feeling the need to right some wrongs."

"I've always told you to go after her. And it seems you are." I stuffed my hands in my coat pockets. "Anyone else going on the trip?"

"She won't arrive for two weeks, but yes, the woman I'm seeing will be joining us. Why?"

"Just trying to get the full picture."

He studied me. "Baby steps, I'm taking baby steps. But I can say this, I'm sorry."

"For taking Annie to Dubai?"

"For what I've done to you. I've never apologized, only defended my behavior. And I'm saying it now: I'm sorry for being such a bad husband. I handled everything terribly wrong. You deserved better from me."

I took a deep breath. "Thank you for apologizing." My emotions felt as if they were tumbling in a dryer. Ed was trying to be a better dad. Not quite sure why it involved taking Annie half a world away from me for the holidays. She wasn't the type to require grand gestures. A hug. Making her feel visible, heard, noticed, not just someone who was put on this Earth to make him proud. That had always been enough for her. I took a step back and looked up at him. If Ed could be a true father to Annie, it would be a wonderful gift to my girl. Who knows? Maybe it would improve her relationships. Maybe she would find the right guy for once. Okay, time to stop the thought tsunami. Baby steps for you, too, girl.

"Have a nice trip, Ed. Be safe and have fun." I smiled. "Just wondering, have you been seeing a therapist by any chance?"

"Yes. For three months. How did you know?"

"Lucky guess?"

"Well, yes, I have. And I can't believe how much I am learning about myself." He stepped closer. "My apology was from the heart, Rose. There was nothing right about how and what I did to you. To us. Can you forgive me?"

"I appreciate you saying it. But, Ed, forgiveness is a tricky thing. If I forgive you, does that absolve you from what you did? That's not for me to decide. So I will stick with appreciating your apology. Please don't ask for anything in return. Let it just be that. You're sorry. 'Nuff said."

Ed combed his hands through his hair. "Well, there's some content for my next session."

I remained silent, wishing I could be a fly on his therapist's wall.

"But, okay," Ed said. "Have it your way. I said it, and I meant it." He exhaled and gazed around the neighborhood. "Weather sure has been lousy. You okay to drive?"

"Yes. I'm a little bit tempted to put the top down and blast the heat."

"Hah. Do you do that? Heat with the top down? Ms. I drive a Prius?"

"*Drove* a Prius," I said. Our eyes met. "Take care of our girl. She's still vulnerable, Ed. Especially with another breakup."

"I promise you."

And with that, I got in my car and started it up, giving it an extra rev on the accelerator. Forty-five degrees glowed on the dashboard. Ed watched as

I buzzed down the top. "See you later," I called. As I shifted into second gear, I decided the next time I saw Ed, I would be wearing leggings, a sweatshirt, and my most comfortable sneakers.

Chapter Thirty

The next day, Glenn and I made arrangements to meet at the café. He had learned Neil Rutherford would be meeting with David Bestman that morning to go over his father's estate. Glenn had suggested Neil stop at the café when he finished.

Feeling organized and in no hurry for once, I decided to check in with Bini before I headed into town. I found her in our freshly built barn with our five newly acquired goats, four females, and one male. Bini sat perched on a small three-legged stool, gently brushing one of the goats.

"I brought you cinnamon muffins from Sunday brunch." I set a white bag next to her. The smell of wet straw dominated the small space.

"Awesome," Bini said. "And did you know Ms. Betty White is pregnant?"

"That's wonderful." I knelt down next to Betty and smoothed my hand over her coat. "She looks radiant."

"We'll let her nurse her kid for a while, but then we can start milking and making goat cheese."

I found another stool and sat near them. "I heard you're taking a class on Wednesdays."

Bini grinned hard as she continued to brush.

Hesitant to pry into Bini's private life, I tucked my hands between my knees.

"His name is Lucas, by the way."

"Oh," I said. "I was wondering."

"I know you were. You don't miss much."

"I hope I'm not being nosy. It's just...you seem pretty happy."

"Something just feels right. I can't explain it."

I noticed small gold studs in her earlobes. "Did you get your ears pierced?"

"Re-pierced. I first got 'em done when I was thirteen. But eventually, I let him close up."

"Why?'

She looked up at me for the first time. "We talking here?"

"I hope so."

"You see, my dad had two girls. First my sister and then me. And eventually, I sort of became the son he never had. And I was cool with that. I learned a lot from him. And I figured I was doing what I love, working this farm, maybe saving up enough to buy my own one day. We checked the box scores every day and watched football together. I don't think the man has ever seen me shed a tear. I've never been an emotional person. And now I guess that's changed."

Betty nudged Bini's leg, and she returned to her brushing.

"If I would have read it in my horoscope," she continued, "that I was gonna fall for someone, I would have stopped reading the paper. It wasn't in the stars for me."

I hugged my knees. "It's not in the stars to hold our destiny, but in ourselves."

"Shakespeare?"

"Yes. Not sure I got it exactly right."

"He was a smart guy."

"Does Lucas live in Devon County?"

"He lives on the shore. Travels from county to county teaching the classes. He really knows his stuff." Bini paused for a moment. "Would you mind if he came by the farm? I'd like him to see what we have, maybe advise us on setting up a space to start making the cheese."

"Can he stay for dinner? I'll cook."

"I know that's your thing, but I'm taking it slow."

"Good idea. Thank you for sharing this with me, Bini. It means a lot. I love it when you're forthcoming and we get to know each other a little better." I studied her, wondering if I should offer to take her shopping, try some makeup, but thought better of it. This man met Bini and liked her just the way she was. But love can do funny things to how we perceive ourselves. "I'm here if you need me for anything."

She frowned for a moment. "I think I've finally realized that."

I took in the moment and felt content. We were finding our way at last.

"Bini? I'm wondering, will this be hard for your father, you in a relationship?"

"I honestly don't know. Maybe I created the situation on my own, and he just went along with it. And we can still do all those things." She pulled a wad of hair from the brush. "I know it's pretty soon to be talking about this stuff, but Lucas feels the same. He's always been a loner too."

"Oh, Bini, quick! Betty found the muffins!"

"Oh, no, you don't, Ms. Betty." She snatched up the bag. "Them are my muffins."

"Everything okay in here?" Tyler stood in the doorway, clutching the top of the doorjamb. My eyes went directly to the bulge of his biceps.

It's difficult to describe the feelings that washed through me every time Tyler was in close proximity. It's a lot like trying to describe food or wine in a new way. There were only so many adjectives available. I could say he's complex and delicious. It would be true. But when it comes to how I feel, let's just agree it's butterflies in my chest and flips in my stomach. There are no other words. And there they were, right on schedule.

I stood from the stool, which wasn't as easy as I'd hoped. "Did you hear? Betty White is pregnant."

"How can you tell, Bin?"

"Her belly is bigger, and she's snoring. She's also more affectionate. I think she's been trying to tell me."

I laughed. "Snoring?"

"Oh, yeah," Bini said in a serious tone. "It's a sign."

"This was really nice, Bini. Let's do it again soon." I glanced over at Tyler. "Walk me to my car? I'm meeting Glenn this morning."

"You bet. Oh, Bin, water heater working?"

"Affirmative."

Tyler ducked outside, and I followed. “How was Annie?” he said.

“We were both a little sad. But I’m really glad I got to see her.”

“And didn’t you go to the country club with Janice on Sunday? How was that?”

“Not at all what I expected.” I hitched my purse higher on my shoulder. “What would you say if I joined?”

“The country club? Why? You wouldn’t want to eat there. You have your own restaurant.”

“You know, it’s different from what I expected. It’s not the least bit snooty. I saw our plumber there.”

“The guy makes a ton of dough.”

“Oh, well, that’s true. Anyway, it was just an idea I was entertaining.” We walked in silence.

He tapped my arm. “Rosalie?”

I looked up, trying to read his expression. “What’s going on, Tyler?”

He combed both hands through his hair. “It sounds a little like going back to your old life in Chevy Chase. Is that what you’re looking for?”

“Oh, no, never. Janice calls it a *country* country club. I just went there to meet a few people.”

Hands on his hips, he said, “Now I’m getting it. You were asking questions about Glenn’s friend.”

“I was.” I stepped closer and wrapped my arms around his waist. “It’s Tuesday. Want to hang out tonight?”

“Affirmative.”

Chapter Thirty-One

When I arrived at the café, I realized I still had time to get my *Post* from Birdie's Shoe Store before Glenn arrived. Since the café reopened, Glenn had been picking up both of our papers on his way in to work. But I hadn't seen Doris for a while, and a visit with her always brightened my day. I buttoned my coat and walked the two blocks to Doris Bird's store.

My breath puffed out in cool clouds as I walked. When I reached the store, I stopped to take it in. Most likely in its thirtieth year of business, Birdie's was Cardigan's version of a vintage shop. It hadn't been updated in all of those thirty years, but was still a favorite gathering place for the locals. Not only did Doris offer a few pairs of shoes, she had consignment doll clothes and homemade crafts, comic books, all kinds of candy, and every major newspaper.

Doris was the first person in Cardigan to remember my name. When I realized I could get that day's *Washington Post* in her store, I became a regular. Doris always asked about my life at a time when I felt alone and invisible, and as the months went by, we grew quite fond of one another. And I will always credit her with giving me the crucial nudge to open the café.

The shop looked different today. Last Christmas, Doris had strung some very old colored bulbs in her front window, sections of it sagging by the second week in December. The peeling letters on her door had always spelled 'Bird e Sh e tore,' but today, it sported a fresh set of letters. Her windows had been washed, and I could actually see through them.

The bell on the door announced my arrival. Doris sat reliably behind the glass counter full of penny candy, arms crossed, her thick glasses low on her nose.

"Happy December," I said.

"I hope it will be," she said. "Haven't seen you around, Miss Rosalie. Mr. Glenn's been picking up your paper. You busy now that the café is open again?"

"Busy enough." I set a to-go cup on the counter. "Mocha latte with chopped candy canes and shaved white and dark chocolate. My holiday special."

"I will sip on this all day and enjoy every minute of it." She pulled the cup closer. "So, any news? How's Annie?"

"On her way to Dubai."

"Where?" She scrunched up her nose.

"Exactly. What will you do for Christmas, Doris?"

"I'll be with family Christmas day. What's left of it, that is. You?"

"I haven't figured that out yet. My Christmas has been totally focused on Annie for the past twenty-one years."

"Let me know if you want to join us." She popped open the lid and passed the cup under her nose. "This here cup is going to be the highlight of my day."

I scanned the room. "The store looks terrific."

"I got a helper. I finally decided to take a few afternoons off to take a senior water aerobics class at the Y. Summer Belle is working three hours in the afternoon."

"That's wonderful. How is she with credit cards?"

"You know kids these days. They were born with buds in their ears and fingers on a keyboard. She's even upgraded my system. And when she's bored, she cleans and organizes. She went through all the shoe boxes in the back and sorted them by size and color."

"Do you know much about her?"

"Quiet as a mouse. But very cordial with the customers." Doris rolled her lips in. She looked over at me. "She's one of those still waters run deep kind of kids. Keeps things pretty close to the chest. At first, it made me nervous. But not anymore. She wouldn't hurt a fly. I think it's more about protecting herself from a world that hasn't treated her so great. At least not yet."

I smiled and picked up my paper. "Those sound like pretty accurate insights, Doris. Maybe I'll stop in and see her this afternoon."

Chapter Thirty-Two

If Neil Rutherford was going to stop by, Glenn and I were on the same page. We needed to get him talking. As was my way, I decided an offer of lunch might entice him to stay a while.

I had been tweaking my egg salad recipe for a few years and now served the final version in the restaurant—sixteen-minutes eggs, mayonnaise, dijon mustard, diced celery, finely chopped cornichons, capers, dill, chives, and pickled shallots. My secret ingredient? A dash of curry powder.

Glenn arrived while I was gathering the ingredients. He peered into the pot on the stove. "Water's boiling."

"How was your day with Gretchen?"

"Fulfilling in every way. Especially my stomach. Between the two of you, I'm wondering if I'm going to need to loosen my belt."

"Do you know what time Neil's meeting is?"

"I believe he said eleven. Are you making egg salad?"

"The longer we can keep him here, the better." I filled a strainer with eggs and lowered them gently into the boiling water. "Do you think he feels comfortable talking with us? He doesn't seem to have anyone else in his life. No kids. And isn't he divorced?"

"He has never mentioned a wife." Glenn bit into a stick of celery. "And I would spill all of my family secrets for one of your egg salad sandwiches."

"Secrets?" I eyed him. "I'm intrigued."

"These things are all relative. What are family secrets for me would most likely put someone else to sleep."

"I'm still intrigued."

* * *

Neil Rutherford burst through the front door. "Is that a real bar?" His overcoat had fallen from one of his shoulders, his hair disheveled.

"Yes." Glenn hopped up. "It is, Neil. Can I get you something?"

"Bourbon. Straight up." He plopped onto a bar chair.

Glenn set a glass in front of him, and we watched him swallow it in one fierce gulp.

Slapping the glass on the bar, he said, "Another."

Glenn eyed me warily. I gave him a small nod.

As Glenn poured a smaller amount into Neil's glass, he said, "What's happened? Did David Bestman have your father's will?"

He finished the second pour. "See what's in this glass? Nothing, right? That's what my dad left me. All these years looking after him. Being his only family member to check in on him. Nothing."

"Was he broke?" I said.

"Looks like he was living on his social security. Apparently, he made some bad investments. And his life insurance? It all goes to some woman named Michele Belle."

"Neil?" I said tentatively. "Michele Belle is Summer's mother."

"Who?" His forehead scrunched up. "*Who*?" His eyes darted back and forth. "You mean the *kid*?"

"Yes. Summer."

Neil shook his head. "He said he would take care of me for being there for him. Gave me all his passwords, that kind of thing. I don't know why. He was as healthy as a horse."

"Was he in some kind of danger?" I said. "Did he have reason to think someone might want to hurt him?"

"You mean kill him? I guess narcissists think that way, don't they? They're so important someone would want to kill them. Here's my take. I'm glad he's gone. He was a thorn in my side my entire life."

"I don't know, Neil," Glenn said. "From what I've seen, your father lived a comfortable life. Didn't he drive a Tesla?"

"Well, it's all gone now. Look, can you pour me another? I'll stay at the old man's house tonight." Neil's eyes pleaded with Glenn. "Could you join me, though? Have a drink with a guy?"

"Of course." Glenn poured a small glass of wine for himself and sat next to Neil."

He swirled his third pour. "Do you two know who hit my father?"

"No one has come forward."

"Do you think it was intentional?"

"I don't know, Neil," I said. "Do you?"

"Something ain't right. That's all I know." He clinked his glass on Glenn's and downed the rest of his bourbon.

Chapter Thirty-Three

Neil wiped his mouth after eating the last of his egg salad sandwich and munched on a potato chip.

"I'll drive you home whenever you're ready," Glenn said. "And you are welcome to stay at my place. At least it will be warm."

"Thanks, Glenn. But I need to process some things. Sitting in my dad's house might give me some insight."

Sheriff Wilgus came through the kitchen door. "I smell egg salad."

"Of course you do," I said. "Sheriff, this is Neil Rutherford, Bill's son. He's here in town settling his father's estate."

Neil eyed the sheriff, his eyes a little less glassy than they had been. "Who hit my dad?"

"Dunno."

"Aren't you the law? Isn't that your job?"

The sheriff placed his hat on the bar. "Your daddy leave you a bunch of cash?"

"No." Neil straightened his posture. "It's been over a week. Someone crashed into my father and is getting away with it. You could probably go door to door in this town and find out."

"I'll let you know when we do." His eyes narrowed. "Who do you think crashed into him?"

"Someone who deserves to go to jail." Neil wadded his napkin. "Look, I've had a bad day, Sheriff Wilgus. I'm not handling all of this very well. Glenn has offered to drive me back to his place, and I'm going to take him up on the offer." He stood, wobbled a little, then regained his balance. "If I can help you in any way to find out who did this, please let me know."

Wilgus nodded. "I'm sorry for your loss, Neil. It was a hell of a way to go for an athlete like him."

"It's December. He had no business riding his bike on that road at night."

"You blaming the victim?" The sheriff had a small smile on his face.

Neil frowned. "Maybe?" He pulled on his coat. "You ready, Glenn?"

"Of course."

* * *

Sheriff Wilgus took a bite of his second sandwich as I fired up the Miele. "That guy's intense."

"He just had a shock," I said. "Any news from the body shops?"

"Nothing."

"Do you know a man who goes by Jonesy?"

"Donny Jones? Yeah. Why?"

"He was part of Bill's golf foursome. I met the other two, let's see, Gunther and, um, oh, Patrick. They played every Sunday, then had a cocktail at the bar. They said Jonesy didn't play this Sunday because his car was in the shop." The sheriff looked up from his sandwich. "They said he hit a deer."

"Let's get this straight. He played golf with Bill Rutherford the day he was killed and had a few drinks, and now he says he hit a deer? Well, his car isn't in a shop around here. I've been checking every day."

"If you hit a man on his bike, would you take it to a local shop? Especially in Cardigan. As Janice says, you can't fart in this town without someone smelling it."

"She says that?"

"You know Janice."

"I like Jonesy. He's a good man."

"Maybe he's afraid," I said. "And very upset. Bill was his friend."

"All the more reason to come forward."

I filled two coffee cups. "Have you forgotten, Joe? Bill Rutherford had a bullet in his back."

Chapter Thirty-Four

I arrived home that afternoon early enough to ensure Tyler would still be working. After changing into the same sweater dress I wore Monday for my visit with Annie and Ed, I headed into the kitchen to open a bottle of wine and slice some cheese and crudités.

Marco Giovanelli, the chef I was fortunate enough to study with a few months ago, said one of the oddest features of American grocery stores was the salad dressing aisle. For Marco, mixing up a salad dressing was as easy as olive oil, an acid, meaning citrus or vinegar, salt, and pepper. I felt the same way about the rows and rows of hummus that were now a part of every store.

Hummus was merely tahini sauce, garlic, lemon juice, salt and pepper. Hate to stir tahini in a jar? It now comes in a squeeze bottle. Enhancing it with swirls of romesco sauce, tapenade, or, like tonight, fresh pesto was easy.

I was slicing a celery stalk when I heard the front door close. "I have a very large egg salad sandwich for you in the fridge," I called out. "But I thought I'd make a few appetizers." I set the knife down and picked up a dish towel. When I turned around, I was face to face with Tyler.

"That's the dress," he said in a husky voice.

"Yes. I remembered."

"I didn't forget."

I dried my hands and dropped the towel on the counter. "How was your day? How is—"

He grabbed my hand and tugged.

"Tyler?"

"Let's start the evening upstairs."

* * *

I slipped into my robe and lit a few candles. Tyler was sitting up in bed, hands behind his head. "I'll get the wine," I said. "Hungry?"

"Famished."

"Don't go anywhere."

"Wouldn't dream of it."

I set a plate on the nightstand next to Tyler, loaded with a sandwich, hummus, and a mound of sliced vegetables. Once I was tucked back under the comforter, Tyler filled our glasses with one of Alessa's delicious chiantis and held one out for me.

"How decadent is this?" I took a sip.

"You were the one wearing the dress."

I smiled and pulled the comforter up a little higher. "I like that you work so close by."

"It's in the benefits package." He slugged back his wine and picked up a carrot.

"Tyler, can I ask you something?"

"What cha' got on your mind, gorgeous?"

With the wine, the blankets, and Tyler's affection, I felt as warm and toasty as freshly baked bread. "I've never asked you this, but how did you start farming here? How did it all begin?"

"You know how much I hate talking about myself."

"It's a piece of the puzzle I don't know." I reached up and twisted his hair around my finger. "We have all night."

He exhaled a long sigh. "Shall I start when everything in my life changed?"

"Most definitely."

"My mother died of breast cancer when I was seventeen." He chewed another carrot. "There you have it."

"I knew she died at a young age, but you were only seventeen? How did the rest of your family handle that?"

"My family began disintegrating the minute we put her in the ground. She was our anchor, and suddenly, we were all adrift. My sister was engaged, so she turned her focus on her new family. My brother Butch was untethered and unchecked. And my dad just kept working. But every night, he sat by the fire and wept.

"I was in my senior year, but there was no talk of college for me, so after graduation, I took every odd job I could find. Earned enough to move out and spent my days working on whatever farm would have me. At night, I found companionship in books."

"When did you meet your wife?"

"At a bar when I was around twenty-two. I thought being tied down with her would stop the drifting. And it did for a while. I liked being married. I liked the certainty of it all. You know who you'll spend Christmas with, who you'll go out to dinner with, and who you'll have sex with. And when you're married, you have a built-in future."

"I never thought of it that way, but it's true. So what went wrong?"

Tyler shook his head. "You know exactly what happened."

"She ran off with the UPS man."

"And never looked back." Tyler refilled our glasses. "So not only was I the joke of the town, what little certainty I had known since I lost my mom was gone. That's when my reading list changed. I needed a purpose. So, I started learning about climate change, farming, ways to help sustain our planet. It's the first time I felt passionate about something. I got a steady job at the spinach farm and saved enough to buy my own house."

"East of Eden." I squeezed his hand.

"That's right. My little piece of heaven."

"And Charlotte?"

"One day, she put an ad in the paper looking for someone to lease her lands. Sick of all the pesticides and herbicides, she was looking to make some changes, too. I knocked on her door, and she invited me to the kitchen table."

"A lot has happened at that little table." I smiled.

"We talked for five hours. I had three cups of coffee and four slices of that bread you make.

"We started slow. I continued to grow soybeans and corn and converted one field at a time to organic. She paid for me to take classes at the community college and gave me a loan to buy my own equipment."

"How did I never meet you?"

"I always kept my distance when Charlotte had visitors. She had the open door policy like you, but I had firm boundaries. I would never have taken advantage of her kindness." Tyler slipped his hand into mine. "Funny, I don't remember seeing you even from a distance."

I caressed his knuckles with my thumb. "I'm sorry, Tyler. For ignoring this place. And mostly, for ignoring your letters. That was an awful thing to do." I sipped my wine. "It haunts me sometimes. That I was so inconsiderate of another human being."

"It happened. You had your reasons."

"I guess I'm ashamed of how much I allowed Ed to control things in our family. Maybe I still am. Maybe I should have insisted on time with Annie, that he not take her away for so long."

"I don't blame you, Rosalie. It's a big farm."

"She wanted you to have it if I decided I didn't. Did you know that?"

He shook his head. "I had no idea. How do you know?"

"She left me a note in her safety deposit box. Asking me to find a way to give Barclay Meadow to you if I chose to sell."

"I like knowing that." He clinked his glass against mine. "Here's to Charlotte Barclay, for who she was and for bringing us together."

I smiled so hard my cheeks hurt. "What would she think?" I said. "If she knew we were sitting in her bed together drinking wine."

I flinched when the bedside light flickered on and off. "Tyler, did you see that?"

He hesitated. "Wires are pretty old in this place."

"That was Charlotte. I think she just winked."

I looked over at him. He stared off, seemingly deep in thought.

"Maybe so, Rosalie," he said. "Maybe so."

Chapter Thirty-Five

When Glenn arrived at the café the next morning, I offered to help him with the menu inserts. "I've had three cups of coffee already, and I need something to occupy myself."

"Should be an interesting morning." He eyed me over his glasses.

"What happened with Neil yesterday? Did you go back to Bill's house with him?"

"He actually came to my place. Seems his father was out of bourbon." He closed a menu and added it to the stack.

"Did he say anything more about the will?"

Glenn frowned. "Bill Rutherford had made an appointment with David Bestman for tomorrow. He wanted to make some changes to his life insurance policy."

"Good lord," I said and handed Glenn the next insert. "Did he say what he was changing?"

"He died before the meeting, obviously, but he wanted to change the recipient from Michelle Belle to her daughter, Summer. But he never had the chance."

"So Micky B. gets the life insurance?"

"It looks that way."

"How do *you* spell motive?" I combed my hair back from my face. "And what was Neil's reaction to this new development?"

Crystal approached. "All done? Want me to put them on the hostess stand?"

"Yes," Glenn said, "and thank you."

Crystal clutched the menus but didn't budge. "You're at it again, aren't you? The man who was hit on his bike, right?"

"Do you have any insights?" I said.

She looked down at the floor for a moment. "There are many factors at play here. I think you need to remember that." She spun around and walked away, silent as a cat in her moccasins.

"Was that really an insight?" Glenn frowned.

"Perhaps." I glanced at my watch. "Do you think I have time to pay a visit to the sheriff before we open? I'd like to share this with him."

"Wednesdays are always pretty slow. I think you're good."

Chapter Thirty-Six

"Joey is with someone," Lila said, a smug smile on her face. "You can't go in."

I stared at the closed door to the sheriff's office. "Do you know who?"

"Yup. But I ain't telling ya."

Stepping closer to the door, I heard raised voices. "Can I just give him his coffee?"

She shook her head from one side to the other. "Nope."

"Okay, Lila," I said in a raised voice. "But the sheriff might need his coffee."

"What in the heck are you yelling for?" She hopped off the chair. "Leave the coffee and go. Come on, now, git." She waved her hands as if shooing away a pesky bird.

"Are you *shooing* me?"

The door opened, and Joe Wilgus stepped into the front office, closing the door behind him. "What's all the commotion, Hart?"

"Is that Jonesy in there?"

"How'd you know?"

"Lucky guess. Anything?"

"He's agitated. Said his Escalade is in a shop in Dover. Swears it was a deer, but he's sweating, and it's twenty-five degrees outside."

Lila stood between us. "I told her to leave."

Ignoring her, I said, "Good cop, bad cop? Maybe on his way out?"

"You think he'll spill?"

"I can be very sympathetic." I gripped his coffee cup.

"I can't take you back there."

"I know. Lila and I will be having a chat. And I haven't given her any muffins yet."

Lila huffed into her chair.

"I'll get him a little more agitated and bring him out."

The door closed, and I could feel Lila's eyes boring through me. I rolled my shoulders back and turned around.

"I thought Joey hated you," she said.

"He did at one point. But a lot has changed." I removed the muffin bag from my purse. "He's letting me help him now. You know I see and hear a lot at the café. In fact, I just learned something that will help him solve this case."

She tilted her chair back. Her sneakered feet dangled in mid-air. "Sounds like he might already know who did it."

I remembered Crystal's words. *There are many factors at play.*

The door burst open, and I was face to face with Jonesy. He was a large man, almost as tall as the sheriff. His hair was soaked with perspiration. His dark eyes bulged, darting around the small room as if looking for the exit.

"Excuse me," I said. "I was just bringing the sheriff some coffee."

"Look, Donny," Wilgus said. "You tell that body shop to not touch your Escalade."

"Escalade?" I said. "Are you by any chance Jonesy?"

"Who's asking?"

"I met your friends at the club on Sunday. They mentioned you. That it was odd you weren't playing golf on a Sunday. I guess I can see why after losing your fourth buddy so tragically."

"Bill was a fool for riding his bike at night."

"I can see that. But it seems he was a pretty generous guy. He had been giving his daughter, who he'd never met, five thousand dollars a month. That's pretty nice. But I guess that all stops now. I wonder what she'll do."

"I want pictures of the damage, Donny."

"Oh, that's right. They said you hit a deer. It's all so sad about Bill. I met his son at the funeral. He's devastated. He just can't make sense out—"

"He was weaving all over the road," Donny shouted. "He came out of nowhere, riding that bike like he couldn't keep it straight. He just rode right out in front of me. I couldn't dodge him." Donny pressed his palms against his temples. "Something was wrong with him."

"So you just drove away?" the sheriff growled.

"No. I pulled over and got out. He was bleeding like crazy. But he was already dead. No pulse. No nothing."

"And *then* you drove away?"

"I wish I hadn't. I'd had a couple of drinks. But I swear to the lord I wasn't drunk. It almost looked like someone pushed him into the road. I never seen anything like it."

I swallowed hard, feeling a little nauseated. I peered over at the sheriff. His frown was deep set.

"I'm going to have to charge you, Donny. And then I want you to walk out of here and hire a lawyer, A good one. You hear?"

I glanced at Lila. She was typing into her phone. "Lila," I hissed. "No!"

She put her phone down and lifted her chin.

Once the sheriff had finished reading the Miranda rights, Jonesy hurried out the door, ball cap in a tight grip.

The room was silent.

"I didn't really think it was him," I said.

"Neither did I," Joe said, hands on his hips.

"Sheriff, if you get a chance, can you stop by the cafe today? Glenn and I have some more information about the will."

"Didn't we just hear a man confess?"

I pulled my gloves out of my coat pockets. "There's more to this, I'm sure of it."

Chapter Thirty-Seven

Welcome to the Day Lily Café
A gathering place offering simplicity and
freshness, with a focus on locally sourced ingredients

Plant-based Wednesday Specials:
Lunch: Butternut squash soup with toasted pepitas and sliced green apples
Dinner: Grilled seasonal vegetables in a Zaatar panko crust
over red lentils stewed with chili crisp

"The act of putting into your mouth what the earth has grown is perhaps your most direct interaction with the earth."
—Frances Moore Lappé

* * *

Janice was at her usual perch at the bar for Wednesday lunch. "What's with you, Rose Red? You seem distracted."

"Maybe a little. Sorry." I smiled. "What are you in the mood for?"

"What's in that soup to make it creamy?"

"Coconut milk. It's really good."

"Any more thoughts about joining the club?"

"Mason gave me a thirty-day free trial." I put a set of silverware wrapped in a cloth napkin in front of her.

I looked up to see none other than Abby, the Fitness Angel, come through the door. She wore a down jacket with a swath of fur around the hood. Glenn met her at the door, and her smile widened.

"Janice," I said. "Do you know that woman?"

Janice turned around and looked back at me with a dramatic eye roll. "She joined the club a while back. Isn't she in Glenn's community?"

"Yup." I frowned. "She's making him blush."

Janice looked over her shoulder again. "You ever hear that song Dixie Chicken by Little Feat?"

"I know it."

"At the end of the song, all the guys at the bar know the same lyrics about Dixie chickens and a Tennessee lamb. Right? Well, let's just say there's a lot of guys at the club who know that there is a Tennessee lamb."

"She's very tan," I said.

"She belongs in Ft. Lauderdale. Not Cardigan, that's for sure."

Glenn escorted her to the bar. He started to seat her next to Janice, but she said, "This seat is reserved for a woman named Gretchen."

I studied Glenn. He looked pained. He was not the kind of man to encourage flirtatious behavior. It took Gretchen at least four weeks to get him to finally have tea with her.

Janice and I watched as Abby slipped out of her coat a few seats down the bar. More spandex. To her credit, she was taut in all the right places, whether by exercise, a little tuck here and there, or both. Nothing jiggled on that woman.

"Have you ever watched any of her TikToks?" I said.

"Do I look like I watch her TikToks?"

"I'll put in your soup order. Side salad?"

"Coleslaw." Janice unrolled her napkin.

Glenn followed me into the kitchen. "I can't stop thinking about what happened to you this morning."

"Nor I. The sheriff read him his rights. But I can't believe this is the answer. There's so much more here at play."

"His description of Bill's behavior is interesting."

I pinched my bottom lip.

"You guys want to take some of these specials out?" Custer said. "We're backing up in here."

"Yes, of course," I said and typed in Janice's order. I stopped. "Glenn!"

Even Custer stopped flipping burgers. They both stared at me.

"What if he had been shot before Donny hit him? What if someone else shot him, and that's why his bike riding was so erratic?"

* * *

I carried Janice's soup out to her and noticed Abby had moved next to her.

"I told you, Abby, this seat is reserved."

"I've been here twenty minutes, and no one has showed up. I'll sit here if I want." She looked at me. "You can bring my salad to this seat." She unwrapped her silverware and placed her napkin over her thighs. Glenn set several dirty plates in a bin and headed into the kitchen.

"That Glenn is a handsome man, don't you think? He's so distinguished."

"Glenn has a girlfriend," Janice said flatly.

"I've never seen him with anyone." She sipped her water. "Waterside Village has a Christmas party coming up. Maybe I'll invite him to be my date."

"Are you hard of hearing, Abby?" Janice stared at her. "He has a girlfriend. Her name is Gretchen. So, mitts off, my friend, you got it?"

Abby straightened her spine. "I've recently lost someone very dear to me. He was going to invest in my business. We had great plans. But he's dead, and I'm very lonely. And now I don't know what to do with myself."

"I'm sorry to hear that, Abby, but there ain't no fish for you to fry in here." Janice wiped her mouth and looked at me. "I'm ready for my check."

Chapter Thirty-Eight

The lunch crowd was light as expected, so before we did the final dinner prep, I walked to Birdie's Shoe Store. Heavy gray clouds hung low in the sky. I wrapped a black wool scarf around my neck and lifted the collar of my coat.

I found Summer behind the counter reading *The Great Gatsby*. She stood when I entered the store.

"Remember me?" I said.

"You were at the funeral." She had woven her long dark hair into pigtail braids and wore the same heavy eyeliner. "But everyone in town knows who you are, Miss Hart."

"They do?"

"You own the café, right?"

"Yes. Okay, so that's why. I don't feel like everyone knows me. But it's Cardigan, and I shouldn't expect anything else." I hitched my purse higher on my shoulder. "Doris tells me you are really helping out around here."

"I gotta make my own way. And Mrs. Bird seemed to need some help, so we are a good fit."

"Your half-brother was in town yesterday for the will reading." I checked her reaction. Nothing. "He's still pretty upset about everything that's happened."

"Of course he is. It's only been a little over a week."

"Summer? Can I ask how you found out Bill was your father?"

She shrugged. "It was about a month ago. Right after I turned sixteen." She scratched her nose. Black nail polish coated her short nails.

"I don't mean to be nosy. I actually think I might be able to help you. So how did you find out?"

"I haven't told anyone but my dad. And my mom, of course. I was going for my driver's test. I needed my birth certificate and some other documents. My mom was at work, so I went into her office to look for them. Her banking statements were in a folder. I saw the automatic $5,000 deposit every month."

"She never told you?"

"Of course not. Have you seen her wardrobe? She's always whining to me that her budget is tight." She rolled her eyes. "I did the math. That's $60,000 a year."

"Did you go to Bill's home?"

"I sent him a letter. He texted as soon as he got it and invited me to meet him for coffee at the diner. I thought he'd be angry, but he was really just curious. I didn't try to impress him or anything."

"No. That doesn't seem to be your style."

"It made him angry to learn my mom hadn't shared the money with me. I mean, part of taking care of me involves spending money for things that benefit her too, for sure, but he was hoping it might pay for a private school or something."

"How long did you two talk?"

"At the end of two hours, he said he liked the idea of having a daughter, that he had never given it much thought."

"Oh my, Summer. That must have been very confusing to hear."

"Not really. Honestly? I can get why he didn't want to get tied up with my mom. That it was easier to just keep his distance. Could I have used his help? I think so. But my take on him is he didn't like to be tied down. He liked to do what he wanted to do whenever he chose to do it, so maybe it's okay."

"Is that the only time you met?"

"We started having coffee once a week. I think it was when he found out I was really good at math that it hit home we shared some of the same genes. He said he was going to help me get into a good college. And that he was going to change his life insurance policy and put it in my name." She stared at her shoes. "I swear, I never asked anything from him." She looked up. "That isn't why I wanted to meet him."

"I'm sorry you didn't have more time with him."

"Why are you so interested, Miss Rosalie?"

"He was Glenn's neighbor, and the police still don't know what happened." I smiled. "And I'm a very curious person, and this is a small town. Something like this happens, I want to know why and how. So I ask a lot of questions, and sometimes I find the answers. I don't know if you agree, but I think it helps people with their grieving once they know exactly how a loved one has passed."

"My dad got hit by a car, right?"

"Yes."

She frowned. I waited several moments before she spoke.

"If you have any more questions, you know where to find me," she said.

"Thank you, Summer. I like talking to you. I'll definitely stop by again. And I have a holiday mocha coffee for you." I set a white bag on the counter.

"Mrs. Bird told me about these." Summer removed the cup, popped the lid off, and held it up to her nose. "She said it's the best thing she's ever had to drink in her whole life other than gin."

I grinned hard. "I hope you like it too."

Chapter Thirty-Nine

I stepped onto the sidewalk, deep in thought about Summer and her mother, when a gust of wind slapped me in the face. Oversized snowflakes swirled around, and I felt as if I were in a snow globe being shaken by a toddler. Snow had already carpeted the sidewalk, and I had to tread carefully. I chastised myself for not paying attention to the weather forecast. My hair was already wet. I would look like little Orphan Annie in no time. I turned the corner, squinting my eyes from the flakes assaulting my forehead.

The lights from A Well-Loved Home twinkled through the blizzard. I stopped and took a deep breath. Snowstorms were a rare occurrence on the Eastern Shore, and I found myself unexpectedly smiling as the flakes swirled in tiny cyclones. It was beautiful. A winter wonderland.

Kneeling down, I gathered up enough snow to form a ball and resumed my stroll. Catching a few snowflakes on my tongue, I marveled at the quiet. It felt as if the world had been hushed for a moment, leaving the senses open to new surprises.

"I brought you something," I said to Glenn and tossed him the snowball.

"You look like the Yeti."

"Isn't it just the best?"

"Hm," he said. "Is someone feeling the holiday spirit?"

"Yes. For a fleeting moment, I am happy it's December."

"It's sticking," he said and set the snowball in the sink.

"Maybe I'll text Crystal and tell her to stay home. She's got at least an eight-mile drive." I hung my coat on a hook. It was drenched. "And I'm pretty sure it will be a slow night."

"Enjoy the white stuff while you can. It's the Eastern Shore. It will all be gone in the morning."

Chapter Forty

Despite Glenn's prediction, the white stuff continued to fall from the sky for the next two hours. Owning only a motorcycle, Custer had to hitch a ride from a friend to make it to work. While Glenn was shoveling the front steps for the third time, I gazed out the window as a snowplow passed by, its headlights casting an eerie yellow glow on the tumbling flakes.

Glenn stomped his shoes and stepped inside. "Do you think we'll have any customers?"

"It's doubtful. Are you worried about getting home?"

"My Volvo has all-wheel drive. I should be fine. Would you like me to give you a lift?"

I smiled. "Tyler just texted that he would come and fetch me when I'm ready. He said these roads aren't safe for a 'Little Tykes' car."

Custer pushed through the door. "Those filets you got look pretty damn good. What do you think about a *bearnaise* sauce?"

"I was actually thinking steak au *poivre*, maybe with a *beurre blanc*. Is that in your wheelhouse?"

Glenn rubbed his chin. "Can you make it steak *frites*? Nothing like a good steak with crispy fries."

"Custer?" I said.

"I'll play around with it." He grabbed a coffee mug and headed for the Mieles.

"*We* could always eat it if no one shows up," Glenn said with a wink.

Custer stirred a heavy dollop of cream into his coffee. "Can I crank up the Mozart?"

"Yes. And I can make my Hollywood salad if anyone orders the steak." I picked up the stack of menus by the door. "We never put in the inserts. Oh, and Glenn, can you add steak *au poivre* to the chalkboard?"

We propped the door to the kitchen open to keep Custer company. The music resounded through the café, and the snow continued to spiral and gust. Glenn sat at the bar while I played around with a French buttercream recipe. I glanced out the window. The snowplows weren't keeping up. "Let's give it thirty minutes and call it a day."

"Sounds like a plan."

"Remember snow days in school?" I said.

"The best. Is that what we're doing here?"

"Yes, let's call it that. And if this steak is as good as I think it's going to be, we can make Thursdays all *Nuit Française*."

"Today is Wednesday."

"I know, but Wednesday is plant-based special day, and Friday is *Notte Italiana,* so Thursday can be steak frites day. And, Glenn? Your phone is vibrating."

Chapter Forty-One

Three middle-aged women hustled in the front door, brushing snow from their parkas with gloves and woolen mittens. Gretchen had texted Glenn that she had three hungry guests and had offered to drive them into town in her SUV. She tooted her horn and waved as she eased her vehicle back onto the road.

"Welcome to the Day Lily Café," I said.

They wiggled out of their coats and sat around the table in the center of the café. I distributed menus, and they opened them immediately.

Glenn arrived with three glasses of ice water and a small basket of savory mini muffins with local butter. "Would you like to take a look at the wine list?"

"Oh my goodness, yes. We are very excited to try out a new restaurant. I'm Vera, by the way." Vera looked as if she stepped out of an LL Bean catalog with a thick fleece, corduroys, and rubber snow boots. She slipped on a pair of pink-rimmed readers and opened the wine list.

"I guess we should all introduce ourselves since we plan to be here awhile. I'm Susie, and this is Mary Beth." Susie smiled at Glenn and tucked her folded hands under her chin. "We'd never even heard of this place before, but Gretchen insisted we come. This is our gals' night out. We do it every December. Stay at cute Inns and Christmas shop for a few days. I'm not sure how we decided on Cardigan, but we did. So far so good." She winked at Glenn.

Susie and Mary Beth were dressed similarly to Vera, but when I looked a little closer, I noticed some inconsistencies. Vera's fleece was zipped, but there was a string of pearls around her neck. And a cherry red Chanel bag sat on the vacant chair next to her.

Vera looked up from the wine list. "Is this a Santorini white?" She pointed with a red polished nail.

"Yes," Glenn said. "And it's delicious."

"Ladies?" Vera said. "Shall we start with that one?"

Susie, who had spiky, short gray hair, nodded her head and buttered a muffin. "Oh, and Glenn? We'll have one of each of the appetizers to share."

"All five?" Glenn said, eyebrows raised.

"All five," she said. "Just for starters."

* * *

Custer was sitting on a stool, one arm on the counter, the other holding a dog-eared, tattered paperback copy of *Zen and the Art of Motorcycle Maintenance*.

"You look so comfortable," I said as I tied my apron around my waist. "But there are three very hungry women out there who are," I made air quotation marks, "starting" with all five appetizers. How can I help? Should I make the mini fish tacos? We usually only put two on the plate, but I'll make three."

"I've been adding an avocado mousse and salsa verde," Custer said as he hopped up and fetched a cast iron skillet. "Why all five? Is that instead of a main course?"

"They're very hungry." I shoved my hair from my forehead. "Snow day's over. It was a short December day, but It's going to be a long night."

Chapter Forty-Two

I had to give these women credit. They were having a fabulous time. I was very tempted to pull up a chair and join them.

"Rosalie," Vera said. "This wine is fantastic. We can't stop drinking it. It's nuanced yet complex."

"I agree. So you've had the stuffed oysters, crispy polenta topped with mushrooms, my signature Hollywood salad, and the Brussels sprouts topped with a gruyere aioli."

"Don't forget the fish tacos," Susie said. "I ate two."

"So are we sated?" I stacked the plates on my forearms.

Mary Beth frowned. She was the slightest of the three with slightly hunched shoulders. "I read on your chalkboard that there's a filet."

"We have to have it," Susie said. "Let's get two entrees. The steak frites and the crab cake."

"Did you see the risotto?" Vera said.

"Okay," Susie said. "Three entrees." She slapped her menu shut. "How about a red wine?"

"I highly recommend any wine from our local winery, Casa Vanelli. Their Italian red blend will go with everything."

"Then bring two bottles," Susie said. "Save you the trip."

I turned around and almost bumped into Glenn. "Custer needs you," he whispered.

"I'm sure he does." I set the dishes in a bin. "They ordered two bottles of Alessa's red blend."

"Two?" A lock of Glenn's silver hair had fallen onto his forehead. "Yes, of course, I'm on it."

* * *

It was after 9:00 when Susie, Mary Beth, and Vera dropped their wadded napkins on the table. After two bottles of the red blend, they asked to end their night with a sparkling. Glenn popped open Alessa's signature prosecco, and they asked to meet the chef.

Custer didn't blink an eye. He removed his apron and bandana and checked his hair.

"You look marvelous," I said.

He smoothed his hands over his black chef's jacket. "Are they going to eat any more food?"

"I cleared their plates. The buttercream is history."

I have never denied Custer was a very handsome young man. He was fit, with the Wells family green eyes and sandy blond hair. When he appeared through the doors, all three women gave him a standing ovation. Susie had to steady herself on the table to keep her balance.

"Bravo!" Vera sang.

"He's so young," Susie said. "Tell me, dear, how did you cook those fries?"

"If I tell you, I will have to kill you," Custer said in his best French accent. "Actually, I cooked them in beef tallow. Gives them some depth."

"Can you sit with us for a bit?" Vera said, a wide grin on her face. "Have a glass of prosecco?"

Custer glanced over at me. "Of course," I said. "I'll open another bottle. This one's on the house."

Custer sat down, forearms on the table. Vera leaned in, peppering him with questions. I'm pretty sure I didn't hear my name mentioned once. Although Custer and I collaborated on every dish that left the kitchen, I always gave him the credit. He had a touch. And I had grown to trust it, which wasn't easy. It was my café. My dream. But I had a budding new chef. Although I had to rein him in, a lot, I knew I was very lucky to have him in my kitchen.

I filled their glasses and one for Glenn and me. "Ladies," I said, "thank you for spending time with us. I feel as if you are already friends, and I hope you return."

Just then, Tyler entered the front door. (Heart flip) He stomped his boots and lowered his hood. "You ready to come home yet?"

The ladies all stared. "Who is that?" Mary Beth said in a hoarse voice.

"He's my uncle," Custer said and sipped his prosecco.

Tyler approached the table. "Sorry to interrupt. I'm Tyler Wells. I farm Rosalie's land."

"So you grew much of what we ate tonight," Vera said.

"Yup. And organically, to boot.

"Good lord," Mary Beth said, fanning herself. "Why is this our first time on the Eastern Shore?"

Chapter Forty-Three

Glenn was often right about things. Thursday morning was a perfect example. That beautiful snow? A slushy, gray history.

I cinched my robe and trotted downstairs, my hair in ringlets from a shower. I found Bini at the kitchen table holding a cat treat in front of Sweeney Todd's nose. I stopped on the bottom step and watched.

"You have to sit first," she said to my cat, whose ears were flat against his head. She pushed on his backside, but Sweeney didn't budge. "If you earn the good things in life, they taste better, make you happier than if they are just handed to you," she said to him and held it closer to his nose.

In one quick swipe, the treat was on the floor, and Bini's finger oozed a pearl of blood. She hopped up and tore off a paper towel. "Don't say it."

I continued into the kitchen. "Wasn't going to."

"If goats, dogs, even chickens, can learn how to follow commands, why can't a cat?"

Sweeney finished the treat and began washing his paw.

I fired up Mr. Miele. "I guess because they don't have to."

She ran her finger under the faucet. "I had cheese-making class last night."

I turned around and leaned back against the counter. "Do tell."

She opened the refrigerator and removed a glass container. "My first batch of goat cheese."

I gasped as she lifted the lid. "Can I taste it?"

"I was hoping you would."

"It's so beautiful and creamy." I found a spoon and dipped it into the cheese. "Oh, my goodness, Bini. It's amazing."

"I thought I could experiment with adding herbs from the greenhouse. We could make several different flavors. Maybe lavender to start." She shifted her weight. "I'll sell it at the farmers' market, but do you think you would serve it at the café? I mean, I'm not trying to tell you how to run your restaurant."

"Oh my goodness, yes. But you know what? I'm not going to use it as an ingredient. It can be a stand-alone appetizer." I tasted another spoonful. "Yes to the lavender, but we need to serve just this plain version. We could serve it with petite crackers and maybe a local honey."

Bini's cheeks had flushed a bright pink. She was never one to seek out praise or the slightest bit of attention.

"When can I put it on the menu?" I said.

"I'll make a big batch today."

"Your teacher must be very good at what he does." I eyed her.

Bini checked her phone. "Yes. That would be true." She looked up. "Maybe I'll bring him to the café. Do you know I've never actually eaten there?"

I sipped my espresso. "Why don't you bring him once I put this cheese on the menu."

"Cool." She slipped into her coat and shoved her phone in the back pocket. "Do you mind if I use your kitchen today to make the cheese?"

"I would be thrilled. Oh, say, Bini, do you by any chance know Michelle Belle?"

"Micky B.? Yeah, we went to high school together. Why?"

"Did you get along with her?"

Bini frowned. "You're at it again, aren't you? That guy on the bike?"

"What was she like? Were you friends?"

"Micky B. decided to call herself that because she thought it was cute. But what she didn't realize is most of us agreed to call her that, but to us, the B. didn't stand for Belle. 'Nuff said?"

Chapter Forty-Four

When I arrived at the café to begin lunch prep, Glenn was already seated at the bar. I tucked my purse away and tied an apron around my waist. "You're early."

The Devon County News was on the bar in front of him. He tapped the headline. "Have you seen this?"

"*Donald Jones Charged with Hit and Run in the Killing of Local Cyclist, William Rutherford,*" I read. "There it is. Jonesy must be devastated. Glenn? I worry if we don't find out who shot Bill, Donny Jones could go to prison for a crime he didn't commit."

"And your theory is Bill had been shot before Jonesy hit him, and that's why he was riding so erratically."

"Jonesy may have hit Bill, but he didn't kill him." I washed my hands and dried them on a towel. "I wish you could have seen him at the sheriff's office. He was still in shock and extremely upset. I just hope he doesn't—"

"Harm himself?" Glenn crossed his arms.

"Some people will do anything to avoid prison." I picked up a tray of mugs and began stacking them on the shelf over the coffee station. I stopped and faced Glenn. "So whoever did shoot him must be assuming they've gotten away with it."

"Well, there is the problem of a bullet in his back."

"Joe Wilgus has a reputation for not looking too hard. When he has his perp, he's done. I'm worried he might end up taking the lazy way out again."

"So the question now is, will he let us continue looking into it?"

"I think so. He told Jonesy to get a good lawyer. I think he's worried about him, too."

Glenn shook his head. "We have to figure this out soon. Neil Rutherford has contacted a local realtor. Everyone involved is ready to move on." He frowned. "We don't really even have a list of suspects, do we?"

I set the empty tray in the dish bin. "Okay, we have Micky B.," I counted with my fingers, "Neil, Jonesy, and maybe Gunther or Patrick, the other two in the golf foursome. And anyone else who was at the club that night, or lives on River Road for that matter. And—Glenn? What's wrong?"

He stood next to the chair, slightly stooped. "I think I did something to my back. I took a yoga class this morning."

"With Abby the Fitness Angel?"

"Yes, she suggested it to me the other day."

"I'm sure she did." I frowned. "Too many downward-facing dogs?"

"I believe that's what they're called."

"I'll get you some ice." I started to go but stopped. My protective radar was on red alert at the thought of Glenn becoming friendly with Abby. "Remember when we found Abby in Bill's house? Have you thought any more about that?"

"Of course. That's why I'm taking the yoga class."

"Wait, what?"

He rubbed his lower back. "Why else? To learn what Abby's motive would be. She made herself a suspect the day she was snooping around."

My shoulders relaxed. "I thought...I thought you *liked* her."

He scowled. "I am a lucky man to have Gretchen for a companion. I would never jeopardize that."

"And I should have never doubted you. I'm sorry." I combed my hair back from my face. "And have you learned anything?"

"Yoga positions are not conducive to conversation." Glenn walked behind the bar and picked up a teacup. "And chatting up women when you are hanging upside down can come across in an odd way. Maybe you could join me."

"If you are sacrificing your back health for the investigation, it's the least I can do. Tomorrow morning?"

"So soon?" Glenn squeaked. "How about Monday."

"Okay. And maybe we could do another search through Bill's house to see what she was after. Will Neil mind?"

Glenn turned on the hot pot. "We can think of an excuse. Maybe I saw something suspicious. Or maybe we can offer to straighten up before the realtor walk-through."

Crystal pushed through the doors and plopped down at the bar without taking off her fringed leather jacket. She clutched her phone and scrolled. Her eyes were moist. Her lips had the slightest tremble.

"Crystal, honey?" I said.

"My mother and older sister are texting. I don't think they realize I'm on the thread, and they are saying horrible things about me. I don't know what to do." She dropped her forehead on her crossed arms.

Custer's motorcycle roared past the window and down the alley.

"I've just started the hot water," Glenn said. "I'll make you some tea."

"I'm so sorry, sweetie. Where does your mother live? I don't think I've ever asked you."

She lifted her head. "My mom lives just outside of Ocean City. She's very tan. Even in December."

Custer came through the door while tying his bandana around his forehead. He glanced at Crystal and headed for the coffee.

She picked up her phone again. "Here's a sample of what they are writing. This is my sister:

Is Crystal going to be at your house for Christmas? Because if she is, then one of my kids would have to sleep on the sofa.

And my mother's response:

She can find somewhere else to stay. Or I can just tell her there isn't enough room this year."

She set her phone face down on the bar. "It gets worse."

Glenn delivered a cup of tea. The scent of chamomile filled the air. "I'm very sorry, Crystal. I wish you hadn't been included."

"Thing is, I'd rather know than not know if this is happening. But it sure feels awful." She placed her hands on her stomach. "Really awful. And now I don't know what to do. Should I tell them I saw this thread? But that could just mean more of the same. Blaming *me* for being on the group text. Like it was my idea!"

Custer stood next to me, a steaming coffee in his grip. "Silence is a great source of strength."

Crystal batted her eyes a few times. "I'm sorry? That sounded condescending, master chef."

"I am the last guy to judge someone's messed up family. Remember when my illustrious father was in town?"

I thought for a moment. "Crystal, I think Custer is advising you to not engage."

"It's the Lao Tzu way," he said. "It's tempting to engage, but your strength is in your silence. Let the hurt wash over you. It will pass, and you will be stronger."

"Don't engage," she said quietly. "I have that choice, right? I can step out of the toxic pattern."

"Exactly," I said. "And Custer's right, feel it and let it pass."

She twitched her lips to one side, seemingly taking in our words. She nodded once and said, "Thank you, Custer. And you too, Rosalie and Glenn. This is my safe place, I think. I still feel rotten, but it's already going away. Oh, and Custer?"

"What's up?"

"I think we need a smaller version of the Day Lily burger for kids. They don't like all that blue cheese and stuff. Maybe a smash burger, fries on the side. And Rosalie? We need more for kids to eat. It's as if we are discouraging families from eating here. It seems snooty. Maybe I'll bring in a jar of applesauce."

I smiled, trying not to giggle at her about-face. "What do you think, Custer?"

He shrugged. "You get a kid in here who wants a smash burger, I'll make it." He sipped his coffee. "But only if you stop calling me master chef."

"I can't promise that. It's too much fun."

I checked Custer's reaction. "I'll just let that wash over me." The door swung back and forth as he went into the kitchen.

Glenn nudged his glasses up his nose. "God, I love my job."

Chapter Forty-Five

Welcome to the Day Lily Café
A gathering place offering simplicity and
freshness, with a focus on locally sourced ingredients

Comfort Food Thursday Specials:
Lunch: Locally-caught Grilled Rockfish Taco
with avocado mousse, salsa verde, and grilled corn
Dinner: Steak Frites and Hollywood Salad
Steak au poivre with beurre blanc sauce and crispy fries
Romaine salad with garlic croutons and parmesan crisps

With enough butter, anything is good.
– Julia Child

* * *

The café was surprisingly busy for dinner that night. Maybe one day of being snowed in gave our customers enough cabin fever to want to get out on the town. Without Nathan on Thursdays, my job included making drinks. I was no mixologist, but Nathan had prepared a cheat sheet for me that I kept under the bar. When that didn't work, I had an app on my phone. I now knew to fill a martini glass with ice water to chill the glass before adding the cocktail, and I had a set of copper mugs for Moscow Mules. So far, even my thirstiest customers have been patient.

Crystal tapped in an order on the Point of Sale. "I got my first smash burger order. The kid is so freakin' cute and polite. He said, 'Thank you, Ma'am,' when I gave him a straw for his water. Oh, wait, there's nowhere to put this."

"Just put it in as a special," I said. "I'll tell Custer."

"Those steaks are coming out beautifully," Glenn said as he waited for Crystal to finish. "I'm salivating."

As I wiped down the bar, I noticed the front door opening. A man stepped inside dressed in khakis and a thick fleece jacket. He wiped his shoes and looked around as if getting his bearings.

"Glenn," I said. "I think that's Patrick. The golfing partner. I met him at the club when I was there with Janice."

"How fortuitous. Shall I seat him at the bar?"

"Yes, please."

Patrick removed his jacket and draped it over the back of the chair. "Hello, Rosalie. We met at the club."

I set a glass of ice water in front of him. "Yes, I remember, Patrick. Welcome to the Day Lily Café."

He sat and folded his hands together. A thick gold wedding band was tight on his left hand. "I've never been here before. It seems I always just go to the club."

"So, what brings you in tonight?"

"I don't know if you saw the paper this morning, but Jonesy is the one who hit Bill. He called me Wednesday night to tell me. He said he came clean with the sheriff."

"How is he?"

"Not good. How could he be?" Patrick frowned. His dark brown hair, flecked with white, had begun an ebb tide from his forehead. His hazel eyes were lined with pain. "It's as if the world's gone mad."

"Can I get you a drink?"

"Oh, yeah. Vodka tonic with no tonic. Not too much ice."

As I was scooping ice into a tall glass, Glenn sidled up next to me. "I need two *winds at my back*, please."

"What are those?" Patrick said.

"It's one of our specials," I said. "We combine vermouth from Vanelli's Winery with sparkling water and a garnish. It's a dark Spanish-style vermouth they spice with herbs from their farm. It's delicious."

"I should probably get out more." He looked around the room. "You keep a pretty nice place."

"Thank you." I set the glass of straight vodka in front of him. He immediately took a long slug.

After I garnished the drinks for Glenn's order with a large Greek green olive and an orange slice, he ushered them to table four.

"How is Jonesy handling this?" I asked Patrick.

"He killed one of his best friends. How do you think? At least the doc has him on a bucket full of tranquilizers."

"It must be hard for both you and Gunther."

He shook his head slowly. "That's the other crazy part. You know what Gunther said when I told him about Jonesy? He said, 'Well, what do you know?' He practically sounded happy. Happy? What the heck is wrong with that guy?"

"Maybe he was just surprised?"

"It was weird. I think his reaction is bugging me as much as everything else. I mean, we played golf together at least once a week. It's intense. We can all hit the ball, but you know, that's a lot of personalities in two little golf carts. But we all got along with Jonesy. He wouldn't hurt anyone unless it was an accident. I know him. His wife still adores him. She acts like a schoolgirl when they're together. Why would Gunther want anything bad to happen to him? Christ almighty Jonesy could end up in prison." Tears rimmed his eyes. "That would kill him. I'm certain of it. He wouldn't last a day. Not even an hour. With a big heart like that?"

"Has he hired a lawyer?"

"Hey, Rosalie?" Crystal said. "We're backing up. Check the POS. I need two cosmos ten minutes ago and a bottle of chianti with four glasses."

"Yes, okay." I briefly wondered if Nathan would add another night to his schedule. "Two cosmos. I know that one."

"Make that three cosmos," Glenn said while filling a cup with ice and diet cola, "and a bottle of rosé."

"Glasses?"

"One," Glenn said.

I set two trays on the counter. One glass? Maybe Gunther was right. Maybe the world has gone mad. At least in December.

Patrick drained his drink and sucked on an ice cube. His face drooped like a basset hound's.

"Would you like some food?" I said as I rattled the cocktail shaker.

"Just more vodka. But take your time. I like sitting here. You folks are nice. And it's a welcome respite from the routine at the club." He sniffled and swallowed the ice. "That years' long routine of mine just vanished in a puff of smoke."

The cosmos were ready, and I set the wine glasses on the trays. "You know, Patrick, Jonesy said Bill's bike was going all over the road. It clearly sounds like an accident. I hope you encourage him to get the best lawyer he can. And they can't say he was drunk because no one did a breathalyzer." I pulled a rosé from the cooler. "Hopefully, he has an excellent driving record. Has he ever had a DUI?"

His forehead was deeply furrowed. "You a lawyer in your first life? And can I please have another drink?"

* * *

My hairline was dotted with perspiration by the time I caught up on the drinks. I checked the POS and headed into the kitchen to get the dinner orders for the customers at the bar.

"She did it," Custer said. "She actually did it."

"Who?"

Custer picked up a jar of applesauce. "This."

"It looks like you had some takers."

"I'm all about catering to families, but this can't happen. Our customers come here for elevated food. If they don't like it, they can take their kids to the drive-thru." He pointed to the jar of applesauce. "I'm not dishing out that slop in this restaurant. I'm trying to make something out of myself. Elevate me too. Applesauce is not on the menu. Understand?"

"Yes, I understand. And I agree." I blotted my forehead with a dish towel. "I'll think of something."

When I returned to the bar, Patrick was on his phone. He looked up. "I just texted Jonesy everything you said. I think it helped. You know? Focusing on solving the problem is a good way to keep moving forward."

"Thank goodness."

"Say, Rosalie, can I get two of those steak specials to go? I'd like to take one home to my Penny. And I'm going to bring her here. Sometimes, we all need a change of scenery."

Chapter Forty-Six

The next morning, Tyler and I scheduled a coffee date in my kitchen. What remained of the two avocado toasts I made for him were the crumbs he was dabbing up with his finger.

"Are you coming to the café tonight?" I said and took a sip of coffee.

"Always."

"How is Betty White feeling?"

"So far so good." He slurped his coffee. "Did you check out the batch of goat cheese Bini made yesterday? Lucas gave her a couple of gallons of goat milk to work with."

I hopped up. Already in my café uniform, I smoothed my above-the-knee black skirt and opened the refrigerator. "Two batches?"

"She used the dried lavender from the greenhouse in one. It's pretty damn good."

"This is going to be a big hit. I need to pick up some crackers from the wine and cheese shop on my way into town."

Tyler pointed to yesterday's paper. "Looks like your murder mystery's been solved."

I sat down across from him. "Can I tell you something? Just between you and me?"

Tyler frowned.

"Bill Rutherford had a bullet in his back. That's why he was weaving around in the middle of the road."

"There's nothing about that in the paper."

"The sheriff is keeping it quiet until we figure out who shot him."

"So you're not finished." He crossed his arms.

"No. Not yet."

"That's a disappointment, Nancy Drew. I thought you might have some more free time."

I played with his fingers. "Always for you."

My phone vibrated. Tyler peered over at it. "It's Glenn."

I swiped it open and pushed the microphone icon. "You're on speaker. Tyler and I are having coffee. What's—"

"You need to get here immediately, Rosalie."

Tyler and I exchanged a concerned glance. "Where are you?"

"At the café. I have something for you to see."

"Is everything all right?"

"Please just come."

Glenn ended the call.

"That was cryptic," Tyler said.

"Why is he there so early, and what on earth is wrong?"

"Um, Rosalie? Why are you still sitting here?"

"Right." I kissed him and began gathering my things, including the two batches of goat cheese. "Tyler?"

"Yes, Rosalie?" a small smile on his face.

"Thank you for being patient with me. I'll text you once I find out what's going on."

Chapter Forty-Seven

I rushed into the restaurant and found Glenn at the bar. "What's happened?"

"Vera from Wednesday night is not Vera," he said. "She's Doris Flatbush."

I gave my head a small shake. "That name sounds familiar. But what about Vera?"

He spun around an open Washington newspaper and tapped on an article. *"Unearthed Eastern Shore Gem."* I slipped on my glasses and began to read. "Is this a restaurant review?" I looked up. "Of the *Day Lily?*"

"It just so happens Vera, or should I say, Doris, is a food critic."

My heart thumped into my stomach. "Is it positive?" I asked tentatively.

He nudged it closer.

Unearthed Eastern Shore Gem

It is often a huge commitment to cross the Chesapeake Bay Bridge from Washington, D.C., just to go out to dinner. But one snowy evening this week, my friends and I decided to explore the Eastern Shore frontier. With low expectations and just hoping to make it back to our hotel in a blizzard, we would have been happy with a glass of red wine and maybe a steaming Maryland crab soup. But when we arrived at the Day Lily Café in the quaint Eastern Shore town of Cardigan, my heart's pace slowed immediately, and I found myself grinning, anticipating what I was hoping would be a lovely evening. The Day Lily Café did not disappoint.

Modeled after the colors of a Tuscan villa at sunset, the interior design is warm and welcoming. The walls are painted a soothing shade of ochre that softens the space and somehow gets you thinking about eating fresh parmesan cheese with some salty olives. We were greeted by owner, Rosalie Hart, who provisions the restaurant with herbs, produce, and eggs from her organic farm just outside of town.

When she suggested a Santorini white wine to go with our appetizers, I was skeptical. But when we ordered one, the crisp, clean, yet complex taste was perfectly paired with locally caught rockfish tacos topped with avocado mousse, pico de gallo, and grilled corn.

Chef Custer Wells, a native of Cardigan who studied at the Washington Institute of Culinary Arts, prepared a perfectly cooked steak au poivre topped with a beurre blanc sauce paired with French fries cooked in beef tallow. The salad, a recipe from Rosalie's childhood, put your accustomed Caesar to shame.

And don't get me started on the crab cake which we paired with a red blend from a local winery. I know, a local winery in Maryland can make your lips purse, but the Casa Vanelli winery in Devon County is another unearthed gem. I have already joined the wine club.

There's nothing complicated here. And yet the dimmed lights and crisp white tablecloths encourage you to put your napkin in your lap and rub your hands together as you look forward to the next dish. I know the Eastern Shore has been called many things, but the friendly, down-to-earth approach to life made our experience feel as if we were dining al fresco with a large Italian family—wine, laughter, fresh loaves of bread on the table. We stayed for over three hours, the evening ending with a charming discussion about food and its narrative with Chef Wells over a glass (or two) of Casa Vanelli prosecco and candied figs.

For those of you making weekend plans, we learned Friday is Notte Italiana at the Day Lily Café, and Chef Wells prepares the original recipe for Fettuccine Alfredo table-side. I will be back for this one. I'm sure he puts on quite a show.

Dining at the Day Lily Café made me feel as if I were Robert Frost arriving home after having chosen the right road. It mastered freshness mixed with originality marinated in a small-town cozy feel on a snowy winter night.

The Day Lily Café
220 Main Street
Cardigan, MD
410-888-8888
Cuisine: New American Comfort
Open: Wednesday - Saturday
Lunch 11:00 - 2:00
Dinner: 5:00 - 9:00
Sunday Brunch
11:00 - 2:00

Rating: 4 out of 4 stars

Where to stay: Devonshire Inn (a third unearthed gem—just wow!)

Atmosphere: Inviting, extremely comfortable seats, no rushing, warm and friendly. The solid mahogany bar is inviting. The television is only on during Ravens games.

Acoustics: We got a little loud, but no one complained

Service: Non-intrusive, helpful, and informative—a perfect blend. When the three of us ordered a shared appetizer that included two mini tacos, they added a third, no charge

Plating: Artwork!

Price: Moderate

Reservations: None

"Glenn?"

"Yes, my dear?"

"What does this mean?"

"You got four out of four."

“I need to sit.”

Glenn patted the seat next to him.

“I can’t breathe.”

“I recommend that you do.”

“Four stars?

“Mm-hm.” He was grinning. Hard.

Chapter Forty-Eight

Once I finally caught my breath, I called Tyler to assure him everything was fine at the café. More than fine. It was time to prep the kitchen, but I was having trouble focusing. "Is business going to pick up, Glenn?"

"We shall see." He stood and put his tea cup in a bin. "I need to get this out on social media. And I've got to tell Gretchen. Doris mentioned the inn. Her business is going to pick up as well."

Just as he was heading back to sit at the desk in the kitchen, Custer burst through the door. "Did you see it?"

"We did indeed," Glenn said.

"I can't believe it." He hugged Glenn, then me. "Monique called me first thing this morning. She's the one who told Flatbush about the café." He clutched his helmet. "She loved it. Four freakin' stars."

"It's incredible," I said. "Please thank Monique for me."

Crystal strolled in, the suede fringe on her jacket swaying back and forth. "What's up? This room is vibrating."

Glenn handed her the paper.

She began to read. "Wait, this is about the Day Lily?" She looked up, mouth agape. "Was this person here the night it snowed?"

"You bet," Custer said.

She continued reading. The rest of us remained silent until she finished. "We are going to have to start taking reservations," she said and returned the paper to Glenn. "It will be too crazy if we don't."

"She's right," Glenn said. "I can download the software. We should get on

'The Best Table' as well so customers can make reservations online."

"Should we wait and see what happens tonight?" I said, knowing this was probably me hating change. It was a thing for me. Or at least it had been. I liked to know what was coming my way, which is one of the main reasons I took my divorce so hard. But a lot has changed since then. I had grown past the need for certainty. I was willing to take risks now.

I clutched my mother's pearls. She had always told me to identify a feeling before I acted on it. Massaging a pearl with my thumb, I frowned.

"Rosalie," Glenn said, looking puzzled. "What on earth could be bothering you?"

I didn't answer. I had to discern what and why this feeling tugged at me. It at least deserved my noticing. I gazed around the room at my intimate café, the recently erased chalkboard still showing traces of yesterday's menu, the sun streaming in the front windows highlighting dust motes. Just like Vera, I loved every inch of this place. My unearthed Eastern Shore Gem.

"It doesn't matter what's happening," I said. "What matters is our response."

"Hey, Boss," Custer said, eyes narrowed as if trying to fathom what I was trying to say. "You're sounding a little nuts again."

"I realize that, but hang on. Do you know why the local country club doesn't have tee times?"

"Rosalie…" Glenn said in a not-so-patient voice.

"Because it's Cardigan," I said. "We have to stay true to the spirit of this café and where we live. So, no reservations. We can figure it out. People love to drop in on a whim. It's a gathering place. I absolutely hate it when I spot an interesting restaurant, and the first thing the greeter says is, 'Do you have a reservation?' And when I say no, that look of disgust, like how could you be so stupid to not have a reservation. It makes me feel wretched."

"I hate that, too," Crystal said.

"I guess what I'm trying to say is, this visibility and praise can't change us. We have to stay true to what this café is all about. We can't get swept away, or we will lose our soul." I looked from face to face, trying to read if they had any clue what I was saying.

"I think I understand," Glenn said. "We can't let this change us. Vera gave us four stars because of the welcoming environment we've created. What did she say? Informative and helpful but not intrusive. And they were here for three hours, and no one asked them to leave."

"Okay, so not to be pragmatic when we are talking about dreams," Crystal said. "Because I'm all about listening to our hopes and dreams. But what do we do if there's a line out the door?"

"Good question." I chewed on a fingernail. "We take their cell phone number and text them when we have a table open. We can suggest they shop at our lovely stores or get a cocktail somewhere. Or if it's not too long, they can wait at the bar. There's enough standing room. We could move some tables around too. Okay, am I nuts as Custer has so politely suggested?"

"Just sounding nuts," he said. "Not actually nuts. Anyway, I'm cool with it. But you better nail the system down now before we open."

"Thank you for understanding." I smiled. "Now, I believe I need to make a boatload of pasta. Are we good?"

Crystal held out her hand. "Come on, group fist bump."

I took a long, deep breath as I headed into the kitchen, comforted by the thought I would be able to cling to some sense of control over whatever outside forces were about to be unleashed here.

Chapter Forty-Nine

Lunch was normal, no throngs of diners. I got the feeling we were all a wee bit disappointed, but it would take some time to get the word out. Once I had finished the pasta, I walked over to Birdie's to see how many extra papers she had. Ours had been handled quite a bit, and I wanted to frame a pristine copy to hang on the wall.

Summer was on Doris' stool, filing a nail coated in dark purple polish. I wondered briefly if she was a Ravens fan.

"Hi there," I said as I removed my red leather gloves. "Doris swimming at the Y?"

She placed the file on the glass counter. "That she is. She's lost three pounds already."

"Wow. That's impressive."

"My mom told me not to talk to you." She held my gaze, eyes unwavering.

"Okay. That's interesting. Do you know why?"

"She said you were nosy and liked to get into other people's business."

I clutched my gloves. "Only when they have something to hide."

"Do you think my mom's hiding something?"

"Do you?"

"She hid the money from me. I know that."

"I'm glad you know that now," I said softly.

"They charged Mr. Jones with hit and run, didn't they?"

I huffed out a sigh. "Yes, he's been charged with involuntary manslaughter."

"Now *you're* hiding something," she said and continued to lock eyes with mine. It was easy to do when we were both not a quarter of an inch over five-four. "Do you think he wanted to kill him?"

"No. Absolutely not." A trickle of sweat traveled down my back as I debated what to tell Summer about how her father died.

"What really happened, Miss Rosalie?"

"You can't tell anyone, do you understand?"

"My English teacher once told me I had integrity. I had to look it up to understand the full meaning. Her saying that has given me my north star. Whatever I do, my goal is to do integrity."

"I can see that about you."

"How did my father die?"

"All I can say is we are still looking into it. I don't think we have the full story."

She plopped down on the stool. "You think it was my mom."

"There are others with motives."

"If it was my mom, I want to know. It would be horrible, but I want to know." She checked the nail she had just filed. "Can I help in some way?"

"Oh, my dear." I shook my head. "I would never ever ask you to do that."

"Okay. Thank you. I like talking to you, Miss Rosalie."

"I like talking to you too. I have a great deal of respect for you."

She stood and picked up a stack of papers. "Doris said you can have them all. No charge. That's really cool about the review. You must be pretty happy."

"I never expected something like this. And I have no idea what happens next. Maybe nothing?"

"Maybe something." She flashed me a rare smile.

Chapter Fifty

Welcome to the Day Lily Café
A gathering place offering simplicity and
freshness, with a focus on locally sourced ingredients

Friday
Notte Italiana
Antipasti: Local goat cheese served with honey and sesame crackers
Pasta: Fettuccine Alfredo
Prepared table-side by Chef Custer Wells
Secondi: One dozen local oysters raw or grilled with garlic
Contorni: Artichoke salad in a parmigiana basket
Dolci: Vanilla ice cream topped with espresso

Menu Insert
Drink Special: Negroni Tramonto
The Day Lily's signature version of Negroni Sbagliato
changes out the Prosecco for Italian Lambrusco.

Tramonto translates to 'sunset' in Italian.

History of Negroni Sbagliato
Legend has it that while mixing
the classic Negroni for a patron, an Italian bartender
noticed a beautiful woman seated at the bar.

Distracted by her charm, he unintentionally
poured Prosecco into the Negroni instead of gin.
Sbagliato translates to 'mistake'
in Italian.

* * *

Nathan gripped the newspaper and frowned as he read the review. "Holy crap," he said. "Flatbush joined the wine club?"

"She loved everything."

"I missed it." He looked up at me with that adorable grin. "Did you at least tell her about me?"

"Yes, Crystal, too. Neither of you were here." I rolled my lips in. "Which brings up another topic, any chance you want to work Wednesday and Thursday nights? I'm getting in over my head. We had a backup last night. Too many cosmos."

"I thought you'd never ask." Nathan's red hair was particularly disheveled that evening, and I was pretty sure he must have worn a knit cap on his way to work.

"Thank you. Do you want to borrow a comb?"

"It's a waste of time."

"I totally get that. I never should have asked."

"Do I look that ridiculous?"

"No. Never. And, thank you. Everything's better when you're here."

We stopped talking while Crystal lit the last candle of the menorah and said the prayer. She spun around and walked over to us. "Miss Rosalie?"

"You don't really need the 'Miss,' Crystal, you can just call me Rosalie."

"For the umpteenth time, I know, but I grew up here, and that's what you call your elders."

"Okay, so, you have a question?"

She glanced down at her moccasins for a moment and took a deep breath. "If we are going to start getting busier around here, and I'm working harder, and you're pulling in more money, I…I think…no, I want a raise."

"Hey, Crys," Nathan said as he wiped down the counter. "You'll be making a ton more tip money too. Did ya' think about that?"

"I didn't ask you, Nathan, but yes, I did think about that."

"I'm not opposed," I said.

"Wait, what? I've been rehearsing this all afternoon. I have the numbers worked out, and I have all kinds of reasons why." She pulled a crinkled piece of paper from her apron pocket. "Do you want to hear them?"

"No need." I smiled. "But I'll take a look at your numbers." I noticed several people outside the door. "And Crystal? It's time to flip the sign." I clapped my hands together. "To quote Samuel Jackson in Jurassic Park, *Hold onto your butts.*"

Chapter Fifty-One

By six the café had begun to fill with patrons but so far we were all keeping up. Only one party of four opted to wait for a table via text and decided to walk over to The Grande for cocktails. Tyler was at the bar drinking a *Negroni Tramonto*.

"What do you think?" I said.

"Four stars."

I giggled. "Is Dickens at my house or yours?"

"The latter." He peered up at me. "That okay?"

"Better than okay."

Crystal approached the POS. "Are we ready?"

"Do we have a *Fettuccine Alfredo* order?" I said.

"Another family of four." She held the door open for Custer and the cart.

"He's not going to toss some more on the floor, is he?" Tyler said.

"He's got it down. Chef Alfredo would be proud." I noticed a couple at the door and hurried over to them. "We're full, but I can take your number and text when we have an opening. Or you can dine at the bar."

"What's going on?" the young woman said, a wide smile on her face.

"Our chef is making the pasta table-side."

She turned to look at her companion. "This sounds like fun. Sit at the bar?"

"You bet."

The lights dimmed, and *Bella Notte* serenaded Custer.

I filled wine and water glasses, and everyone was mesmerized as Custer did his thing. I noticed another woman at the hostess stand and walked over to her.

"Welcome to the Day Lily Café. Would you—"

She waved me away. "I'm watching," she said in a thick French accent, eyes focused on Custer. She was dressed in all black—tight pants, tee, and leather jacket topped with an expensive floral scarf. She was short and thin but wore spiky black leather boots.

"Can I bring you a drink?"

She shook her head. I remained next to her, and as far as I could tell, Custer hadn't noticed this woman, who was, without a doubt, the infamous Monique. She watched his every move, nodding and gasping, her face animated, her lips a deep burgundy. Custer had indeed mastered his routine. Since his debut, he began shoving his sleeves up to his elbows, exposing his rock-hard arms. He took more risks as his confidence grew, and he somehow managed a little wiggle into his routine that was ridiculously cute. When he plated the pasta, he swirled it expertly with a set of tongs into a rich, creamy mound.

"Excellent," Monique whispered. Custer bowed, and she yelled, "Bravo!" at the top of her lungs.

He noticed her and broke into a wide grin. After swiping the rims of the plates with a towel, he set them in front of each patron, grating extra Parmesan on each.

"*Buon Appetito,*" he said to the family, "enjoy our *speciale.*" He turned and hurried over to Monique, hugging her hard. "You're here."

"Of course, my darling. I'm so proud of you."

"Boss? This is Monique."

"Welcome, Monique. And thank you for the referral. That review was absolutely amazing."

"I wanted her to experience my protege's talent."

"Come back to the kitchen with me." He grabbed her hand and called to Nathan as he passed, "Hey, dude, can you bring us a bottle of champagne and a couple of glasses?"

I stood next to Tyler.

"Who's the woman in the black leaving a trail of French perfume in her wake?"

"Custer's teacher."

"Say no more."

* * *

When I stepped into the kitchen to ask Custer what he needed from me, I stopped in my tracks. Monique was wearing an apron, and they were both huddled over a frying pan. The room was filled with the scent of crisped bacon.

"What's going on?" I said.

Custer glanced over his shoulder. "We're elevating the oysters. It's amazing what she's doing."

"Oh, my darling." She brushed a finger under his chin. "It is so wonderful to see you." She planted a wet kiss on his lips.

I started to ask Custer how I could help but decided I needed a better word choice. "What's backing up? The pasta orders are flying in."

"Always the salad," he said and dipped a spoon into whatever they had going on in that pan. *"Oui, Oui, Mademoiselle."* He wiped his hands on his apron. "The goat cheese orders are piling up, too." He took a long sip of champagne.

My eyes widened, and I tried to process every detail of this very odd and unexpected twist in the evening.

"Two more fettuccines," Crystal called through the door. "Step it up, you guys."

Monique turned to look at me. "Is she your manager?"

"No," I said with a sigh. "She's Crystal."

Chapter Fifty-Two

Glenn unlocked the door to Bill Rutherford's home Saturday morning, our collars turned up, our breath vaporizing into clouds. Remembering the initial chill in the house the last time we were here, I was dressed in jeans, fur-lined boots, and a cozy turtleneck sweater. It was early enough that I would have plenty of time to change for work before we opened.

"It smells musty," I said as we stepped inside. "Neil has his work cut out for him."

"He's coming out Monday to go through some things. I said I would stop by with a sandwich or something. And bourbon, of course."

"You okay after last night?" I said. "We were pretty busy. Maybe we should hire another server."

"I'm fine. It was a great deal of fun." Glenn turned up the thermostat. "I went home last night and did some googling on Abby."

"Can we sit for a minute, gather our thoughts?"

Glenn went into the family room and eased himself onto an oversized chair. I sat across from him and peeled off my gloves.

"That is a very large television," Glenn said. "I don't think I would need my glasses to watch it."

"Agreed. So, anything interesting about Abby?"

"Oh, yes. It turns out she was a talented gymnast and a contender for the Olympic team."

"That fits, doesn't it? Her body type, her drive. Did she qualify?"

"There was a meet before the trials. Her team was winning the group all-around event. Abby had twisted her ankle during her floor routine, but her coach made her get on the balance beam anyway, saying they couldn't win without her. She did a flip and missed her landing. Compound fracture in her ankle and was in a cast for months. And her gymnastic career? Poof."

"How awful," I said. "What's her life been like since?"

Glenn slipped out of his shoes and propped his feet on an ottoman. "It's not really clear. There's something online about a fitness program that's associated with her name. Like some sort of combination of Zumba, yoga, and tumbling." Glenn frowned. "I may not have that right."

"That must be the business Bill was going to invest in. Has she ever married?"

"I don't know how to find that out. I do know she's had several addresses all over the East Coast."

"Great research, partner. A gymnast who went through some tough times. Wonder if her luck changed as she grew older?"

"I'm also wondering how she can afford to live in this community if all she does is teach yoga. She's only sixty. Not eligible for social security."

"I'm getting the feeling there is a little devil in our fitness angel. Where do we start?"

"Isn't there always money involved? I mean, really. How often is it not the reason?"

"Certainly for Micky B., and now maybe Neil and Abby. Glenn, tell me more about Bill. I know he was an acquaintance, but any insights? Was he thrifty or a big spender? Did he have a lot of visitors, or did he spend his nights alone?"

"All good questions. Most of our interactions were on one of our patios. We liked to have a martini on Monday evenings when the café was closed. At least in the summer. Let's see. He was a fidgety guy, you know? I don't think he liked sitting still. But I enjoyed spending time with him. He certainly wasn't ever boring. Do you know we were at the same Bruce Springsteen concert in 1980? Anyway, like I said, he was very social, but there was something in his eyes, a distance, I would say." Glenn rubbed his chin. "As if part of him was longing for something he knew he would never have." He frowned. "Good lord. How did I come up with that?"

"It's what you saw in him." I smiled. "And I wonder what that something was."

"Yes, yes, I do too." Glenn stood and brushed off his khakis. "I hope Neil gives me some time on Monday. I think you're right asking questions about Bill. The more we learn about him, the more we will understand the killer's motive."

Okay," I said. "I'll go back to his office. I don't think I was thorough enough. I hit the jackpot with Micky B. and stopped my snooping."

"I'll check around the kitchen and bedroom to see if there are any photos of Abby and Bill together. There's something she doesn't want us to find. And then I'll join you in the office." Glenn pushed up the sleeves of his sweater. "Warming up nicely in here. I wonder what sort of heat pump Bill had." He stepped into his shoes. "Are you all right, my dear? Should I go to my place and make us a coffee?"

"Why not? That's a fabulous idea. And Glenn? I believe we are going to find out who shot Bill. Someone was lurking along River Road that night. I wonder if anyone heard a shot?"

"It's deer season. We hear shots all the time. I doubt anyone would remember or think it odd."

"And they could have had a silencer, I guess."

"Looking for witnesses probably isn't the best course. Now, I'll get us some coffee. Be right back."

Chapter Fifty-Three

I was at Bill's desk again, but this time, I decided to be still for a moment and focus on what it would feel like to be Bill in this chair. A framed picture on the wall in front of me was of a waterman hauling in a bushel of oysters on a hazy, gray day. Neil said his father grew up in the D.C. area. Maybe Bill had embraced his new home. Or maybe this is what an interior decorator suggested for artwork in a home on the Eastern Shore.

"Who were you, William Rutherford," I said softly. I looked around with a different eye. No framed photographs of family or friends, unlike Glenn's sideboard crammed with loved ones. I felt lonely in his chair. *As if longing for something he knew he would never have.*

I hopped up and went into his bedroom. The Love Me wall must have something for us to go on. Yes, he was a runner and a cyclist, both solitary sports. Is there a diploma? Ah, George Mason University, bachelor of science. That doesn't tell me much. Above it was a framed newspaper article from 1968. *Willy Rutherford of Fairfax breaks school record with a cross country win* by Henry Rutherford.

The smell of fresh coffee preceded Glenn. "What are you doing in here?"

I accepted the mug and faced the wall again. "Trying to learn more about Bill. His father was a journalist for the local paper. At least when Bill was in high school."

"Will you look at that? Broke the school record." Glenn closed the door a little so we could see more. "What about those small photos up there? Looks like one is with Bill and his parents. I wonder if he was an only child. Oh, and the one below is of Bill and Neil, and that must be Neil's mother."

"She's lovely. But Bill isn't smiling in either of them. What was he longing for, Glenn?"

"We may never know."

I crossed my arms and frowned. "We're missing something. It's right under our nose." I slapped a palm on my forehead. "Good grief, Glenn. There won't be any interesting photos or documents around here. Did Neil ever pick up his father's belongings?"

"I don't believe so."

I checked my watch. "I need to make a stop on my way to the café. And Glenn?"

He was smiling. "Yes?"

"I want some time with Neil on Monday, too. Maybe we could take him to the Tavern for a beer and a burger. Do you think he would do that?"

"Yes. I believe that man is struggling. And I want to know why."

Chapter Fifty-Four

"It took me five tries today," I said to Joe Wilgus as he glared at his phone. After running home to change into my uniform, I stopped at the café for his coffee and headed to the Sheriff's Department. Happy to see Lila was off duty, I strolled into his office and sat across from him.

"Doesn't mean it will take me that many." He punched in five letters on the Wordle app. "Damn. I got the 'a' and the 'e' in the right place but not a single consonant."

I crossed my legs. "It's one of those words. You need a throwaway word with a bunch of possible letters."

"I don't have it in me. Waste of a turn. And I'm not a throwaway kind of guy." After a moment, he set his phone on the desk. "What's up?"

"Do you have Bill Rutherford's phone?"

"Yeah. It's pretty banged up."

"I can't believe I haven't asked to see it before."

"You know I've charged Jonesy."

"Donny Jones didn't shoot Bill in the back."

"So, who did?"

"I have suspects."

"How are you going to open his phone?"

"I have no idea."

He folded his hands over his stomach. "What exactly are you looking for?"

"Texts and photos. Emails would be harder to hack into." I crossed my arms. "Joe, you don't really believe it was Jonesy, do you? He was so distraught the other day."

"Maybe because he got caught. Ever think of that?"

"Patrick said he wouldn't last an hour in prison. That he has too big of a heart."

"Then he shouldn't have run over his friend."

I scowled. "This is an act. You don't believe it any more than I do. Listen, I'll do the heavy lifting, just give me a chance to keep looking. You don't want an innocent man to go to prison."

"He's not innocent. He hit the man with his SUV and didn't tell anyone and tried to hide the evidence by going to a body shop in Dover."

"Well, there's that." I dropped a couple of creamers on his desk. "Forgot these."

He picked one up and flipped it around in his palm. "You're right, Hart. I don't want Jonesy to go to prison."

I cleared my throat, trying to suppress a smile. "I'm sorry. Did you just say I'm right?"

"Get over it." He stood. "I'll fetch his phone."

Chapter Fifty-Five

I parked my car in the alley behind the café and gathered my things, including a large container of lavender-infused goat cheese. The temperature had dropped quite a bit in the last few hours, and the air was so cold it dried my nostrils. Hitching my purse on my shoulder, I stopped short when a woman stood between me and the door to the café.

She was slight but had a fierce look on her heavily made-up face. Her blond hair had streaks of pink.

"Can I help you?"

"Stay away from my kid," she hissed. The intensity in her eyes caused me to step back.

"Who are you exactly?"

"You know who I am, you nosy bitch."

"You said daughter. You mean Summer? Are you Michelle?"

"The name's Micky." She moved closer. "And nothin' else. Stay out of my business, or you'll regret it." She punched the front of my shoulders with her fists. I stumbled backward. "Got it?"

I stared. "Do not touch me again," I said, trying to quell the quiver in my voice. "Now get out of my way."

She didn't move. So much for my attempt at bravado.

"What do you want with my daughter? She's sixteen, for chrissakes. What could you possibly need from her?"

"What does everyone want? The truth."

"It's overrated."

"I need to get to work. I have nothing more to say to you."

"I'm watching you. I can get a restraining order."

I rolled my eyes. "Good luck with that, Michelle." I pushed past her and went into my restaurant, closing the door hard.

"What the heck was all that?" Custer said. "She just shoved you. I was about to go out there, but then you totally handled it. I never took you for an ass-kicker."

"That was terrifying." I dropped my purse. "Is she gone?"

Custer looked past me. "Yeah."

"Darling," Monique came through the door. "I have the foie gras and the caviar from FedEx. It smells amazing." She noticed me. "Hello, Rosalie. You look as if you've seen a ghost."

"Oh, don't mind me. But did you say foie gras?"

"I'm cooking with Custer tonight. It's going to be a feast. Your patrons will love it."

"Foie *gras?*"

"Darling," she said, "maybe you should gather yourself. It's almost time for lunch."

She stood next to Custer and nuzzled his neck. "Let's make some herbed butter. We can slather it on everything."

"What's cooking in that pot?" I said.

"Prime rib." Custer rubbed his hands together. "I started it at 6:00 AM."

"Oh." I turned to go but stopped. "Custer?"

"Yes, boss?"

"One special for lunch and one for dinner. That's it. The rest of the menu is the same."

One of Custer's eyes narrowed in an annoyed wink. "Got it, boss," he said and turned away.

Glenn and Crystal were seated at a table when I entered the restaurant.

"I have no idea what to write on the chalkboard," Crystal said. "What are we even serving today? And I have no idea how to spell the words coming out of her mouth. I don't even know what they mean."

"Rosalie, are you alright? You look pale."

"Yes, that's what I've been told."

* * *

Welcome to the Day Lily Café
A gathering place offering simplicity and
freshness, with a focus on locally sourced ingredients

Saturday Specials:
Lunch: Gruyere soufflé with champagne vinegar dressed greens

Dinner:
Appetizer: Lavender goat cheese topped with caviar and a side of foie gras custard
Main Course: Prime Rib with French potato salad and French green beans

Good food is the foundation of genuine happiness
*—**Auguste Escoffier**, 'king of cooks'*

* * *

I stared at the chalkboard, hands on my hips. *Simplicity with a focus on locally sourced ingredients.* Caviar and Foie gras? I shook my head and took a long, deep breath. Patience, Rosalie, patience. This was all happening for a reason.

Crystal emerged from the kitchen. "Mr. Glenn, you have to help me. They just gave me the specials, and it ain't no grilled cheese."

"Did they write it down?"

She handed Glenn a piece of paper. He read it and looked up at me. "Apparently Saturday is *Journée Français*."

"French day?" I said.

"Yes."

"Well, this is going to be interesting, to say the least."

Chapter Fifty-Six

My day improved when Janice and Gretchen were seated at the two chairs at the end of the bar.

"You seem buggy, Rose Red," Janice said.

"I'm just happy you are both here."

"My inn is sold out tonight," Gretchen said. "I hope you're ready for the onslaught."

"Not even close." I filled their water glasses.

"I'm certainly not complaining," Gretchen said.

"Hello, my dear," Glenn said to Gretchen. "Finally have your head above water?"

"Not for long, but it's lovely to see you." They clasped hands.

"What's all that gobbledygook on the chalkboard?" Janice said. "Are you seriously serving caviar?"

"I'm going to try that," Gretchen said. "This will be fun. And I would like to toast to that fabulous review. Do you have a prosecco split?"

"I'll drink to that," Janice said.

"Of course we do," I said.

"You might want to have a little sip, too," Glenn said, eyeing me. "You seem a little tense."

I motioned for Glenn to follow me over to the wine cooler under the bar. "Micky B. shoved me in the alley," I said in a low voice. "She wants me to stay away from Summer."

"She assaulted you?" Glenn said. "You should tell the sheriff."

"And I have Bill's phone. I'm charging it now."

"Is it locked?"

"I don't know yet. But if it is, Maybe Neil will have an idea of what his password is. Remember he said his dad had given him all his passwords?"

"She actually shoved you?"

"And called me a B."

Monique walked into the room. "Did I hear something about prosecco, Rosalie? Please tell me you also serve champagne, as in the Champagne *region?*"

She was dressed in tight black slacks and a black scoop neck tee, also skin tight, with large gold hoops in her ears. Her hair had a henna tint, and it was slicked back from her face.

"Yes, we have champagne, Monique."

"Oh, thank god," she said dramatically. "May I have one, please?"

I gave her a puzzled look.

"I'll buy." She rolled her eyes. "This place needs to loosen its corset." She noticed Janice and Gretchen. *"Bonjour, Mesdames,* I'm Monique, Custer's teacher."

"Oh." Gretchen sat up a little straighter. "I'm Gretchen. And I'm ordering the foie gras for certain."

"Nice to meet you. And do I detect a British accent?"

"Yes, I'm from southern England. Would you recommend we have champagne with that appetizer instead of prosecco?"

"Yes, of course. A blanc de blanc if we have one. Now see?" She shot me a look. "Someone here knows how to appreciate the concept of pairing food and wine." She gazed around the room. "Filling up nicely. Will you bring the champagne back to us, Rosalie? Custer and I are very busy. *Au revoir, mesdames,*" she said to my friends and blew them a kiss.

The door to the kitchen swung back and forth like an exclamation mark.

I knelt down and examined the champagne selections in the cooler. None of the French champagnes were cheap. I peered over the counter at the smiling faces, the full tables, the buzz in the room. Monique helped make this happen. I pulled out two bottles of *Perrier Jouet Blanc de Blanc Brut* and stood. "Ladies," I said to my friends. "The champagne is on me."

Chapter Fifty-Seven

We survived dinner, and once the door was locked and the sign flipped, I felt as if we all let out a collective exhale. I sent Glenn and Crystal home as soon as the dishes were cleared and the tablecloths tossed in the laundry. Crystal had counted her tip money, and a high-pitched squeal followed the last dollar bill. As always, I gave Custer and Nathan the tips from the customers who ate at the bar to split.

As I wiped my hands on my apron, my feelings tumbled around inside me like a dryer full of towels. The prime rib was a tremendous hit, and taking phone numbers when we were full worked like a charm. I got a text from the owner of The Grande, who thanked me for sending customers over to them for a cocktail. I'm certain some got so comfortable they stayed for dinner instead, but that thought made me happy. It's a small town. We have to support one another, and I have no doubt the staff at The Grande would feel the same.

I stood next to Nathan. "Champagne."

"You got it."

After a loud pop, Nathan set a glass in front of me. "Where's yours?" I said.

His grin widened. "Coming up next."

"I'll take the rest of the bottle back to the kitchen. Feel free to open another. We need to celebrate. This is a night to remember."

I pushed through the doors with my glass in one hand, the bottle in the other. Custer and Monique were huddled over a bowl. How could they possibly be still interested in food?

Unlike me, whose hair was damp with perspiration, my apron askew, and I had changed into a pair of sneakers, Monique looked completely comfortable in her low heels and not a stain to be seen after at least twelve hours in the kitchen. Maybe that's why she wore all black. Duly noted.

"You two have been on your feet all day," I said.

"Not all day." Monique looked over her shoulder and smiled. "We had a nice break after lunch."

Custer placed his hand on her lower back.

I set the bottle on the counter. "Rats. I forgot the glasses."

"No worries." Custer picked it up and took a slug. "Chef?" he said to Monique.

She read the label and took a long sip, her Adam's apple bobbing.

"What are you guys doing?" I said.

"Come and see," she said.

I walked over and sat on a stool next to the stove.

"I'm showing Custer how to make the perfect omelet."

I narrowed my eyes and looked closer. "Do tell."

"We have blended the eggs and cream, and the oil is at a perfect temperature. So now we pour the mixture through a sieve, like this."

"Custer," I said, "have you ever—"

"No, boss."

The eggs spread out into a perfectly thin, evenly mixed puddle in the pan.

"You know how they always tell you to lift up the sides of an omelet to ensure there is no runny egg?" she said. "There's no need when it is the perfect thinness. So, no messiness. Just a beautiful, perfectly round disc. Custer and I have already mixed up a crab and herbed cheese mixture for the filling."

"Maybe we should add a little lemon or zest to give it some freshness," Custer said.

She gazed up at him and kissed him on the mouth. "I will be working for *you* one day."

Another gulp of champagne, and I was mesmerized. These two people had given me a huge gift. I couldn't believe they were standing in my kitchen.

CHAPTER FIFTY-SEVEN

The events of the past few days overwhelmed me with joy: the review, Monique, the overflow of enthusiastic customers. Happy holidays to me.

I sniffed and wiped my nose with the back of my hand. Custer and Monique looked up. "Boss?" Custer said.

"I'm okay."

Monique's red-coated lips curved into a smile. "I get this," she said.

"Thank you, both." A fat tear spilled down my cheek.

Custer stuffed his hands in his front pockets, reminding me for the first time that day he was only twenty-five. "We're good," he said.

"You're welcome," Monique said with an uncharacteristic trace of warmth. "May I cook tomorrow? I'm here all weekend."

I coughed out a laugh. "Um, yes. Hell, yes."

Chapter Fifty-Eight

Some odd sort of nostalgia was with me that Sunday morning that I couldn't quite label. But it felt nice. My mind was drifting to cozy thoughts and comforting memories. Watching Monique and Custer reminded me of my love of the creative side of cooking. It's easy to forget while running and provisioning a restaurant. I was struck with an idea for a dish. I checked my freezer and found a puff pastry. Maybe I will have the café kitchen to myself for a bit to experiment. I scratched Sweeney's ears and headed to my car.

The morning sky was still a pale gray. It was less than two weeks until Christmas and as I rounded the bend into town, Cardigan looked like a holiday card with garlands and wreaths and twinkling lights. It was beautiful, and yet it reminded me that Annie wouldn't be with me. I was receiving daily texts and pictures from Dubai. Their accommodations were clearly top notch, and the place looked exotic and so unlike the world I was occupying for the holidays or otherwise.

Crystal said I would see Annie, but that seemed more a Christmas fantasy than icy reality. Maybe it was some sort of metaphor. Perhaps a Zoom call on Christmas. Rats, I thought, and forced myself to switch gears.

The sky hung low and looked as if it was ready to unload several truckloads of snow as I walked toward the café. I hoped it would hold off until brunch was over. Monique's omelet would wow the crowd.

Once I deposited my things, I got to work on my idea. I knew the puff pastry would thaw quickly, so I started a mushroom crema. I sautéed chopped baby bella mushrooms in butter and garlic until they began to sweat and soften, then I added cream and thyme leaves. I played around with other ingredients, debating between red wine or balsamic, and mixed and concocted until the room was filled with savory aromas, perfect for a cold winter day.

I lined a cylindrical metal cup with the pastry, added pie weights, and baked it until it was golden brown. When it had cooled, I removed the pastry from the cup, and it was a perfect little basin for the mushrooms.

"Why, Rosalie," Monique said as she strolled into the room. "What have you done?"

"I've been feeling creative."

She peered over my shoulder. "Will you look at that? What an amazing idea. It's a perfect cup, almost a soup bowl but savory and crispy, and will you put those mushrooms in it?"

"That's what I'm thinking."

"Let's do it." Still in her jacket and scarf, Monique spooned the mushroom mixture into the pastry. Custer's entry was followed by a burst of cold air, and she said, "Darling, come and see what Rosalie has done."

He picked up a spoon and slurped up the mushrooms. "Whoa. So when you get close to the bottom, do you start eating the cup?"

"Yes," I said tentatively.

Monique selected a second spoon and tasted. "This has to be on the menu today. The weather is wretched, and this is a taste of home, is it not?"

"We are pretty low on puff pastry, unfortunately."

"Custer, my darling man, get on your motorcycle and get us some pastry dough. How are you on baby bellas?"

"We could use some more of those as well."

Custer slid his helmet back onto his head. I reached for my wallet and stuffed a bunch of cash in his hand. A year and a half ago, this would have made me nervous, not really understanding Custer's true nature, only knowing he had a troubled past. But today, I didn't give it another thought.

"I'm so glad you like it. And you," I said to Monique, "must be ready for coffee."

Chapter Fifty-Nine

Monique and I settled at the bar, sipping coffee and nibbling on some lemon mini muffins I had thawed earlier that morning. The sky had brightened, and a ray of sun that had escaped through the wall of clouds warmed the room.

"I'll bet you make amazing crêpes," I said. "Maybe—"

"No crêpes." She moved her index finger back and forth like a metronome. "No crepes."

"Oh," I said, surprised. "Okay."

"Thank you." She took a sip of coffee and eyed me over the rim.

"There's a story here."

Her eyebrows lifted. "Excuse me?"

"Tell me your story. Everyone has one. How did you end up in this café on a wintry morning in Cardigan, Maryland? Did you grow up in France? And, most importantly, why no crêpes?"

She took a long sip of coffee. "Yes, to France. I grew up in a small village outside of Paris. With four brothers, I might add. Which is why I've never had children." She set her cup onto the saucer. "I was the youngest. I stayed by my father's side as much as possible to protect myself from them."

"What did your father do for a living?"

"He was a vegetable farmer. He would take his produce to the food markets in Paris and sell it to chefs. I liked to go along, and I became obsessed with the chefs—what they chose to buy, the way they fondled and smelled the vegetables. I used to watch what they bought and imagined what dish they would concoct that night in their restaurant."

"And your mother?"

"A school teacher. Someone needed to earn a decent wage."

"So, the market, is that where you first fell in love with food?"

"Not necessarily the food, it was more the chefs. Their world seemed so romantic to me. And I vowed to become one and live in Paris and be famous and adored." She pursed her lips. "That would show my brothers."

I finished my coffee. "They sound like rascals."

"Heathens is the word. Don't get me wrong, they never hurt me. But the constant chaos and clutter and earthy smells were too much. It overwhelmed me." She recrossed her legs. "I was a very nervous child, as you could probably guess.

"Thus, I wanted to get out of the house as soon as humanly possible, so one day, I asked a chef if he would give me a job. I was seventeen and said I would work harder than anyone on his staff."

"And did he?" I said, smiling with anticipation.

"Oh, yes. But I didn't get to cook. I was the maid." She shook her head. "The second one liked to stand behind me while I chopped the onions and garlic. His hand would inevitably land on my ass." She looked up and seemed to be getting her memories straight. "Oh, and the third one said I had promise but made me the hostess. He said I was too pretty to be hidden in the kitchen. You see, I had no idea I was pretty. It was all news to me. But that was a horrible job. People were snooty and rude, and I wanted to cook. And, of course, the chef was constantly ogling me. It was only a matter of time before, well, you know, I'm sure."

"And was there a fourth?"

"He had me make the crêpes." She closed her eyes for a moment. When she opened them, they were more distant and narrowed, as if the memory was painful. "Crêpes were their featured dish. They served all kinds, sweet and savory, so it was an important job. I was relieved to finally be at a stove."

"I'm intrigued," I said and tore off a bite of muffin. "What went wrong?"

"The restaurant had an open layout, the type where the diners can see what's happening in the kitchen. After many failures, I finally learned how to make the perfect crêpe. So the chef put me front and center so everyone could watch me. Then he told me to buy some makeup and do something with my hair. And when I showed up for work, he made me unbutton a few more buttons of my blouse. And so I made crêpes. All night long. The heat from the stove was brutal. Sweat would soak my hair, and my face was always red. And when my crêpe wasn't perfect, he screamed at me and would say horrible, demeaning things."

"While the diners watched?"

"Oh, yes. Of course. Some would laugh, others would show no emotion. It was abuse, and it took its toll, and I finally gave up. I went back home and worked long hours in a small bookshop that sold coffee and Pâtisserie. No crêpes," she added and smiled. "When I saved up enough money to go to culinary school in New York, I got on the first plane I could. I haven't been back to France since."

"What about your parents?" I brushed my hands free of crumbs. "Don't you miss them?"

"Three of my brothers still live at home. Two have their families living there as well. My parents have enlarged the house. My mother is exhausted. And there is no room for me. You see, Rosalie? There never was." She hopped off the chair. "There is your story. I have never told it to anyone."

I allowed silence to settle over us, honoring her willingness to confide in me.

"And now—" Her voice caught in her throat. "It is time to prep the kitchen. Because that is what we do after a moment like this. Food is orderly. Food is balance. Food, if done right, is predictable." She picked up her cup. "Food, at least for me, is solace."

Chapter Sixty

Brunch was hectic and busy, but we all worked together beautifully. It was fun having Monique among us. She added a new energy and enthusiasm that was contagious. It seemed as if we were all folding the napkins a little tighter, straightening the plates so they offered the best view of the food, brushing crumbs from the tables, anything and everything to enhance our diners' experience.

Glenn joined me behind the bar and filled his water glass. "Did you know Gretchen has invited Monique over later today to teach her this new omelet technique?"

I crossed my arms and smiled. "I love that."

"Is that so? I didn't think you were very fond of Monique."

"Just a little wary. I've been trying to figure out why a successful forty-something-year-old woman would be dating a twenty-five-year-old man."

"Um, that shouldn't be terribly hard." Glenn smiled.

"Well, there's that." I laughed. "I mean, it is Custer, after all. She just seemed so brash at first. An interloper. But now I realize she has her own story and is a survivor just like the rest of us. We have to be careful not to judge too quickly living in a small town."

"To not become small?"

"Oh, yes, exactly."

Crystal approached. "Do we have any candy canes?"

"Maybe, I put them in the latte," I said. "Why?"

"This kid is really cute, and it would be fun if we could give him something."

"Crystal," Glenn said. "I had no idea you were so fond of children."

"You know, Mr. Glenn? I never realized it, either. It's so weird."
"What do the stars tell you?" I smiled.
She stuffed her hands in her apron pockets. "To stay on birth control."

Chapter Sixty-One

I sat at the island in Glenn's kitchen, Bill's phone in my grip. "It's charged. But we need a password. Is Neil still coming out today?"

"Yes. Let's hope he has this password. But I'm not sure I want to mention that we have his father's phone. What do you think?"

"The sheriff can return it to him once we've finished. And we are going to have to finesse the password from him somehow."

Glenn set a plate with scrambled eggs and buttered wheat toast in front of me. "Don't tell anyone, but I didn't strain the eggs."

"This is just what the doctor ordered. I'm famished."

Glenn sat next to me with a legal pad and a pen. "I've been trying to get us organized. Let's go through the suspects. First, I have Neil. But other than an apparent alienation from his father, I haven't detected any real animosity. Or motive. Maybe some disgust when he learned about Summer, but I believe he had no idea about there being so little in the will, and even if he did, killing him would be the last thing he would do because the will would never change. What do you think?"

"Agreed." I sipped some orange juice. "Let's poke around a bit today. Is he coming to the Cardigan Tavern with us?"

"Yes. After he meets with the realtor."

"Next?"

"Micky B. She showed aggression toward you, and she knew he was about to change his life insurance and that the money would stop anyway when Summer turned eighteen, so what's to lose? If she was going to get the insurance by killing him, she'd be set for life. Also, she warned you to stay away from her daughter. So she is worried you will tell Summer something that her mother doesn't want her to know."

"All legitimate motives. I would talk to Summer again, but I don't want to make her life harder than it already is. So what's next?"

Glenn scratched his chin. "Maybe draw Micky B. out somehow? Scare her that we're getting close?"

"We could go to the bar where she works. Talk loudly?" I smiled.

"One martini, and that will happen either way."

"I'll drive."

"I like it when you drive."

"Okay," I said. "I have learned one of the foursome Bill played with at the club, Gunther Langford, has a reputation for being a mean guy. Plus, the Langfords are a powerful family in this county and are considered real locals. Although Bill lived here for twenty years, he was considered to be from 'away,' not a true Eastern Shore guy. Sometimes, there is animosity toward guys like Bill. Especially since he slept around and got boisterous at parties."

"Again, we need to draw him out." Glenn made a few notes on the pad while I stuffed my mouth with a bite of eggs piled on a slice of toast.

"And lest we forget Abby, the illustrious Fitness Angel," I said once I finished chewing.

"We need to get into that phone." Glenn wiggled the pen back and forth. "Have we completely ruled out Jonesy?"

"He's well-liked. But no, I think he's very scared. We know he hit Bill and then tried to cover it up. He confessed to that."

"But how do you shoot a man and then hop in your truck when he's wobbling around in time to hit him? It doesn't add up."

I piled more eggs on the toast with my fork. "I hadn't thought of it that way, but that's really good. The only way it would have been him is if he shot him after he plowed into him. But again, why would Bill be riding so erratically if he hadn't been shot yet?"

Glenn crossed his arms. "Jonesy could have made that part up. And you said he was upset. But he could have been upset that he was getting charged because he's guilty, not just that he hit his friend."

"Okay. Keep him on the list."

Glenn made a few more notes.

I stood and straightened my sweater. "Alright, my friend, I'll pick you up at five."

Chapter Sixty-Two

I stopped at the café on my way home to let in some deliveries. "Hey, Sam," I said as his diesel engine idled in the alley.

"I'm supposed to tell you we didn't have the fancy roquefort you ordered."

"I didn't order any roquefort."

"Somebody did." He stacked the boxes in the corner of the kitchen.

"Fancy roquefort can't be local."

"That's why we didn't have it. Sign?"

I scribbled my name with my finger on his tracker. "Do you like roquefort, Sam?"

"I like a Cobb salad with lots of bacon, tomato, and blue cheese dressing. Does that count?"

"Yes. Thanks for everything, and stay warm. Oh, say, can I make you a quick cup of coffee to go?"

"Why do you think I'm still standing here?"

Once I gave Sam the coffee and shut the door, I immediately headed back into the restaurant. While making Sam's coffee, I noticed a white envelope affixed to the front door. After slipping on a pair of latex gloves, I opened the door. I waved to Mary across the street, who was sweeping the sidewalk in front of her shop, and grabbed the envelope. It had been taped shut, and inside was a folded piece of paper. Typed in a Times New Roman font, it read: "Mind your own business. Donny Jones killed Bill Rutherford. The case is closed. Stay out of it. This is your first and final warning."

I sank into one of the dining room chairs, feeling enervated. Part of me knew this was a clue, but it was the fifteenth of December, and instead of shopping for Annie and baking cookies and sitting with my family and Tyler by the fire, I was receiving threats. Who were we really helping here? Bill? He's dead. As Charles Dickens said, dead as a doornail. Neil wasn't particularly interested in how his father died, and Abby would probably find whatever she was looking for in the long run. And then I thought of Summer. What if it was her mother? Would she be better off if Micky B. got away with it? I thought back on our conversations. She believed in integrity. It was vital to how she lived her life. And Summer said she wanted to know, even if it was her mother. That was it, then. She deserved to know how her father died. Not to mention an innocent man could go to prison. We had to see this through.

Feeling a chill pass down my spine, I looked out the window. Mary was still sweeping. No one else was on the street. I pushed myself up to a stand and dropped the envelope into a Ziploc. I needed to get home to get ready for our meeting at the tavern. After double-checking the locks and scanning the alley, I got into my car and drove to Barclay Meadow, my eyes darting between the road and my rearview mirror.

Chapter Sixty-Three

A year and a half ago, Glenn and I visited the Cardigan Tavern for the first time in search of information on an investigation we were conducting. Chuck, the bartender, was warm and welcoming, but we soon learned he didn't give up information freely. He prided himself on his discretion. "You can't tell tales out of school about your customers, or they'll stop coming in."

I had no doubt many a patron cried in their drinks as they confided in Chuck. And it wasn't until one of his favorite patrons had been threatened that he agreed to help us. His one soft spot—he hated injustice. I vowed to never take advantage of his willingness to compromise his prudence and was happy tonight was just about talking with Neil, no need for an insider's tip from Chuck.

The bar was quiet when we arrived, just a crack of a pool ball now and then and a Luke Bryant song in the background. Business wouldn't pick up until the Monday Night Football fans crowded the large, square bar. Glenn and I selected a table in the corner. I waved to Chuck and pulled off my leather gloves.

Ducking through the hinged section of the bar, he approached our table. In his late forties, Chuck had been shaving his head for as long as I'd known him. The first time we met, he rubbed his head and said, "Decided not to wait for nature to finish the job and took matters into my own hands. Or should I say my own razor."

Chuck had a square patch of beard on his chin and wore round wire glasses. Of average height and weight, he reliably had the sleeves of his flannel shirt rolled up to his elbows and a kind smile on his face.

"What brings you two in?" He placed thin white napkins on the table that read, "Fill up or pay up."

"We're meeting a friend," I said. "He should be here soon, but we would love to order a drink."

"The usual?"

"Yes," Glenn said. "That would be most welcome."

Chuck straightened and looked from Glenn to me and back to Glenn. "I detect a mystery."

"Well," I said, "there's a little bit of that. But I don't think any of your patrons are involved."

Rubbing his chin, he said, "I don't know of anything fishy going on around town." He thought for a moment. "Okay, I'll get your beverages and some menus."

Once Chuck was on his way back to the bar, Glenn said, "I'm not sure if you've noticed."

"Noticed what?"

"The word is out. People in this community know we are a bit; how should I say it, snoopy? I think that's why Micky B. shoved you. She knows if anyone can uncover her wrongdoings, it would be you and me."

"Not such a great way to make friends," I said. "No wonder we never get invited to parties."

"We don't get invited to parties because we work every Friday and Saturday night."

"At least we're closed from Christmas to New Year's. Oh, and Janice is having a party." I hesitated. "You're right."

"About what?"

"The word is out. There was an envelope on the door of the café this afternoon. A first and final warning to stop the investigation."

Chuck set our drinks on the napkins, a martini for Glenn, and a frosty pint for me. "That guy who got hit on the bike."

I glanced at Glenn, hoping he would stay mum.

Glenn took a sip of his drink. "You are very astute."

"Jonesy hit him with his truck. He's been charged. So what gives?"

"You know, Chuck," Glenn said, "I didn't think we would be involving you this time, but there's a chance you might hear something, maybe even a confession. You see, we believe someone else is involved. The sheriff agrees."

"But that's all we can say." I shot Glenn a look. One sip of his martini, and off he goes.

"I'm intrigued," Chuck said. "I'm a 'like to know but won't tell' kinda guy, so if you decide to tell me more, I'm all ears."

"I like that about you," Glenn said.

I looked up to see Neil in the doorway, his overcoat loose, his eyes adjusting to the dim light. "Here's our friend."

Chuck studied him. "He ain't from around here."

"No," Glenn said. "He isn't, but I can guarantee he'll want a drink."

Neil shrugged out of his coat and tossed it on an empty chair. "Name's Neil," he said, and Chuck shook his hand.

"What can I do 'ya?"

"Bourbon straight up."

"We got fried rockfish sandwiches on the menu tonight if you get hungry."

"Definitely one of those whenever you get around to it." Neil settled in.

"What did the realtor say?" Glenn asked.

"There's a waiting list in the community, and Dad's house will sell for pretty much anything I want to ask. He had a mortgage, though. I'm not going to become rich overnight. Not even close. And that house is the only thing he left me. So, cheers to you, Dad. Oh, wait, here comes the bourbon."

Chuck returned with his bourbon and a small wooden bowl full of popcorn.

"What are you going to do with his things?" I said.

"I may pay one of those companies who gets it all done, and I don't have to know how they do it." He scooped up some popcorn. "I'll be glad when it's off my hands."

"What about his personal things?" Glenn said.

"I was trying to find the lien on the house, so I went through his safe this afternoon."

"He told you the combination?" I said.

"The guy was not original. All of his PINs and passwords are 8-7-3-5. It's 'T-R-E-K,' you know, the bike brand?"

I felt Glenn's foot pressing down on my toes.

"Oh," he reached into his coat pocket, "and I found this." He unfolded a check. "Looks like it was never endorsed, but it's fifty-thousand dollars to a woman named Abigail Harrington. Why does that name sound familiar?"

My eyes widened. "May I see it?" I studied the check. FFF was written on the memo line.

"She was a gymnast," Glenn said. "She was in the news back in the 80s when her coach forced her to do a balance beam routine on a sprained ankle. She ended up fracturing her foot and was never able to compete again."

"What did she have to do with my dad?"

"She lives in their community," I said. "She goes by Abby the Fitness Angel. We caught her in your dad's house when we were checking for leaks and spoiled food. She may have been looking for this." I passed it to Glenn and pointed to the memo.

"FFF." He frowned. "Remember I told you Abby was trying to launch her own fitness program? I think it was called Fitness For Fun. That must be the FFF. She said something that afternoon about him investing in her new business."

"But apparently he didn't," I said. "Who writes a check and then puts it in a safe?"

"Something must have happened," Glenn said.

"Well, I don't care now." Neil took the check and started to rip it in half.

"Wait—" I touched his arm. "The sheriff might want to see this. Abby has a, how should I say it, questionable past?"

His thumbs remained on the check for a moment, then he gave it back to Glenn.

"I'll keep it at my place." Glenn tucked it in the front pocket of his shirt.

I noticed Chuck watching us carefully. I had no doubt he was trying to figure out what Neil had to do with the guy on the bike.

"Neil, can I ask you more about your dad?" I said. "How was his childhood? Carefree, happy, miserable?"

He finished his bourbon and motioned to Chuck. "He was an only child. My grandparents were nice enough people, but he was alone a lot. His dad wrote for the local newspaper, and his mom sold real estate, so they both worked long and odd hours. He was left to his own devices, way too much, if you ask me."

"Why?" Glenn said. "Did something happen?"

Chuck set the drink on the table. "You're Bill Rutherford's son, aren't you?"

"Yes, that would be me."

"I'm real sorry about your dad. That's a rotten thing to have happened. Drinks are on the house."

Neil watched him walk away. "Everyone is nice around here."

"You were talking about your dad's childhood." My brain was in full gear. "Left to his own devices?"

Another slurp of bourbon. "You see, when a kid doesn't get a whole lot of supervision, it can go two ways. One, they figure out how to be a good kid on their own. They do their homework even if there's no parent to remind them. They figure out a way to eat an adequate meal, feed the dog, and get by in an honorable way. They take pride in who they are, what they do."

Neil was beginning to look more and more pained. His forehead was deeply furrowed, his hair askew.

"The kid I'm describing was me."

Glenn sat straighter.

"You would think after being raised without a whole lot of adult supervision, my father would have been the opposite kind of parent. But instead, he was the, *I turned out okay, so why can't you?* kind of guy. But see, he didn't turn out okay. With no one around to expect him to tell the truth, he told lies. With no one to watch, he cheated at games. If he could, he took the easy way every time.

"It drove my mother nuts. She thought he was this successful guy and fun-loving and a little thrill-loving, from what I'm told, which is why she married him. But he eked his way through college and decided to sell cars. Worked his way from a Chevy to a Lexus dealership. And then hit it big with Tesla. Started making a ton of dough. Thing is, he didn't just cheat at games. He would sleep with any woman who would fall for his charms, married or not. My mother left when I was eleven. I didn't want to leave my school and friends, so she gave him custody without so much as an argument and moved to Boca Raton." He shook his head. "I love my mother, but that was a pretty rotten thing to do. She saw through him, and yet she was unwilling to stick around long enough to see me through high school. She let a guy she learned to loathe raise her only child." Neil picked up his glass. "You don't need to think too hard about why I never married, let alone had a kid. It's all pretty obvious."

Tears formed in my eyes, I was so deeply moved by Neil's story. I finished my beer and glanced at Glenn. He had been riveted on Neil's story, too.

"Thank you for sharing with us," I said. "I agree 100% with what you said. There are two ways to go in that situation. It's true in so many parts of life. With no one to watch, it's up to you and your conscience which person you choose to be."

Glenn patted Neil's hand. "So much makes sense now." He tucked his hand back in his lap. "This was an important conversation to have."

Neil stared down at his shoes. "I found something else in the safe." He looked up. "It was a note to me from my dad. It was attached to this." He removed a key from his shirt pocket. The key had a wire through the top fastened to a round piece of paper rimmed in metal. "Do you know what this could be?"

"Maybe a safety deposit box?" Glenn said. "What did the note say?"

"Something about people going after his money and some bad investments and that he didn't want to leave me with nothing, so he emptied all of his investment accounts and left me this. Even his lawyer doesn't know about it. Apparently, he still had a checking account, which he wanted me to have to settle any unfinished business. The checkbook was in the safe, too. There's a sizable balance, so I think I'm good."

"Enough to cover this check?" Glenn patted his shirt pocket.

"Definitely."

"Oh, and Neil, is that a number written on the tag?"

"Yes."

"Next time you're out, we can go to every bank in town and find out where the box is," Glenn said. "And let's hope there's some cash in it."

Neil gazed over at Glenn. "If I forget to thank you for all you've done to help me out since this happened, I'll say it now: Thank you."

Glenn nodded and smiled. "You're welcome."

Neil shook his head and wiped his nose with his knuckle. "You two are easy to talk to." He looked around the room. "Now, where the heck is Chuck? He tells me the drinks are on the house, and then he quits coming around."

* * *

Glenn ended up joining Neil in a fried rockfish sandwich. I wasn't feeling particularly hungry, so I sipped on another draft beer. Having eaten the sandwich and a large side of fries, Neil appeared sober enough to drive home. He offered to give Glenn a lift on his way out of town.

The check had been paid, the tip given, and the tavern was filling up. Chuck had dimmed the lights and upped the volume of the country music. Glenn excused himself to, as he said, answer Mother Nature's call, and I had some time alone with Neil.

He seemed spent yet sated, the furrows in his brow not as deep, and I wondered if telling his story lifted his burden, as it often does. "I've been thinking about everything you said, Neil. And I know someone else who is currently living a childhood very similar to yours."

Neil frowned. "Who?"

"Your half-sister. Summer Belle."

He inhaled slowly and sighed out a breath. "Why do you think that?"

"She works afternoons at Birdie's Shoe Store. We've become friendly, but it's clear she is left to her own devices. Your dad and Summer had started having coffee together. He liked her, thought she had a good head on her shoulders. Remember when you found out from your dad's lawyer that he had wanted to change his life insurance policy so that it would go to Summer? As I think you know, the money went to her mother instead; he died before David Bestman could change the will. Her mother also hid the fact from Summer that your dad deposited $5,000 in her account every month to support her daughter."

"What makes you think she's a good kid?"

I folded my hands on the table. "She works hard at the store. Doris, the proprietor, is getting on in age, so Summer cleaned up the place, decorated for the holidays, and you can see through the storefront windows for the first time in years." I smiled. "She also said something that stuck with me. With no one to supervise her, she decided to let integrity be her guiding light. She learned the word in middle school and liked it. She's only sixteen."

Glenn arrived. "Are we ready to launch?"

"Sure." I stood and slipped into my coat.

We called goodbye to Chuck and headed for our cars.

Once outside, Neil tapped my arm, and I turned to face him.

"This shoe store is in town?"

"Right on Main Street."

"She works afternoons?"

"After school so Doris can take a water aerobics class."

He shook his head and stuffed his hands in his coat pocket. "I just don't know. My goal is to sell this house and move forward without looking back. I think that's best for me."

"I understand, Neil. You've been through a lot." I fished for my keys and gave them each a quick hug goodbye.

Chapter Sixty-Four

Tuesday morning, I was up early preparing for Glenn's arrival. Bill Rutherford's phone was charged, and we had the password. At least, we hoped we did. But I wasn't going to find out without Glenn.

I had flipped on every light in the house before going to bed the night before. Wide awake for several hours, I longed for Tyler. I kicked myself for not inviting him to stay as soon as I found the letter. And he probably would have wanted to give me a little 'kick' as well for not telling him I had been threatened. Be that as it may, when we shared our coffee that morning, I still didn't tell him about the note and I'm not really sure why. My investigations seemed to be the only uncertain issue between us. Maybe I should have told him, promote openness, that sort of thing. Or maybe not. Maybe just keep it out of our relationship.

* * *

Glenn and I had finished our breakfasts and cleared the table. I topped off our coffees and sat down. Bill Rutherford's iPhone was on the center placemat like a laboratory specimen waiting to be examined.

"What do we check first?" I said. "Texts? Photos?"

"I say texts," Glenn said. "Who is going to do the honors?"

I nudged the phone over to him.

"All right. It's T-R-E-K, is that correct?"

"Let's hope so."

He typed carefully. I held my breath.

Glenn gripped the phone tight in his hand. He peered at me over his glasses. "We're in."

"Yes!" I whispered.

He placed the phone in the middle of the table and scooted his chair closer to me.

"I have an idea." I hopped up and picked up the prop stand I used for recipes. "Let's put it on here so we can both see."

Glenn tapped on the screen. "The last text was to Pamela Langford."

I just beat your husband in golf again. Want to come over tomorrow afternoon? I'll pick up some bubbly.

"Langford?" I said. "Could she be married to Gunther Langford?"

"He says he beat him in golf. Who else could it be? And it was on the day he died. Of course, that's who he played golf with."

"Was he sleeping with her? Doesn't he know the rule?"

"What rule?"

"Janice told me. Don't mess with a Langford. It's rule number one."

"Sounds like Devon County to me." Glenn frowned.

"Look at her response," I said.

I made a mistake. I was hurting that night, and you comforted me. Thank you for that. You were a gentleman. But this isn't my style. I have been loyal to my husband my entire life. I wish you well.

"So it was just the one time," Glenn said.

"This is strange, isn't it?" I said. "Here we are looking at his life; it's hard to believe he's dead. It's like when a Facebook friend has passed, and you still get notifications of their birthdays."

"I guess you never die on social media." Glenn sipped his coffee. "Gunther Langford had a solid motive—revenge."

"Who else is there?"

"Here's one with Neil. Looks like it's from a week before his father died."

Weekly check-in. How's your blood pressure? How's your handicap? I'll be laying low for the holidays, but if you want to come to DC to grab dinner, that would be fine.

Glenn straightened his cup on the saucer. "Doesn't sound like someone who is about to kill his father."

"No," I said. "Agreed. "I think we can tell him about the bullet. But I'll run it by the sheriff first." I clicked out of the text and noticed a thread with Summer. "This will be telling. Summer said they became friendly."

See you at the diner next Saturday, kiddo. Looking forward to it.

Glenn sighed. "The kid is legit, but we already knew that."

"Maybe one of us can go through these in more detail, but there's one more I want to see for certain." I studied the names. "There it is. Abby Harrington. Okay, the last one is from Bill on November thirtieth."

I hired a private investigator to look into your business venture. I think your fitness program has potential. And you have an internet presence that's impressive. I thought it would be a good investment for me if you agree to provide dividends and a spreadsheet. I've written the check, but I need you to explain something. My PI linked you to an ex-con named Freddy Bucks. I don't know what to make of this, but we need to talk before I hand over the check. I'm golfing this afternoon, but can meet for a little fun in the sack on Tuesday. The check is for $50,000. I really do believe in you.

I gasped.

"My god," Glenn said. "We have another motive. She knew he had written that check."

"Can she still cash it if he's dead?"

"It's dated November thirtieth, before Bill died. So I would say yes. Remember, Neil said the checking account was still open."

"This is intense. An ex-con? If we've learned anything here, it's that we are on the right track. We just don't know where it will lead. What do we do next?"

"We have to draw them out some way. But I'm not sure how." Glenn stood. "I'll take this phone home with me and do some more sleuthing."

"Check to see if there's anything from Jonesy, too."

"And what will you be doing today?"

"Oh, I don't know. I guess I'll look at more pictures of Annie and her dad in Dubai." I rimmed my coffee mug with my finger. "Yesterday, they went on a picnic in the desert on camels. The day before, they ate at a local restaurant where she had to wear a burka. And the day before that, she was by the pool with her dad, sipping a very large and fruity drink. She's very tan, and it makes her teeth look really white, and her brown eyes stand out and—"

"Oh, my dear." Glenn shook his head. "I'm so very sorry."

"Anyway, I need to meet some deliveries at the café, and then I'll check in with the sheriff. We've learned a lot. It's time."

"Well, that certainly won't improve your mood, now, will it?"

Chapter Sixty-Five

I said goodbye to Glenn and walked to my car. Despite the cold, I allowed my coat to flap in the bitter breeze. I stopped in my tracks when I noticed a deer munching on some leaves next to my Mercedes. She had shiny chocolate-brown eyes and a twig in her mouth. She didn't run away.

"Hello," I said.

She blinked.

"You're beautiful."

The deer held my gaze. I realized my shoulders had been tensed all morning. I took a deep breath and relaxed them, feeling at peace for the first time in weeks. Tears filled my eyes and streamed down my cheeks. I couldn't stop crying. "I really miss my mom," I said. "And my girl. And—" I heaved in a sob. "I hope you are safe. Be careful out there. And you can eat my hostas if you want to, and there are a few pumpkins on the vine. Do you like herbs?"

She skittered away.

"Oh," I said, shoulders slumped. I heard footsteps on the gravel. I wiped my eyes as quickly as I could and turned around to face Bini.

"Who were you talking to?"

"Um, well, there was this deer."

"I get that," she said. "You okay?"

"Not really, but I will be." I managed a smile. "But thanks for asking, Bini."

She jammed her hands into the front pockets of her jeans. "There's something my dad used to say to me that might be relevant here."

"I'm listening."

"You know, Bini, my girl, you don't always have to be so brave."

* * *

After receiving multiple deliveries, I did some prep work for tomorrow and checked on supplies, toilet paper, most importantly. As I went about my chores, a feeling nagged at me. Glenn and I were working hard on the investigation while keeping up with our other responsibilities. But what exactly had the sheriff been doing?

I poured a to-go coffee, leaving the sweets behind, and walked briskly to his office. Lila was rocking in her chair and watching something on her phone when I arrived. Not bothering to get her permission, I breezed right by.

"Hey," she said. "You can't—"

I held up my hand to shut her up and continued, slamming the coffee on his desk so hard droplets popped out of the hole in the lid.

If I'm not mistaken, I do believe the sheriff was dozing. His feet were propped on his desk, hat over his eyes.

I cleared my throat. He snorted awake and shoved his hat back. Bringing me into focus, he said, "Hey, Hart. That coffee is just what the doctor ordered."

"How's the investigation going?" I said.

"Jonesy's car had blood on the bumper."

"Have you forgotten Bill Rutherford was shot in the back?"

"Must'a been Jonesy, sad as that may be. He didn't call in the accident because he shot Bill in the back after he hit him."

Still standing, I gripped the back of the chair opposite his. "Why was Bill riding so erratically, then?"

"That's just Jonesy's word. There's no proof."

"Have you found a gun?"

"Nope."

"So, case closed?"

He folded his hands over his stomach. "Looks like it is. Prosecutor said we have a strong case."

"I thought you cared about Donny Jones. Didn't think he had it in him to kill a man, especially a friend."

"Don't know what you're talking about, Hart." He chuckled. "But that's not so unusual."

I tossed the Ziploc containing the letter onto his desk. "Then why would I find this on the café door yesterday?"

He unzipped the baggie.

"Sheriff Wilgus!" I shouted.

He startled. "What?"

"Perhaps you should use a pair of gloves?" I took a deep breath.

"What is this?"

"It's a letter threatening me to stop looking into Bill Rutherford's death. If Jonesy killed him, why would he care? He would *want* me to keep investigating." I snatched it from him. "This did not come from Donny Jones."

"So, who's it from?" he said sarcastically.

"The murderer, of course."

"How do I know you didn't write this yourself?"

"What?" My face was heating up. "Why? What's *my* motive? Remember those? Motives? Let me reeducate you on this part of an investigation. For instance, Abigail Harrington was swindling Bill for cash. There was a check for fifty-thousand dollars in his safe, but apparently, she has a boyfriend who is an ex-con she was in cahoots with. And how about Michelle Belle, who accosted me in the alley behind my café, warning me to stay away from her daughter, who is also Bill Rutherford's daughter? And, the illustrious Micky B. learned Bill was about to switch his life insurance from her to her daughter, but, hm, he died before that happened? Oh, and what about Gunther Langford, whose wife slept with Bill Rutherford? How—"

He jumped forward in his seat and bellowed, "You leave Gunther Langford out of this."

I reared back. "What did you say? Wait, what is going on here?"

"You're off the case."

I took another step back. "You're protecting him," I whispered. "Rule number one."

"You're done, Hart. And bring back that man's phone."

My breath had left my body as I stumbled out of the Sheriff's Department, gripping the pathetic Ziploc. I placed a hand on my chest and tried to breathe. Bracing myself on Lila's VW with the eyelashes over the headlights, I tried to get oxygen back into my lungs. It didn't work. I slumped to the ground and dropped my head onto my knees.

Chapter Sixty-Six

Turns out, the Culinary Institute of Washington D.C. was closed until January, meaning Monique Dujardin was still with us. Once I heard Custer's motorcycle roar into the alley Wednesday morning, I looked out the window and saw them both huddled together, smoking cigarettes.

When Glenn arrived, he seemed to know immediately something was wrong. He stored his belongings and hurried over to me as he tied his black apron around his waist. "What's happened?"

"We're off the case. And," I held up the Ziploc, "I received an anonymous note threatening me to stop the investigation. First and final warning."

"Did you wear gloves when you read it?"

"Yes, thank goodness I thought of that."

"The sheriff will want to run a fingerprint text." He filled the hot pot with water. "Wait, did you say we're off the case?"

"Yes. And the sheriff wants Bill's phone back. Did you get a chance to go through it again?"

"I have it in my coat pocket. There were a few interesting things, but I think we already had a pretty good idea of who this man was. There were photos of him with Abby but nothing with Pamela Langford. He had dates scheduled with Abby Tuesday and Wednesday night."

"Didn't you say he had Viagra in his medicine cabinet?" I smiled.

Glenn laughed. "Yes, there's that." He filled a mug with hot water and dropped in a bag of peppermint tea. "What happened with the sheriff?"

"He's decided Jonesy killed Bill. I confronted him with all that we've learned, and he became enraged when I mentioned Gunther Langford."

"What is it with this family? Now they've scared the sheriff off." Glenn frowned. "You don't think he's drinking again, do you?"

"I haven't noticed any signs, but who knows?"

"What are you two whispering about now?" Crystal said. Her hair was in the usual braid, but I noticed her earrings were each a cluster of bells with bows on top.

"The usual," I said. "You look festive."

She smiled and gave her head a small shake. The tiny bells chimed daintily.

"I'll get started on the menus," Glenn said. He picked up a manila envelope, and headed over to the hostess stand.

"Crystal, did you mean what you said about Annie, or was that just some sort of trope? You said you knew I would see her. Did that mean I would see her in photos or maybe a Zoom call? Or maybe even through a spirit animal?"

"Say, what?" Crystal said, scrunching up her petite nose.

I shrugged. "I don't know. It's just...I had a conversation with a doe yesterday."

"Well, this is all interesting on so many levels, but for the record, when I said that to you, I meant in the flesh."

"At some point during the holidays?"

"Correct. Don't lose faith." She studied me. "Miss Rosalie, I didn't tell you this because I wasn't sure how you would take it, but your mother is the one who told me."

I placed my hand on my chest. "Oh, my goodness."

Chapter Sixty-Seven

Welcome to the Day Lily Café
A gathering place offering simplicity and
freshness, with a focus on locally sourced ingredients

Plant-based Wednesday Specials:
Lunch: Caramelized leek and potato soup topped with thyme
Dinner: Sherried mushroom and butternut squash risotto
with miso roasted Brussels sprouts

The difference between a flower and a weed is a judgment.
—Unknown

* * *

I was texting Tyler, inviting him to stay the night, when Janice plopped down on the chair in front of me. I hit send and looked up. "Hey, Snow White. Happy Wednesday."

"Is it?" She eyed me. "What's going on with your kid?"

"Crickets today. I haven't heard a word. But she did send me a photo of her in a burka while out to dinner the other day."

"There's nothing right about that picture. What's with your ex-husband?"

"That's a loaded question. How's your flock of young men?"

"They made iced sugar cookies with Trevor's mom on Sunday. They came back looking as if they'd been tie-dyed from all the food coloring."

"That sounds like a lot of fun. Did they bring you any?"

"Unfortunately, yes. I can't have those things in the house, I'm telling you. I want to lock 'em up and give the kids the key."

I filled a glass with ice water and set a menu in front of her. "Interesting parenting strategy."

"Oh, I was thinking of it as more of a 'don't gain twenty pounds in December' strategy for me." She drummed her thumbs on the bar. "Okay, I won't be having the soup. Um, I'll take that big burger you guys make. So far, I've only had four cookies. I can swing the burger."

"Glenn says it goes great with an IPA."

"I gotta pick the kids up from school. But, yeah, I'll have one of those. It's Christmas."

When I returned from placing Janice's order, Abby was already sitting next to her. With her ears back and jaw clenched, Janice looked like an annoyed cat.

"Hello, Abby," I said and placed Janice's beer in front of her. She took a long sip.

"Is Glenn here?"

"Are you ordering anything?" I said.

"Um, whatever salad you have. Small salad. Oh, there's Glenn." She motioned him over.

"What is it, Abby?"

"Did Bill's house sell?"

"Not that I know of. Why?"

"You said you would ask if I could retrieve some things that were mine. Is there any way you could let me in for just a few minutes?"

I set a glass of water in front of her and caught Glenn's eye. We would have to draw them out, he had said. I willed him to be on my wavelength.

"You wouldn't happen to be looking for a check, would you?" Glenn said.

Her eyes widened. "Well, um, as a matter of fact, yes. Bill owed me some money. You must have found it. That's wonderful news. Poor thing died before he could give it to me." She took a small sip of water. "You're so sweet to be taking care of things for Bill and his son." She forced an awkward, unbalanced smile.

"I still have the key, Abby, but I can only use it if Neil asks me to do something for him."

"But if you have the check, there's no need to involve Neil, right?"

"Yes, I have the check, but I still can't give it to you without Neil's permission." Glenn shook his head.

"Oh." She pursed her lips. "Well, then, if you could ask Neil, maybe text him right now, then we're good, right? I get what's rightfully mine, and you are being loyal to Bill's son."

"I'm working right now, Abby. I will have to deal with this at a more convenient time."

She looked down at her lap as if hatching her next move. "Um, I changed my mind. No need for a salad." Another sip of water, and she hopped off the chair. "And Glenn? It's lovely to see you. There's a happy hour at the clubhouse Friday afternoon. I could show you some dance moves?" She held eye contact with Glenn those few seconds too long and left.

Janice glugged some beer. "She shouldn't have dirtied the water glass if she wasn't going to eat anything."

Glenn watched as Abby scurried down the sidewalk. "Rosalie, I have two beer orders. Shall we?"

We went to the other end of the bar. "You have to be careful, Glenn. She wants that check, and she'll get it any way she can. She knows you have it and—"

"That's the idea, remember? Draw them out."

I crossed my arms tight against my chest. "Of course, I remember. I was hoping you would say what you did, but now I'm worried."

"I'm a little worried about myself too. What was that flashlight trick of yours?"

"Blind them, then hit them over the head."

"I'll stop at the hardware store on our break."

I filled two glasses with a light beer, and Glenn walked away. My phone buzzed. Tyler: *I will never say no to that question. I'll bring wine.*

I looked up to see Monique in the center of the restaurant, a wide grin on her face. "Welcome all of you lovely people," she said, arms wide. "I am Monique Dujardin, a visiting chef here at this *magnifique* café. Tomorrow night, we will be serving only French cuisine, and I invite you all to join us. Tell your friends! It will be a night to remember." She blew a kiss and retreated into the kitchen.

Janice scowled. "Who the heck is she?"

Chapter Sixty-Eight

Dinner had been beyond hectic, with a waiting list most of the night. At the end of our run, my blouse looked as if I'd been in a paintball match, and a hole in my black tights that started at my ankle became a run that worked its way up to my thigh by closing. To my surprise, Glenn, Crystal, and Nathan shooed me out the door as soon as we flipped the sign.

"I can't leave you with all this work," I said.

With his palm on my lower back, Glenn gently ushered me back to the kitchen. "Get some rest, my dear," he said and closed the door behind me.

I found Tyler in the living room by the fire, a bottle of burgundy wine half empty on the coffee table.

"Hey," I said, attempting to give my hair some semblance of order. "Sorry about my appearance."

"You're gorgeous." He smiled and patted the cushion next to him.

I gave Sweeney Todd a small piece of cheddar from the charcuterie board Tyler had put together and sat down. "The wine and cheese shop must be loving you lately."

"I'm a regular."

I filled a glass and sat back. "Mm, this wine is yummy."

He played with my hair. "Rough day?"

"Rough couple of days."

"Any more pics from Annie?"

"Not a single text today." I shook my head. "I just hope she's okay." I stared at the fire, the flames low and even, an occasional snap and pop here and there. I realized I was wallowing as I noticed the stocking-free mantle, the missing tree in its usual spot in the corner by the window. But I was sinking into it, feeling hopeless about Christmas and the investigation. Based on his interaction with Abby, Glenn seemed driven to continue despite the sheriff telling us to stop. One suspect challenged. Two more to go.

Tyler topped off my wine. "Where are you, babe?"

"The sheriff kicked us off the investigation."

He scooped up a handful of shelled pistachios. "I'm sorry, Rosalie. I know you want to find out what happened to Bill Rutherford. But I gotta say, I'm also relieved."

I took a long sip and realized I was wrong to keep anything from this man. "I got a threatening note on Monday warning me to stop looking into who killed Bill."

"Now that's a development."

I looked over at him. He was deep in thought, as if considering what he was going to do or say next. I once heard someone say there is such a thing as an unexpressed thought. Tyler was a master at it.

"I almost didn't tell you," I said. "But I don't want there ever to be secrets between us."

"Who do you think it was from?"

"We have three solid suspects. Micky B., Abby, a woman in Glenn's community, and Gunther Langford."

"Langford?" He sounded alarmed.

"What's with that family, Tyler? Why is everyone afraid of them? Are they like the Devon County syndicate?"

"All I know is they always get their way. They do what they want and worry about permits, laws, zoning, later. Hunter Langford built a huge house right on the Cardigan River in a protected area. When the county found out, the house was already finished. So, what happened? Nothing. It's still there. Hunter has since added a large dock and riprap along the shoreline, also illegal on that part of the river."

I picked up a throw pillow and held it in my lap. "Has a Langford ever killed anyone before?"

"That family is pre-Revolutionary. I believe they were loyalists to the crown. But, as is their way, they stayed and acted like nothing ever happened. Now they're practically royalty around here. Perhaps they are still loyal to the crown in their own stubborn way."

"Bill slept with Pamela, Gunther's wife."

"Now that was a bad idea."

I sipped more wine. "The sheriff was so angry when he found out Gunther was a suspect, he wouldn't even check my threatening letter for prints."

"I suppose you're going to keep at this."

I twisted the fringe on the pillow. "Maybe."

Tyler's shoulders were hunched, his head low. After a few minutes, he stood and tossed another log on the fire. Sparks flew up like confetti as he poked the lower embers. Once the log took hold, he said, "You stay put. I'm going to open another bottle."

Hugging the pillow, I rested my head on the back of the sofa and closed my eyes. It wasn't fair for me to ruin Tyler's Christmas. I had to get a grip, stop making it about me. Maybe we could pick out a tree tomorrow before the café opened.

"Give me the pillow," Tyler said.

I opened my eyes. "I'm sorry?"

He held out his hand, and I gave it to him. "Sometimes, I like to hold a pillow."

He socked it a few times and propped it at the end of the sofa. "Get comfy and hand me your glass."

I complied.

After refilling my wine and placing it in my hands, Tyler picked up my legs and sat down. Removing my shoes, he began to stroke my feet, softly scratching, then adding pressure with his knuckles.

"Is this really happening?" I said.

His thumb found the perfect spot on the arch of my foot. "Have I ever massaged your feet before?"

"Mm," I said. "No. This is definitely something I would remember."

The logs shifted, I sipped more wine and closed my eyes. Tyler's touch on any part of my body caused me to melt on contact. But what he was doing to my feet was a whole new level of bliss. I've had a few professional massages in my day, probably not enough, and Ed was good for a few back scratches that ended so quickly, it was more like a mean-spirited tease than something pleasant.

"Want to pick out a tree tomorrow morning?" I said as he cupped my heel. Wow. Why did *that* feel so good?

"I don't think you're ready," Tyler said. "But in time. Just so you know, I'm going to sleep here until this whole Bill Rutherford thing is over. And I'm going to go home and get my gun tomorrow morning."

I lifted my head. "Okay."

"I wonder what happens if you shoot a Langford?" he said, pulling on my toes.

My pinkie popped into place. "Why do I feel as if I don't deserve this?"

"Because you're you." He looked at me, his eyelids heavy. "You okay if I stop for a bit?"

"Of course." I tucked my legs underneath me while Tyler filled his glass. "Thank you. That was amazing."

He sat sideways on the sofa and popped a slice of gouda into his mouth. "Rosalie?"

"Yes?"

"It's your turn."

"You want me to massage your feet?"

He shook his head. "Tell your story."

"I'm sorry?"

"Tell your story." Those green eyes burned like the embers in the fire.

I sat straighter. "No one has ever asked me that before."

Tyler sipped his wine. "I know."

Chapter Sixty-Nine

"I don't know where to start."

"I was born?" Tyler smiled that crooked grin.

"Well, yes, that happened."

"Thank the lord."

I laughed. "I don't like to take up a lot of space."

"That I know. Now, your story. And I am going to keep pouring the wine. It seems like a good idea."

"Are we going to get hammered together?"

"You were born. Three years after Oliver on a farm in Virginia."

"And I think my parents would have been happy with just Oliver." I slapped my hand over my mouth.

"Whoa," Tyler said.

My mind raced. "I mean, I know my parents loved me. But I think my dad found me to be a little annoying, talking all the time, coming up with all kinds of pretend games, and my mom was a good mom, for sure. But I've said this before, the family rule was, don't interfere with Oliver because he's going places. And I wasn't? How messed up is that?

"My father laughed when I got a scholarship to UVA and said it must be them trying to keep their quota up for students who weren't from Northern Virginia. But when I was in middle school I got so many A+'s the kids around me would roll their eyes when we got our quizzes back, 'oh, Finnegan got another A+, big whoop.' So, I deliberately answered questions wrong on the next quiz. My teacher was on to me. He pulled me aside and said, 'it's cool to be smart when you get into the real world, Rosalie, don't ever forget that.'"

"You felt invisible?" Tyler said.

"Maybe. Or at least second class. But it never felt as if my parents were sexist. It was more like, we knocked it out of the park with Oliver, Rosalie is just fluff." My eyes widened. "I was fluff!"

I gripped my glass, an ache filling my chest. Tyler remained silent.

"I never really thought about why we stopped having children after Annie. Ed wanted to try for a boy, but I never wanted a second child for fear I would do to that child what my parents did to me. I don't think I realized it at the time, but I was adamant. One kid, and he finally acquiesced. Mothers have a bigger vote in that department, by the way. We're the ones who transform our bodies and, well, you know the rest."

"But you always say wonderful things about your mother," Tyler said.

"She was kind and loving and smart and an incredible grandmother. So, yes, she was amazing, and I miss her every day. None of this was mean-spirited. But it was there, Tyler." I shook my head slowly. "Even Oliver didn't take me seriously until he was here a couple of months ago."

Tears spilled from my cheeks. "And I think that's what I am to Ed. Fluff. Oh, Rosalie won't stand up to me when I take her daughter to the Middle East for the month of December. Even if she does, who cares?" I blinked a few times. "Maybe that's why I hug pillows."

"I'm sorry?" Tyler said.

"My mother ship. Fluff!"

To his credit, Tyler let a few moments pass before he coughed out a laugh. I looked up at him, a little offended at first, but then I burst into one of the hardest laughs I'd had in a long time. When I recovered, I climbed into his lap and wrapped my arms around his neck, head on his shoulder, and snuggled.

He held me for a long time before he said, "I know I've said this before, but I see you, Rosalie, and you are an amazing person. I am so lucky to have you in my life."

Chapter Seventy

I woke up feeling a little fuzzy, but after a double espresso and an avocado smoothie, I was back on track. Tyler had gone home to shower and pack for the next few days, which of course would include his gun. I noticed Bini's coffee mug in the sink and decided to check in on her.

She was mucking out the goat barn with a pitchfork when I found her, stabbing the straw with all her strength.

"Morning," I said and pulled my coat tighter. "Is the heater still working out here?"

She sunk the pitchfork into the bale of hay and nodded.

"I thought you and Lucas were going to stop by the café yesterday. You said you would try to come on a Wednesday. Was it too crowded when you got there?"

"We never tried." She placed her hands on her hips and looked down at her boots. "I haven't heard from him in three days."

"What? Did something happen?"

"Beats me. The last text I got was on Monday. He said he had classes down in the Ocean City area for the next week."

"Is that normal? For him to not text while he's traveling?"

She looked up. "I don't have a normal with Lucas yet. But this is the longest we've gone without communicating in some way." She kicked at some straw. "Maybe he got bored. I mean, it's been two weeks. Stuff happens, I guess."

At a loss for words, I knelt down next to Cal Ripken and gave him a scratch. "How's Betty?"

"Good. She's really showing." She clicked her tongue, and Betty stood and walked over to Bini. "Check out this belly."

"How many kids do goats usually have?"

"Two is normal. The vet is coming out next week."

Cal Ripken butted my arm, and I landed hard on the ground. "Was that really necessary?" I said.

"You okay?" Bini was smiling.

"I should have expected that, I guess." I pushed myself up and brushed off my coat.

"Ty said I should keep an eye out for strange cars, that sort of thing. Are you in some sort of trouble?"

"I think Glenn and I have uncovered some things that are making our killer uncomfortable. So, yeah, if you could be vigilant, that would be great." Cal started over to me again, and I jumped out of the way. "Is he protecting Betty White?"

"Most likely. He's not used to you yet."

"Bini, I'm really sorry about Lucas."

"Yeah, me too."

I thought about saying something optimistic, that maybe he would reach out to her soon, but platitudes are the last thing someone wants to hear when they are hurting. "I'm going in to work now, although I think I need to change my tights first. Thank you, Cal. That's two pairs in two days." I studied Bini. "I'll catch you later, okay? And hang in there, Bini."

"I'm trying."

Chapter Seventy-One

Welcome to the Day Lily Café
A gathering place offering simplicity and
freshness, with a focus on locally sourced ingredients

Thursday's Special: *La Cuisine Française*
It's all Special!

* * *

Crystal climbed down from the step stool and brushed the chalk dust from her hands. She strolled over to the bar where Monique and Custer were going over the dinner menu, her earrings jingling as she moved. I was busy scrubbing the coffee machines and worrying about Glenn. He was already twenty minutes late.

"We're serving oysters tonight. Is that right, master chef?"

"You got it. Oh, Monique, we need to make the meunière sauce."

"What if we give away a free plate of French fries when someone orders a dozen oysters?" Crystal waited expectantly for their response.

"I actually like that idea," I said. "What do you two think?"

"That's kinda cool," Custer said.

The kitchen door slammed. Glenn. I ran out to meet him. "Are you okay?"

"I never received the menu for today, so I brought the special paper, and we can print them out here. How's your ink cartridge?"

"I was worried."

"About your ink cartridge?" Glenn smiled.

"About you, of course." I rolled my eyes.

"You should be. Abby was outside my house last night with a bottle of Jack Daniels. She said she wanted to come in, and we could see what happened. I wonder if she spiked it in some way, like one of those date drugs, knock me out and search my house." Glenn shimmied out of his coat.

I took it from him and hung it up. "I'm very glad you didn't let her in."

"I drove past her house this morning. There's a beat-up Ford truck in the driveway. Remember Bill's text about an ex-con? Freddy Bucks? I think it must be him. Now that Bill is dead, there is no need to hide the relationship. Oh, and I returned Bill's phone to the sheriff on my way in."

"Did you see him?"

"His door was shut, so I gave it to Lila. But I was able to download the relevant texts and call records onto my computer."

"What did you say to Abby?"

"I'm keeping it friendly, so I told her I reached out to Neil but haven't heard back. As long as I'm semi-responsive, there's no need for her to make a move."

"Hey, Mr. Glenn," Custer said. "Here's the lunch menu. Sorry for taking so long."

"No problem. It smells of onions and butter in here. Please tell me French onion soup is on the menu?"

"Good guess." Custer smiled. "Topped with gruyere."

"I know I've said this before, but I really love my job."

Chapter Seventy-Two

For dinner that night, Monique uploaded some sultry French music, and had dimmed the lights a little darker than usual. She found a box of votive candles in the storage room and set one in the center of each table.

Glenn approached and said, "I feel as if I should be wearing a beret. You?"

"Dark red lipstick."

"I never asked you, but have you had any more threats?"

"No, but I've been lying low, too. Tyler is going to stay at the house for the foreseeable future, and he's bringing his gun."

"Excellent."

"Maybe you should join us?"

"I would really like to have this resolved by Christmas. December is hard enough." Glenn filled a tray with water glasses. "When are we paying a visit on Micky B.?"

"Soon. Oh, here we go. Crystal is flipping the sign."

"And we have customers."

* * *

The champagne was flowing, and Custer was having a hard time keeping up with the oyster shucking. Crystal's idea of offering free French fries was a winner, and Monique had whipped up one of the best aioli sauces I ever tasted. There wasn't a single request for ketchup.

Nathan walked up next to me while drying a glass with a dish towel. "We have a patron. And she sure is cute."

I looked up and couldn't believe my eyes. "Annie?!?"

"Mom!"

She ran into my arms, and I picked her up, spinning her around. "Oh, my girl. Oh, my girl." I couldn't control the sobs. "How did you get here?" I said into her hair. "Is everything okay?"

"Is she *the* Annie?" Nathan said to Glenn.

"The one and only."

"She sure is cute," he said again.

I set her down and smoothed her hair. "How did this happen?"

"It's a long but good story. I'm here through Christmas. I hope that's okay."

"I'm going to pretend you didn't say that. Here, sit at the bar. I'll get you a menu."

Annie hung her bag on a hook under the bar and hopped on a chair. Crystal stood next to me. "Hey, Annie," she said.

"Hi! It's great to see you, Crystal."

"Same. And I believe I'm the only one not surprised to see you here." She gave us a warm smile, her earrings tinkling as she walked away.

Nathan hadn't stopped staring at Annie. "Hello, I'm Nathan." He extended his hand.

"Oh, hey," she said. "I've heard all about you. It's great to finally meet you."

"Same."

I eyed Nathan. His eyes were dancing, and that smile of his was broader than ever. "Would you like the drink special?"

"Yes, please. You don't even have to tell me what it is. Everything is good here."

"Okay," I said, "I know we're busy, but why are you home from Dubai so soon?"

"After two weeks and the arrival of Karen—"

"Her name is Karen?"

"Yes," Annie said. "Unfortunate name. Anyway, he saw me texting with you all the time and said he had made a mistake taking me away the whole month. So he changed my plane ticket. I got home this morning, took a long nap, and drove out here."

I squeezed her hands. "I have so many questions!"

"Just do your thing, Mom. I'm having the drink special." Annie drummed her fingers on the bar.

Nathan delivered her a Negroni Tramonto. "Want to know the story behind this drink?"

"Of course," Annie said and took a sip. "This is delish."

I grabbed a bottle of French chablis from behind Nathan and listened while I twisted the corkscrew.

"Have you heard of a Negroni?" he said.

"Sure. I'm not a big gin drinker, but I know they're popular."

"Well," Nathan rested his elbow on the bar, "legend has it that a handsome Italian bartender," he pointed his thumbs at his chest, "was making a Negroni when a beautiful woman," he pointed at Annie, "sat down at the bar." He winked. "He was so distracted by her beauty, he accidentally poured Prosecco into the drink instead of gin. That is a Negroni Sbagliato. Sbagliato means mistake in Italian."

"That's so cool."

"My specialty drink uses Italian Lambrusco instead of prosecco and—"

"Can I take another sip now?" Annie grinned.

"By all means."

"Hey, Nathan," Crystal called. "You plan on working tonight?"

"Oops." Annie giggled.

Custer pushed through the door with two trays of oysters on ice. "Which table, Crys?"

"Sixteen."

He rushed past us, not acknowledging Annie. She stared after him. When he came back to the bar, he said, "Hey, boss, can you pop open a champagne for Monique and me? Or just bring the bottle if you're too busy," and disappeared into the kitchen.

Annie gulped. "She's here?"

"Yes. She's been here all week."

Chapter Seventy-Three

Annie and I huddled under the covers in my bed. After Tyler and Annie had time to catch up, he offered to sleep on the sofa to give Annie and me some time alone.

"What changed your dad's mind?" I said and sipped some Sleepytime tea.

"Seeing us together. And realizing that if this was his attempt to understand me better, really get to know me, going to Dubai for a month would only alienate me more." She glanced over at me, picking up her own tea cup. "Did you say something to him when he walked you to the car that night?"

"I don't think so." I frowned. "No. We have to give him full credit for this one. So tell me everything. What's Dubai like?"

"So completely different from anything I've ever experienced. It was eerie. I mean, everything was beautiful, and we were staying at this really elegant place, but all that lushness in the middle of a desert gives you some serious cognitive dissonance, you know? But, Dad showed me a good time, which was cool, but what really mattered was that at every meal, he asked me a new question. He said he wanted to learn everything he could that he didn't already know about me. Breakfast, lunch, and dinner, he started out with a new question. The first one was, what's your favorite color?"

"How did he not know it was blue? Your entire bedroom is shades of blue."

"But he asked, right? Then, the questions got more serious. He asked about my dreams, my favorite songs, my classes, everything. It was a brilliant idea. A new question every meal where I had his full attention."

"Do you feel more visible to him now?"

"Yes. Most definitely."

I hugged her. "This is all wonderful news."

"And how about you, Mom? What's going on with the café?"

"Too much. You know that review I texted you? Now people from all over the D.C. metropolitan area are coming here and staying at Gretchen's Inn."

"Are you okay with all the publicity? I mean that review. Dad and I read it on his phone. It was incredible. Four out of four stars!"

"I know, right? Part of me is thrilled to have the validation. We've all worked so hard to create such a welcoming space with good service and food, and to have a critic really get what we're doing. It's more than I could have dreamed of."

"Oh, yeah."

"But the other part of me doesn't want us to lose what we have, the small town feel, the friendliness."

Annie was quiet for a moment. "I think if anyone can walk the line between the two, it's you. And it will be amazing."

I couldn't stop smiling. "God, I'm so glad you're here. There has been a piece of me missing since the holidays started."

Annie wiggled her feet under the covers. "I have an idea."

"I'm listening."

"Let's ambush Tyler. Tell him he has to watch a movie with us. It's only 10:00. You can make popcorn."

I tossed back the covers and tucked my feet into my slippers. "Let's do it."

We found Tyler stretched out on the sofa doing the crossword in yesterday's newspaper. Annie plopped down on the end cushion. "You have two choices. *Talladega Nights* or *Pitch Perfect*."

Tyler sat up. "That's it?"

She nodded. "Pick one, or I get to choose. Mom's making popcorn."

"Well, that's easy. Ricky Bobby, it is."

Annie hopped up and walked over to the remote. "'If you ain't first, you're last.'"

Chapter Seventy-Four

On Friday morning, Annie, Tyler, and I had a raucous breakfast full of laughter and great stories, leaving me energized and optimistic for the first time that month. It seemed now that Annie and her father were growing closer, she was able to be looser in her relationship with Tyler. Even Nathan, for that matter, as if she felt more confident and comfortable with men in general. Way to go, Ed, I thought as I drove into town.

Lunch felt a little more normal. Monique had stayed at Custer's place to get some rest but promised to be back that evening. We served up a lot of grilled cheeses and burgers and sides of kimchi. Custer had decided to elevate the coleslaw. So far, no one had complained.

During the afternoon lull, I was sweeping the dining room and noticed Summer Belle outside on the stoop. I unlocked the door and invited her in.

"You haven't picked up your paper in a few days, so I thought I'd bring them to you," she said. "You don't have to take all of them if you only want today's."

"Thanks, I'll take them all. I know someone who likes crosswords." I set them on a nearby table. "How have you been?"

"I'm sorry my mom pushed you. That is not okay."

"She told you?"

"Bragged about it, actually. I have no idea why she's so down on you. And I miss our talks. They have, um, what's the word, substance?"

"I like talking to you, too." I gripped the broom handle. "Summer, remember when you said I could ask you questions? Well, I have one. I know you just said you don't know why your mom doesn't want me in your life, but is she hiding something? I don't know what it could be. Everyone knows she got his life insurance even though Bill intended to change the recipient to you. And no one is challenging that; she probably already has the check."

"My mom is a secretive kind of person. Back before all this was happening with my dad, she was meeting someone at night. Just a few times, but she would be out for three or four hours. I could always tell she'd been drinking, but I didn't ask with whom."

"But that's stopped?"

"I think so. She pretty much comes home every night after work."

I debated about asking another question but thought better of it. "How about some hot chocolate?"

"No thanks. Maybe next time."

"I'm glad you stopped by. And I won't be staying away. I love that you are working with Miss Doris. Hey, maybe we could start our own little book club or something. If you are reading a book in English class, maybe I could read it too and we could discuss it when I pick up my paper."

She smiled, something I had rarely seen her do. "That's a good idea. I'm in honors English this year. I'm pretty sure our next book is *A Separate Peace* by John Knowles."

"Oh my gosh, they're still teaching that? I read it in high school, too. I would love to read it again, see if I have a different take on it."

She turned to go but stopped. "Miss Rosalie?"

"Yes?"

Her hands were deep in the pockets of her black puffer jacket. "I have to tell you this, and I don't know if it means anything. I hope it doesn't, I really do, but it's been eating me up inside."

"Of course. I'm listening."

"The night my dad died? My mom was meeting that person. She didn't get home until around seven."

Chapter Seventy-Five

Shortly before we opened for dinner, Annie texted and asked me to save her a seat at the bar next to Tyler. I reminded her Monique was still here, but she said it would help her desensitization therapy to get used to seeing Custer with Monique and not herself. Annie and Custer's flirtation had ignited in the café and lasted two years. It would take a while for her to get over the hurt.

It was another *Notte Italiana,* and the *Fettuccine Alfredo* orders were piling up. Annie and Tyler were enjoying glasses of Alessa's chianti and buttering slices of Italian bread.

"What should we eat, Mom?" Annie said.

"Yeah, what should we eat?" Tyler added.

"Monique is doing something amazing with chicken. Butter, lemon, capers, garlic, the kitchen is so redolent I start to salivate every time I go in there."

"Sold." Tyler slapped his menu closed. "Annie?"

"Ditto that."

Custer emerged from the kitchen, pushing the cart.

"Table eight," Crystal said.

Custer's performance received a roar from the crowd, and he took a diminutive bow. He walked over to Crystal and handed her the tip money one of the women had stuffed into the pocket of his chef's jacket.

"That belongs to you," she said.

Not noticing Annie again, he stuffed the money in the tip jar on the bar, and headed back into the kitchen.

Annie, who had dressed up for the evening, her hair in smooth waves, a tint of pink on her lips, looked like a tossed-aside puppy.

"Annie?"

"What was that, Mom?"

"Just something I learned about *Fettuccine Alfredo*. It's been a big hit. Is it too much?"

She shook her head. "It's amazing. Custer did a really good job."

"Your glass is empty," Nathan said, elbows on the bar, gazing at Annie.

"I hope you're about to change that." She forced a smile.

"How about some of the goat cheese, Rosalie?" Tyler said. "Bini made it," he said to Annie. "And Betty White is pregnant."

Annie's shoulders relaxed, as if Tyler had grounded her back into reality. She was here, in Cardigan, with the people who loved her. "That sounds really good."

"Phew," Crystal said, the back of her hand on her forehead. "So many pasta orders. I think you might need to get back there to help Custer with the other orders."

"Go, Mom," Annie said. "I'm just happy to be here."

Nathan delivered her drink. "And I'm happy *you're* here."

I gave him a wry smile. I had never seen him in active flirtation mode. Apparently, subtlety wasn't part of his style. But maybe that's just what Annie needed. A straightforward chatting up. And maybe that's exactly what Nathan was trying to accomplish.

Chapter Seventy-Six

The sign had been flipped, the tables cleared, and Nathan was wiping down the bar and washing glasses while Annie sat across from him, chin in hand. I walked over to them and puffed at a piece of hair that had stuck to my lip. "You guys okay?"

"Better than okay," Nathan said. "Busiest night I've ever seen as a bartender, and the adrenaline is still pulsing through my veins. I've heard about nights like this. I felt sort of like Tom Cruise in *Cocktail*."

"Is that a movie?" Annie said.

He shook his head. "Any bartender who claims to be able to make a decent margarita has seen that movie."

"I'll check it out." She smiled. "Have you seen it, Mom?"

"A long time ago. Nathan, I've been watching people drink champagne all night. Let's open another one. A good one."

"I'm in," Annie said.

I walked over to her and rubbed her back. "Did you have fun tonight hanging out here?"

"Very much. I've been helping. Is there such a thing as a sous bartender?"

"You've been making drinks?"

"No, just chopping garnishes, and I learned how to smoke an orange zest for Negronis. I did okay, right, Nathan?"

He grinned. "More than okay. You saved my butt tonight."

"How about you?" Annie said. "Did you walk the line, Johnny Cash?"

I thought back on our conversation from the night before. "Yes," I said. "I think I did."

Annie's phone vibrated on the bar. She picked it up. "Oh my god. Mom, we both just got a text." She looked up. "Uncle Oliver's coming for Christmas. He'll be here Christmas Eve!!!"

Chapter Seventy-Seven

Once the café closed the following night, I hurried home for a quick wardrobe change. Janice's party must have been in full swing already, but Tyler and I still planned to attend. Glenn had opted out, saying the last thing he needed was to be in a room full of people. Instead, he planned to spend a quiet evening with Gretchen.

I decided on a little black dress, pearls, and kitten-heel pumps. Not original for me, but it was a go-to, and I had no time for a wardrobe crisis. I found Tyler in the kitchen, Dickens slumped in his bed. As I admired Tyler's faded jeans and black V-neck sweater, the butterflies took flight. He wrapped his arms around me, and I breathed him in. Sandalwood soap and Tyler's strong arms and the rest of the world evaporated.

"You're so snuggly," I said. "Have I ever seen you in a sweater?"

"My sister gave it to me for Christmas last year. I thought I would up my game a bit tonight."

I rested my head on his chest. "Mm. I think it's cashmere."

Tyler stepped back. You look nice. You smell pretty damned good, too." He walked over to Dickens' food dishes and topped off the water and kibble.

"So what did you do today?" I said as I transferred my essentials from my purse to a small black clutch.

Tyler scratched Dickens' ears and stood. "Let's see, I worked out, took a shower, then laid on the couch and read *A Christmas Carol* from cover to cover."

"Marley was dead, to begin with. There is no doubt whatever about that," I said and smiled. "What a wonderful way to spend a December afternoon.

I'm jealous."

"The guy can write. Were you swamped again?"

"Busy but not crazy. A few parties had to wait, but we are getting better at this."

Tyler pulled on his coat. "Is Annie coming?"

"I heard that." She shuffled into the kitchen in slippers, a loose sweatshirt, and plaid, oversized flannel pants. "I'm staying in. Still a little jet-lagged. But I am locking the door behind you, so take your keys." She hugged us both, filled her water bottle, and returned to the television.

Tyler took my elbow and escorted me to his truck.

Chapter Seventy-Eight

Janice and Trevor Tilghman lived in an elegant, historic home on the Cardigan River. On one of the oldest farms in Devon County, the house had been expanded and upgraded over the years. They both came from Eastern Shore aristocracy, such as it is and lived simple lives on their trust funds and investments. Trevor worked hard managing the farm, and Janice spent much of her time serving on boards and volunteering. Although a year older than me, Janice had struggled with getting pregnant. But once the problem was discovered and resolved, she gave birth to three healthy young boys in four short years.

The Tilghman family story of how Janice and Trevor got together by 'accident' was legendary. Janice, in her junior year at a private high school, was the star of the field hockey team. That year, they made the playoffs, and when a women's team made the playoffs, everyone showed up, including the school mascot, the Turkey Vulture. That role was always given to one of the tallest boys in the school.

The score was five to zip, the Vultures in a strong lead, but that didn't stop Janice from keeping her foot on the gas. After ramming into one of her opponents, knocking her to the ground, she hit the ball with everything she had. The crowd let out a simultaneous gasp when it landed in the Turkey Vulture's groin, crumpling him to the ground.

Janice ran over and knelt down next to him. The fans roared to life when the Turkey Vulture at last sat up. Trevor removed his mask and said in a weak voice, "Nice shot."

Relief washing through her, Janice popped out her mouth guard and kissed him on the lips. After that day, the athletic department began issuing cups to the mascots, and the three Tilghman offspring often said they were very glad their father's costume had so many feathers.

The lane to their home, which was long and tree-lined, had rows of cars on either side. Tyler slipped his pickup into the first available opening and killed the engine. Their grandiose house sparkled in the dark, cloudy night before us.

"Did she invite the whole county?" Tyler said as he narrowed his eyes at the shadowed figures inside passing by the floor-to-ceiling windows. "Crowds make me a little buggy."

"I guess when you know everyone in the county, it's hard to be selective."

"Stay by my side?"

"Always." I squeezed his hand.

We had to work our way through the congested foyer before we made it to the living room. Pine garlands and tiny white lights were draped throughout the room, and a twelve-foot tree graced the far corner. A uniformed bartender was busy serving a line of guests while a waiter passed by with a tray of glasses filled with champagne.

"Hey, Marky Mark," Tyler called out to him.

Mark turned around. "Wellsie. How ya' doing, bro?"

"Making some extra cash during the holidays?"

He held out the tray for us. "I don't work for Katie's Catering much anymore, but no one in their right mind would turn down this gig."

After introducing me to Mark, Tyler and I clinked our glasses, and Mark eased his way through the partygoers. I took in the room, noticing several familiar faces. I waved to Trevor, who stood on the opposite side of the room, his head higher than most. He lifted his glass and smiled.

"Mark and I used to play football together," Tyler said.

"Football? You've never mentioned you played football. What position did you play?"

"Wide receiver," he said while scanning the crowd.

"Were you good?"

"I got some interest from a few recruiters, including the University of

Maryland, but remember my story? It all went to hell when the last scoop of dirt landed on her casket."

"Of course, I remember," I said softly. "I wish I could have seen you play."

Champagne slopped out of my glass when the person behind me bumped my elbow. I stiffened when I turned to see the profile of the sheriff. Joe Wilgus had been sober for over three years after being bribed by a crooked John Adams College president. But his recent behavior had made Glenn and I curious if he had relapsed. I glanced down at his glass. It was filled with a dark carbonated beverage garnished with a slice of lime, but I had no idea what else was in it.

"Hart," he said gruffly. "When did you get here?"

Tyler inched a little closer, and my shoulders relaxed. "The café had a long day."

He took me in but said nothing. I couldn't read his face, but it was clear he was working through something in his mind. Refusing to ease his discomfort by saying some sort of pleasantry, which was normally my go-to, I turned away, and Tyler and I moved into the dining room.

"Looks like you're still off the case," Tyler said as he picked up a toothpick of prosciutto and cantaloupe.

"I forgot the number one rule." I chose a bruschetta topped with some sort of melty cheesy mix with diced shallots sprinkled on top.

"And what rule is that?"

"I'm sure you know." I picked up a gold napkin. "Don't mess with a Langford."

"And have you?"

"Not yet."

* * *

"'Bout time," Janice bellowed as she crossed the study. She passed by the piano player who had begun a jazzy version of "Have Yourself a Merry Little Christmas." After snatching up a glass of champagne from a waitress, she stopped before us. She pecked a kiss on each of our cheeks and said, "At least you're here now."

"What a party," Tyler said. "Is there anyone you didn't invite?"

"Um, let me see." She tapped her chin with her finger. "Um, nope. Oh, Rose Red, Micky B. is here, so don't let her push you around again, okay?"

"Literally or figuratively?" Tyler said.

"Literally."

"Where is she?" Tyler set his empty glass on a passing tray. "Let me at her."

"Over by the fireplace." Janice motioned with her head. "Go for it."

I looked toward the massive fireplace at the end of the room. Micky was indeed there. She wore a red dress with bell sleeves and was in a conversation with Gunther Langford.

"How do those two know each other?" I asked Janice.

"No clue."

Micky looked up and noticed me staring at her. I gasped as she slid a finger across her throat. Gunther followed her gaze and narrowed his eyes. He turned away from her and walked into a different room. Micky left in the opposite direction.

"You know I was just kidding, Wells," Janice said. "Don't start a fight in the middle of my party."

Tyler studied me. "Seems they made a hasty exit."

I clutched my glass. "Janice, is Gunther's wife here? I think her name is Pamela."

"Of course, she's here. Why?"

"Could you point her out to me?"

She studied me. "Absolutely not."

"Pretty please?" Just then, I noticed Gunther at the far end of the room, his hand on the elbow of a small but elegant woman. Her white hair was in a chignon, and a pair of tear-drop diamonds dangled from her ears.

"Okay, fine," I said. "Be that way."

"Now, could you please just have some fun, Rose Red?" She stuck out her bottom lip. "It's my party. Don't make me cry."

"Hey, Janice," Tyler said. "Do you have a preference which bathroom I use?"

"The one off the foyer."

We watched him go.

"I need to check on the caterer." Janice looked at me, one eyebrow raised. "You stay out of trouble?"

"No problem." She spun around and headed for her massive kitchen. I noticed Pamela leaning against the wall near the bar, arms tucked behind her. She looked subdued, as if her husband may have just chastised her in some way.

Despite Janice's admonition, I approached Pamela.

"Is this the line for the bar?" I said.

"No, dear, it's over there. I'm just waiting for my husband."

"Me too. I mean, he's sort of my husband." I stood next to her. "Nice party."

"Janice is a talented hostess. I look forward to this party all year."

"Are you by any chance, Pamela Langford?"

"Yes, that's me. Why do you ask?"

I mirrored her stance. "I met your husband at the country club the other day. Janice is encouraging me to join. He was at the bar with Patrick Delaney. They had just finished a round of golf."

Unexpected tears welled in her eyes. She quickly brushed one away. "Yes, he spends a lot of time there."

"They had just lost their golfing partner. It was odd, he played golf with Bill Rutherford every week, but he didn't seem sad he died. Were they not friends?"

She stared ahead. "Gunther hated Bill Rutherford from the first day Bill joined the club twenty years ago."

"And yet they played golf together at least once a week?"

"Normally...wait, what is your name?"

"Rosalie."

"Normally, Rosalie, I would tell you to mind your own business, but for some reason, it's a huge relief to talk about this with someone."

"Talk about what?"

The tears let loose. "I think my husband may have done something awful."

"Honestly, Pamela, I think he may have too."

She stared at me. We took each other in. "He can't know we've talked."

I slid a Day Lily business card into her hands. "Let's find a way to meet on Monday morning. Are you free?"

She slipped the card into her bra. "Yes." Her eyes darted around the room. "But let's pick a place. Quick. Before he comes back."

"Riverside Park. Nine a.m." I snapped my evening bag closed. "I'll bring coffee."

She nodded, and I slipped away. As I went into the foyer to find Tyler, I came face to face with Joe Wilgus. I tried to duck away, but he said, "Hart. I have something you probably want to know."

I looked up at him, anger at his negligence simmering in my gut. "What might that be?"

"I just got a 9-1-1 call. Seems someone ransacked your friend's house."

"You mean Glenn?"

"Deputies are over there now."

My anger hit full steam. "And after hearing this, do you still believe Donny Jones shot his friend in the back?"

"Keep your voice down, Hart," he growled.

"There's a killer out there who thinks they got away with it," I said through gritted teeth. "This is on your hands." I pushed past him. "Now I have to go to my friend."

Chapter Seventy-Nine

Lights from two deputy sheriffs' SUVs illuminated Glenn's neighborhood, swathing the tidy houses in eerie blues and reds. I hopped out of Tyler's truck and ran down the sidewalk, regretting the kitten heels. Several neighbors huddled in the street in robes and heavy coats. I hurried toward the door, and a deputy stopped me.

"I'm a close friend of Glenn's. Can I see him?"

The deputy was tall and gangly, dark curls popping out of his hat. "He narrowed his eyes. "You're Hart, right?"

"Yes, I'm Rosalie Hart."

"I'll send him out, but we're still checking for prints, so I can't let you go inside."

Tyler caught up to me. "Do they know who did this?"

"There's no question who did this," I said.

"What were they after?"

I hugged myself. It had to be less than twenty degrees outside. "They were looking for a check for fifty-thousand dollars."

The deputy had stopped writing. "What did you just say?"

"I said, I know who did this."

"You gonna be here when we finish up?"

"Yes, of course."

Glenn and the deputy passed one another in the doorway as Glenn stepped onto the sidewalk. My heart ached when I saw the dazed look on his face. Pale and exhausted, dark circles ringed his eyes.

"Are you all right?" I said.

"I don't know the answer to that question. But I'm glad you're both here."

"Did they find the check?"

Glenn tapped his front pocket. "I keep it with me at all times."

"Did they take anything?" Tyler asked.

"No. They were only after one thing."

I tucked my arm through his. "I'm so relieved you weren't home."

He adjusted his glasses. "Gretchen makes the best hot toddy I've ever had." He inhaled deeply and shook his head. "When I unlocked my front door, I felt a cold breeze. I knew instantly the back door was open. I went outside and called the sheriff."

"Busted lock?" Tyler asked.

"Yes. I believe it was a crowbar."

"Mr. Breckinridge?" The deputy returned. "Looks like we're about done here. Are you going to be okay?"

"You can stay at my place," I said.

"No. They didn't find what they're looking for," Glenn said. "Why come back?"

"I don't like this," I said. "What about your lock?"

"These men were kind enough to install a padlock," Glenn said. "I should be fine. And I have some melatonin and brandy. A fine mix indeed."

"We plan on driving by here every hour or so," the taller deputy said. "It's a quiet night other than a couple of Christmas parties. Keep your phone charged and next to your bed. But if you believe whoever did this will come back, you might want to reconsider staying here."

"Wait," I said. "I have an idea. Glenn, what if you call Neil and tell him to close that bank account first thing Monday morning? Or sooner, if possible." I chewed on a nail. "Hang on, it's coming to me. Then you tell Abby you talked with Neil, and he gave you the okay to give her the check. You can say you're sorry you kept it from her, blah, blah, blah, and when she cashes it, the bank is on alert, and boom—they're caught."

Tyler's head reared back a little. "Did you just now come up with all that?"

"Mm-hm." I nodded my head. "We need to get Glenn out of the middle." I looked over at the deputy. "I know you. You're the one who was so nice to me in jail. Jason, right?"

"That's me. And I like your plan." He looked at Glenn. "Can you text this person tonight? Tell her you'll put the check in her mailbox first thing tomorrow. That way, you can close the account and she won't have a reason to come back tonight. Take a picture of the mailbox with the check inside, too. But don't be obvious." He pulled out a pad. "And can someone please give me this person's name?"

"Abigail Harrington," I said. "She lives in this community. And there's a chance she's with a man by the name of Freddy Bucks. He's an ex-con, so he certainly has a record."

The deputy continued to write.

"My head is spinning," Glenn said. "Would you two like to come inside?"

Jason flipped his pad closed. "You take care, Mr. Breckinridge. Make sure you text this person tonight. And, like I said, we'll be doing our rounds. Oh, wait a sec, which one is her house? We'll keep an eye on that, too."

Glenn pointed. "It's in the next block. One of the duplexes on the left. Gray with black shutters. She's got a very annoying wind chime on the front porch that I can hear from my backyard."

They shuffled away. "Oh, Jason?"

"Yes, ma'am?"

"When will the sheriff receive your report?"

"We write it up when our shift is over." He tipped his hat and climbed into his vehicle.

Chapter Eighty

Glenn's living room looked as if a giant had lifted his house off its foundation and shook it like a magic eight-ball. The cushions of his chair and sofa were tossed about, every drawer open, pencils, several decks of cards, and a pair of scissors were scattered on the carpet.

I picked up the cushions of his recliner and tucked them into place. "Why don't you sit, Glenn? Can I get you a glass of something? Maybe that brandy you were talking about?"

"Yes." He eased himself into the chair. "But I hate to drink alone."

"I would love to join you, but I'm behind the wheel tonight," Tyler said, hands in his back pockets.

"The sheriff spilled most of my champagne, so I couldn't be any more sober," I said. "If you don't mind me driving your truck, Tyler, I'll pour you some brandy as well."

"Watch her on those turns," Glenn said and smiled.

"Good to know. Mind if I look around first?" Tyler said. "I'd like to check that padlock."

The kitchen floor had the appearance of a disorganized yard sale. I had to tip-toe over spoons and utensils and several broken plates. I found the brandy and filled two glasses. When I returned to Glenn, I set them on the side table and tucked the remaining cushions on the sofa. "Do you have your phone?" I said before I sat down.

"It's on the table by the front door. Why?"

"Let's send that text before we forget." I covered him with a crocheted Afghan that had been tossed in a corner and put his glass in his hand.

Glenn took a long sip of brandy, eyes closed. It hurt my heart to see my friend so frazzled and afraid. As I walked to his phone, I wondered, had I put him in this danger? He said it was time to draw out our suspects. Well, we certainly had done that. We knew Abby was capable of breaking and entering. But was she also the killer? I picked up Glenn's phone and headed back to the living room. I hoped the deputies had found some sort of evidence to prove Abby was the one who upended Glenn's home and his well-being.

I sat on the sofa. "How do we prove it was Abby who did this? What if there aren't any prints?"

Glenn set his glass down. "We have the texts Bill sent her, for one. And she was in Bill's house that day. But, yes, prints would seal the deal."

"They seemed to be experienced. Maybe Abby has a record, too."

"Our good sheriff will have to be on board for us to find out any of that." Glenn took another sip. "I feel as if I've aged ten years."

I patted his hand. "I can't imagine how upsetting this is. I'm going to do some cleaning once Tyler returns. Now, shall I type?"

"What do you think?"

"I think it's the only way to guarantee your safety. We have to get you out of the middle."

"I agree." Tyler walked into the room and sat next to me. I handed him the other glass.

"How's the lock?" Glenn said.

"Solid. Your screen door is busted up, but that's an easy fix."

"Okay, here we go." I typed with my thumbs. "Abby, I have just spoken with Neil, and he said it is okay for me to give you the check from Bill. I know you have searched my home for it, so I will happily put it in your mailbox first thing in the morning. All the best, your neighbor, Glenn." I looked up. "What do you think?"

"I like the part about me knowing it was her who was in my home. That's very smart." Some color had returned to Glenn's face.

"Tyler?"

"You two are the detectives. I'm just a farmer who minds his own business."

Glenn chuckled.

I rolled my shoulders back and hit send.

Chapter Eighty-One

On Sunday morning, I texted Annie during a lull in brunch to see if she wanted to do some Christmas shopping that afternoon. After today's brunch, the Day Lily would be closed for two weeks for the holiday break. Not long after, I received her response.

That would be great, but I was thinking we could invite Nathan and Tyler over this evening. I can make some food. What do you think?

My response: *Of course!*

Once Crystal flipped the sign, I gathered everyone together and distributed gifts. Although I had insisted Glenn stay home that morning, he refused. After rising early and placing the check in Abby's mailbox, photo following, he said he had too much adrenaline to stay home.

Monique had started to duck away but I waved her over. "You are part of us, now. So please stay."

"We have an opened champagne from brunch," Nathan said. "Shall I pour us all a small glass for some holiday cheer?"

"But of course," Monique said.

I passed around new aprons for everyone, rolled into a tube, and tied with a ribbon. Although they were still black waist aprons, these had a new and improved Day Lily Café logo on the top left-hand corner in white, their names underneath. We had all agreed the first day we opened that full aprons were cumbersome. With just a few pockets, the aprons could sit on our hips and give us freedom to move around. And just like everything else in the café these past few weeks, our aprons were now elevated as well.

As they unrolled the tidy bundles, I heard sounds of approval, an ooh, and an ahh here and there. But the enthusiasm increased when the end-of-the-year bonus envelopes tumbled out of the middle.

"Thank you, boss," Custer said, envelope tight in his grip.

For Monique, who had also been given her own personalized apron, I enclosed the following note on a small white card:

Dear Monique,

Thank you for the past few weeks. Your knowledge and enthusiasm and talent have elevated us all in the best of ways. Please know you are always welcome here to cook, to dine, to share in the fun.

I am awed by your talent and instinct and am touched that you shared your story with me. You are a remarkable woman, and I hope I have found a new friend.

Most Sincerely,
Rosalie Hart

Monique held the note to heart. "You have, Rosalie, my dear. You most certainly have."

"Happy holidays!" Crystal shrieked, and we toasted our glasses together.

Chapter Eighty-Two

Tyler and I stood in the kitchen. Nathan, having already arrived, was in the living room with Annie.

"How is Glenn?" Tyler said as he slipped out of his jacket.

"He delivered the check, and Neil has canceled the account, so the plan is set. And he just texted that her mailbox is now empty."

"And our guest is Nathan, the bartender?"

"Yes. He and Annie have been having fun together, and now she is curious if there will be a spark." I shrugged. "She's on the rebound, but I hope they have a nice time."

"My nephew's infatuation with all things French is getting to her?"

"I honestly don't blame Custer. He's making something of himself, and he's a really good cook, or should I say, chef. I hate seeing Annie this way, but I kind of get why Monique and Custer found each other." I laughed. "I never thought I would say those words, but there it is."

"There isn't anything you just said that doesn't sound like Rosalie Hart. You believe in people and see the best in them. And you've just done it again."

* * *

A few hours later, the fire reduced to embers, Annie's onion dip and flatbread seriously depleted, and the wine, after having reddened our cheeks, was almost gone. "Nathan," I said, "you grew up in Cardigan, right?"

"Born and raised."

"Is your family still here?"

"Has been for three generations, so, yeah."

Annie inched closer to him, both perched on an ottoman. "Do you live at home?" she said.

Nathan's head fell forward. "Damn. You get invited to a super cool girl's house, and she asks you that." He looked over at Annie. "Yes. I live with my parents. I'm paying off my student loans."

"Nathan!" Annie said. "That's what just about everyone does these days. No judging."

"I'm not sure why I'm asking you this," I drained my wine glass, "do your folks belong to the country club?"

"Again, for three generations."

"Do you golf?" I said.

Nathan shook his head and smiled. "I had a scholarship in college. I've been the club champ twice, so the answer is, yes, I," he made air quotation marks, "golf."

Annie squeezed his bicep. "So this right here isn't from shaking cocktails."

"I can't believe I didn't know that about you," I said. "I don't ask enough questions."

"Um, actually, you do," Tyler said.

"So club champ. If you played in tournaments, you must have known Bill Rutherford."

"Oh, yeah. That's pretty crazy what happened to him."

"What happened to him?" Annie said.

"He was riding his bike home after a round of golf and got hit by a truck."

"Is he *dead*?" Annie said.

"Anybody mind if I open another wine?" Tyler stood.

"I brought home a couple of Casa Vanellis from the café. You could open one of those."

"Was he on River Road?" Annie said.

"Yeah, one of his golfing buddies hit him on his way home."

"That's so awful." Annie stared into her empty glass.

"Nathan, what was your impression of Bill?"

He leaned forward, elbows on his knees. "My dad said something to me when I first showed an interest in golf that I will never forget. He said, 'Nathan, you can learn everything you need to know about a person by playing a round of golf with them.'"

Tyler stopped in the doorway and turned around. "I like that." He thought for a moment and smiled. "I like that a lot."

"And that's how it was with Bill. I first met him in a tournament. I was paired with my dad. Bill was with Gunther Langford. We ended in a tie, so we broke it with a three-hole playoff. I watched Bill move his ball at least two times."

Annie looked up. "Is that against the rules?"

"Hell, yes. Not only is it against the rules, it's a violation of the integrity of the sport. Especially in a tournament. They beat us by one stroke."

"I met Gunther once," I said. "Did he cheat, too?"

"Not that I saw in a tournament, but I've played with him casually when he fudged his score or took a second shot at a putt without counting the stroke. My dad doesn't like him. He said he wouldn't trust him as far as he could throw him."

Tyler returned with a bottle of pinot noir and filled Annie's glass. "You okay to drive, Nathan? Or are you sleeping on the sofa?"

His eyes brightened. "I can always call my dad to come and get me. But it would be great not to bother him. If it's okay with you guys, I would love to sleep on the sofa. I'll leave as soon as I sober up."

"Mom?" Annie said, her eyebrows lifted in hopes I would say yes.

"Of course."

"Alrighty, then." Tyler filled Nathan's glass. He walked over to me. "Have you finished your investigation for the evening, Madam Clouseau?"

I held up my glass but said nothing.

"Wait," Annie said, sitting straighter. "Are you and Glenn at it again, Mom?"

"Glenn lived next door to Bill Rutherford. He was the first to notice he hadn't come home that night."

"But Nathan said he got hit by a car. Didn't you just say that?"

"It was in the paper," Nathan said. "Donny Jones hit him. Which makes it even more awful because Donny's a really good guy. I can't imagine how he's handling this. They played golf together every Sunday afternoon."

"Mom?" Annie said.

Maybe it was the wine, or maybe it was the wine, or just maybe it was so Tyler might understand, as he promised he always would, that it was important to find out what really happened to Bill Rutherford that night.

"You are sworn to secrecy."

Annie zipped her lips.

"He had been shot in the back. And we don't believe Donny Jones is the one to have done it."

"Wait, what did you say?" Nathan gave his head a quick shake. "How do you know?"

"My mom helps Sheriff Wilgus on investigations. She's really good at it." Annie looked back at me. "Do you have suspects?"

I slugged back some wine. "Yes. And that's all I'm going to say."

"I hope you have Gunther Langford on your list," Nathan said.

"Why?" Annie said.

"One afternoon, we were playing a round, and someone's Lab was loose and running around on the fifteenth hole. When it was Langford's turn to hit, he faced the dog and swung at his ball with a pitching wedge. Ball hit that poor dog right in the side."

"Oh!" Annie slapped her hands over her mouth.

Holding the wine bottle in one hand, his glass in the other, Tyler took a long sip and said, "Asshole." He set the bottle down. "You better get to work there, darlin', cuz if it's him, I hope they toss him in prison and throw away the key."

* * *

Once the kitchen was clean and Nathan tucked into his bed on the sofa, Tyler and I climbed under the covers. He lay on his back, staring at the ceiling, hands behind his head.

"Tyler?"

"Yes?"

"I thought you said you understood my curiosity. That I do these investigations because it ultimately helps people." I rolled onto my side and propped my head on my hand.

He blinked a few times and frowned. "I'm trying. I honestly am. But it's all getting too real. And when you reminded me the guy was shot in the back, it got to me. Who does that? A bad son of a bitch, that's who. And what about Glenn getting his house ransacked? And—"

"And?"

"And—" He turned and pulled me into his arms. "I can't stop thinking about what happened last time." He pulled me closer and said into my hair, "You could have died."

I held him tight, my cheek warm against his bare chest.

"I don't want to live without you. This all scares the shit out of me."

"I'll be careful," I said. "I promise."

"God, I love you."

"I love you."

He was quiet for a moment. "And why does your hair always smell so damn good?"

Chapter Eighty-Three

I sat on a bench in Riverside Park overlooking the Cardigan River, ankles crossed, two cardboard coffee cups in my hands. Pamela arrived exactly three minutes later. My guess was she had been sitting in her car waiting for me.

She sat down and accepted the cup, wearing a large pair of sunglasses, a scarf tied over her head. There wasn't a hint of sun, only heavy gray clouds. I looked over my shoulder at a very large white Range Rover in the parking lot. The vanity plate read: Langford2. Was she seriously trying to go unnoticed?

I faced the river again. We both gazed at the lapping water sipping our coffees with gloved hands.

"I'm not sure why I'm here," she said.

"I make pretty good coffee."

After a small laugh, she took another sip. "Yes, you do." She cleared her throat. "What happens after I tell you?"

"Hopefully, I will be able to share it with the sheriff and gain his cooperation. But I'm not really sure what it is you are about to tell me."

"But you have an idea."

"Yes. I have an idea."

"I love my husband. I always have. But our relationship has been on the decline. Our only son has cut us off. He says he hates his father and will pretend I don't exist as long as I stay married to him."

"That's harsh," I said, still looking out at the river.

"I was devastated. I still am. I can't eat, I can't sleep, I'm so angry with Gunther I can't stand to be in the same room with him. He refuses to reach out to our Jackson and make amends. It's all out of pure arrogance and stubbornness. My god, he's our only son."

"It sounds awful. I can't imagine that pain." I looked over at her. "I'm very sorry. It sounds intolerable."

"I ran into Bill at the 'Christmas in Cardigan' meeting at the end of November. I'm on the parade committee. Bill was always Santa. He sat next to me that night and asked what was wrong. He was so sweet and kind. He invited me to take a walk, and sure enough, we ended up at his place. We split an entire bottle of wine before I agreed to go into his bedroom. I've never done anything like that in my life. I should have known when I saw the wall of pictures of himself winning races, riding his bike with no shirt on, dumping water over his head. I mean, who does that? The man lived alone.

"But at the time, I needed a distraction and maybe some sort of twisted revenge. When we finished, I got out of bed as fast as I could and said thank you and that I would never sleep with him again. Little did I know, Bill did it to get under my husband's skin, not because he felt any sort of affection for me. Bill and Gunther were vicious rivals in every way. Not long after, Bill bragged about sleeping with me at the country club bar. And now I can barely show my face in town."

She lifted her sunglasses and dabbed at her eyes with a lace handkerchief. "I know I am the one who has wronged my husband. And I feel wretched. But I also know I'm not the reason my husband has done what he's done. I was just the tipping point he was waiting for."

"Are you saying he killed Bill Rutherford?"

"He didn't come home at his usual hour that Sunday. And when he finally did, he downed several glasses of whisky and began screaming at me about sleeping with Bill and, for the first time in our marriage, backhanded me across the face." She placed an involuntary hand on her cheek at the memory. "But you see, it wasn't about me sleeping with Bill. It was about him. His humiliation."

"Don't mess with a Langford."

"Yes, that's what he believes. It's what everyone believes."

"So, do you know for certain?"

She nodded. "When he passed out, I went out to his truck. The gun was wrapped in a towel under the seat."

"Did you keep it? Or even hide it somewhere?"

"Oh, no. He would have known it was me. And I feared if I meddled in any way, he might kill me, too. I'm sure he has disposed of it by now. But I would testify if I needed to. I can't live with a murderer."

"Do you want me to tell the sheriff?"

She peered over at me. "Do you trust him?"

"Honestly? I don't know anymore."

"I'm so afraid. I'm thinking about sneaking off to my son's house in Easton. But I don't want to involve him if his father should go on a rampage."

"I haven't spoken to the sheriff in a while. At least not in a rational way. You see, he is as afraid of your family as everyone else." I drained my coffee. "But some things have happened that might nudge him out of that stance."

"Donny Jones is a nice man. I know he hit Bill, but I believe my husband had already shot him."

"Pamela, do you think there's a chance he had an accomplice?"

Her head popped up. "You mean that woman he was whispering with Saturday night?"

"Yes, that's who."

"I wondered who she was. I asked Gunther, and he said he didn't know, that she had started up a conversation with him, but he wasn't interested, that he got away from her as soon as he could."

"Do you have somewhere to lay low? Are your parents still alive?"

"No. Unfortunately. I could really use my mother about now."

"I know that feeling all too well."

"My sister is in Baltimore. Maybe I should pay her a visit. Gunther knows I'm upset. I could say I'm giving us some space." She stood quickly. "Yes, that's what I'll do." Checking her watch, she said, "Gunther's hunting this morning. I don't need to pack. I'll leave him a note. No, better yet, shoot him a text." She paused. "Did I just say *shoot* him a text?" She placed her hand on her chest. "Okay, I have a plan." She crumpled her cup and tossed it in the trash. "Thank you, Rosalie. You be careful. That rule is there for a reason."

As she hurried away, the click of her boots sounding on the sidewalk, I realized I was feeling a bit like a human dumpster.

Chapter Eighty-Four

Annie was sleeping in, so I went back to the café to prepare for our holiday hiatus. My mind raced with what I had just learned. According to Pamela, Gunther Langford murdered Bill Rutherford. But how to prove it? And how to get Sheriff Wilgus to even care?

I checked in with Glenn, who was thankfully sounding more like himself, and he confirmed Abby hadn't cashed the check. I wondered if she was on to us. Maybe she and Mr. Bucks would just skip town. After my meeting with Pamela, I was pretty sure Abby didn't kill Bill. But she had the motive and I was beginning to believe she was some sort of scam artist with the drive to do just about anything to get what she wanted.

I made a coffee and sat at the bar, anxiety pulsing through me. How did Pamela unload all of that on me so efficiently and then skip town? The only way out of this was to solve the crime. But how? There were too many constraints. If I did indeed draw Micky and Gunther out, as Glenn and I had planned, there was no way to know if the sheriff would back me even with the facts laid out in front of him. Langford existed in some gilded force field that no one was willing to penetrate. Even his wife and the county sheriff. But maybe if we put pressure on Micky, she would opt for a plea bargain. That might—"

Feeling a presence behind me, I turned around and gazed out at the street. A large black pickup was parked just outside the café; a high-speed rifle rested in the gun rack, barely visible through the tinted windows. I tensed as Gunther Langford climbed slowly out of the truck. I narrowed my eyes. A doe lay in the back bed, her head at an odd angle, her eyes open wide.

Nausea inched up my throat as I watched Langford hitch up his camouflage pants and gaze in the front window of the café. I almost toppled out of the chair when I heard a knock at the back door. My eyes shot to the kitchen door. Another knock. I looked back out the front window, and Gunther was gone.

* * *

Deputy Jason was on the stoop in full uniform, hat in his hands. I opened the door. "Hey," I said, my voice shaky. "Come on in." He stepped inside, and I peered out at the alley one way, then the other. No one.

I flipped the deadbolt. "Coffee?"

"Sure. That sounds good."

We went into the restaurant. "Aren't there laws about driving around with dead animals in your truck bed?"

"There are guidelines." He sat on a bar chair, hat on the counter. "But that doesn't mean anyone follows them. You just see a dead deer?"

"Oh, yeah." One of the Mieles spat out a latte. I dusted the coffee with cinnamon and set it in front of him.

"What's this? I was just expecting a leftover coffee from the morning's first pot."

"They call me a coffee whisperer. I thought you might like something to warm you up."

"You joining me?"

"Um, I think I've had enough caffeine for the day." I waited while he stirred a heavy dose of sugar into his mug. "Any prints?"

"No, but we found some hair samples. We sent them off for DNA."

"The sheriff agreed to do that?"

He set his spoon on a saucer. "Are we talking here?"

"Yes." I stood straighter. "Definitely, yes."

"You know, Ms. Hart—"

"Please, call me Rosalie."

"Mm, yeah, okay. I didn't grow up around here. I'm from the Midwest, so

I can do that."

"You didn't grow up in Devon County?"

"Moved here when I was sixteen. I still haven't forgiven my parents." His smile was infectious.

"Let me see if I have this straight. The sheriff allowed you to send off the hair samples because it could be a way to arrest Abby, clear Donny Jones of intentional manslaughter, and let Langford walk free."

Jason looked over his shoulder. "Do you ever feel like someone is following you?"

"Yes. Absolutely. And someone is most likely following you right now."

He took a deep breath. "Are we still talking here?"

"What do you know?"

"After the riverkeeper found Rutherford, I asked the sheriff if he wanted me to look around. I found two sets of tire tracks off the side of the road just before the spot where Bill was hit. But there were no skid marks, nothin'. Two vehicles, no hurry, no avoiding a deer, just drove in and out. When I told the sheriff, he said it didn't mean anything. Someone was probably fishing. But it rained real hard that afternoon. Washed it all away."

"Did you take photos?"

"Of course."

"Two sets of tracks?"

"One set was definitely a truck. The other was something small and sporty. I could get an ID if I had permission to follow through."

"Jason, if we had a way to prove Gunther Langford shot Bill Rutherford in the back, what would you do?"

"See, that's the thing. I don't know. I'm not from around here. And something smells real fishy. The sheriff ain't acting right. Something's eatin' at him."

"Why are you telling me this?"

"I think we're on the same page. It ain't right a man can just walk away from killing another man. Or woman, for that matter, but that goes without sayin'."

"Is he drinking again?"

"No, ma'am. I know that for certain."

"Good. I have an idea. It makes me a little scared, or a lot scared, but if I know you have my back—"

"One hundred percent. I'm probably headed back to Ohio at some point. I'm tired of being from away. I want to go back where I fit in. But if I can leave having done something honorable, it would be a good way to go out."

"Pamela Langford said she knows for certain her husband killed Bill. She even saw the gun."

"What did she do with it?"

"Left it under the seat."

"Why did she tell you all of that?"

"I've been asking myself the same question. After she finished, she left town. She's allegedly going to her sister's house in Baltimore." I crossed my arms. "Why *did* she tell me? She doesn't even know me."

"Here's my personal cell phone number. Let's stay in touch. Oh, and don't do anything risky without me." He winked and put his hat on his head.

Chapter Eighty-Five

It took me most of the afternoon to take inventory, check expiration dates, and ensure the café would be ready to go on January second. Tyler had texted he was going to be at his sister's most of the evening helping her move furniture. And helping his sister with something always meant he was required to let her feed him a big fat dinner with a decadent dessert.

When I arrived home and stepped into the foyer, my hunger grumbled to life. Garlic and melted butter, and what was that herb? Rosemary? I found Annie in the kitchen standing over a skillet, sautéing mini Yukon potatoes.

"Wow," I said. "I'm famished." I peered over her shoulder. "What an aroma to come home to."

"Good. I also made roasted salmon and green beans. And I'm very glad you're hungry."

I hung my coat and scarf on a hook. "Should I open some wine? Chardonnay? I have a good one from Sonoma County."

"Say no more." She smiled.

After filling our glasses and a quick clink, I set the table with Sweeney Todd's assistance. Apparently, he didn't like the way I folded the napkins. "When did you start cooking?"

"My roomie and I have been reading cookbooks and making nice dinners for ourselves. Now that we live off campus, we don't have to eat in a cafeteria." She picked up two pot holders and removed a baking dish from the oven. "I'll let this rest, and we can eat in five." After covering the salmon with a dish towel, she sat next to me and sipped some wine. "I mean, come on, Mom, I am your daughter. Oh, and on Sundays, Lexie and I make a big dinner for our friends. It's so much fun. Lexie's vegan and has come up with some amazing dishes."

"I want to know what they are. Wednesday's specials are always plant-based."

"Cheers to that, mother of mine!" Her smile was dazzling.

I set my glass on the tablecloth. "Did you hear something?"

"No. why?" Her eyes darted around the room.

"I think I heard movement outside the front door."

"Geez, Mom, is it locked?"

I stood. "I don't think so. I can't believe I forgot."

"Oh, I just heard it. Someone is definitely out there." Annie hurried over to a drawer and removed a large flashlight. "Remember what I taught you?"

I took it from her, my heart pounding so hard I couldn't hear myself think. "Yes, blind them, then bash them over the head."

"And run." She tucked behind me, and we tiptoed to the door.

"Maybe you should hide," I whispered.

"No way I'm leaving you alone," she said as we reached the door. "And why are there no windows on this door? Not even a peephole." She squeezed my shoulders. "I'm getting you one for Christmas. Tyler can install it."

"Maybe we need the fire poker."

Annie hurried into the living room and returned with the fire poker and the ash shovel. I glanced over my shoulder. "Your Uncle Oliver would be proud."

Both of Annie's arms were in the air. "Plant your feet," she said. "Keep your balance."

"Ready?" I said.

"Maybe make sure the flashlight works."

I switched it on. "Okay."

"What if it's an animal?" Annie said.

"That we can handle. One...two...three!"

I whipped open the door and aimed the light at a set of startled green eyes.

"Custer?" We said in unison.

Bringing us into focus, he said, "What's with the freakin' flashlight? And is that a fire poker?"

"What are you doing here?" Annie said, weapons still over her head.

"Can I come in? It's twenty degrees on this porch." He scowled at Annie. "And maybe you could do an 'at ease'?"

Annie lowered her weapons, and I switched off the flashlight. We followed Custer into the kitchen and stood side by side.

"What did you have for dinner, boss? It smells pretty good in here."

"We haven't eaten yet," I said. "And Annie made it."

Annie stepped forward and said tentatively, "Do you want to join us?"

Custer slipped out of a fleece-lined denim jacket and sat down. "I'm in."

I retrieved three dinner dishes and set them on the counter. "Why don't you plate it?" I whispered to Annie. "Maybe a lemon wedge?"

She nodded.

When we were all seated around the table, I swelled with pride at Annie's dinner. The salmon was crispy and topped with herbs with a side of creamy dill sauce. The beans were mixed with shallots and a red wine vinegar dressing, and the potatoes' buttery goodness wafted up my nose. She garnished the plate with lemon wedges and several sprigs of parsley.

Custer began eating immediately. Stabbing a fork into the salmon, he held it up and examined it. "Very well-cooked, Annie. Nice." After swiping the salmon through the sauce, he stabbed a couple of potatoes and popped what looked to be the perfect bite into his mouth.

I could sense Annie's tension next to me. As much as I knew she was her own person and could survive just fine without a man's validation, this was different. This was Custer.

She hopped up. "I forgot salt and pepper."

"No need for that," Custer said.

Annie had her back to us. She stood stock still.

I watched her carefully, willing her to gather herself.

"Got any bread?" Custer said, seemingly oblivious to Annie's impending meltdown. He slugged back some wine and popped a green bean into his mouth. After wiping his hands, he looked at Annie. "What's up? It's okay if you don't have bread, but I know that's unlikely in your mom's place."

She finally turned around. "Custer," she said, "It's really nice to see you, but why are you here?"

He leaned back in his chair and flattened his hands on his thighs. "Come back and sit down. I can explain."

A very large tear had escaped down Annie's cheek. After a moment or two, she brushed it away and returned to her seat. I nudged her wine closer, and she took a sip.

"Maybe I should go out to the dining room," I said.

"No, boss, you need to hear this too."

"You didn't even notice I was there," Annie said.

"Yes, I did," he said. "Are you kidding? I love looking at you."

More tears.

"I didn't know what to do or say," Custer said. "I was shocked to see you. Your mom said you were in the Middle East with your dad. And there you were. Annie Hart. Who can't notice Annie freakin' Hart?"

"I was there to surprise my mom. I wasn't expecting anything from you. But—" She wiped her nose with her cloth napkin. I wondered briefly how much cat hair might be on it. "I don't know. I thought you would at least say hi."

"I'm a slow processor, if that makes any sense. And a wee bit emotionally stunted until I can find my center, meaning, and purpose. For a guy like me, that takes a while. And I didn't want to say something I would regret. That's why I'm here now."

"And what did you come up with?"

He scooted in his chair and looked Annie in the eyes. "I am finally making something of myself. I am driven and on a path. I came from nothing. And I have a chance to be something."

"You were already pretty great," she said.

"Monique and I have a connection that hits many levels. We share a passion that is hard to explain. It wasn't that I stopped loving you; it's that I found a way to elevate my life, my entire being."

I stood slowly and picked up my plate. After topping off my wine, I excused myself and went into the living room and flipped on the TV, keeping the volume loud enough so as not to overhear the rest of their conversation. I decided to try my hand at Jeopardy. By my estimation, after losing Final Jeopardy, I ended up with negative four hundred dollars. There was an entire category about rivers in Asia. I rest my case.

Chapter Eighty-Six

On Tuesday, the next morning, I found Annie in the kitchen, a cup of steaming coffee on the table. "You're up early," I said.

"Habit. I had two eight o'clock classes this semester." She slumped into a chair. "I thought only freshmen got stuck with those time slots."

"How did it go last night with Custer?"

"Really good. You know, the guy underestimates himself like nobody's business."

"Except about his cooking," I smiled.

"No, that too, but he'd never let you see it. I think that's why he is with Monique. It's like she doesn't have the patience for him to waste his time not being his best self."

"That sounds about right. Are you okay?"

"I'm still a little sad, but I think it's time for us both to move on. He was really sweet, though."

I poured a coffee and sat down. "Thank goodness."

When she lifted her cup, I tried to warn her, but it was too late. Sweeney Todd's chin bump was perfectly timed.

"Thanks, buddy," she said and looked at me. "How could I have forgotten?"

I passed her several napkins. "Do you have anything going on today?"

"I'm wide open. Want to shop?"

"I'm thinking more along the lines of some sleuthing."

* * *

We decided to drive in Annie's ten-year-old Volvo instead of my ridiculously conspicuous red sports car. Glenn was in the passenger seat, and I felt like a small child in the middle of the back seat. Glenn had his navigation app open on his phone and was directing Annie to the Bayside Bar and Grille.

"Right turn in one thousand feet," Glenn said. "So, what exactly is this adventure about?"

"We need to figure out what kind of car Micky B. drives."

"Isn't there an easier way?" Annie asked, her hands gripping the wide steering wheel.

"I don't want to involve her daughter any more than I already have. Thus, the road trip. I called ahead this morning to see when she would be working. I told the guy I was at the restaurant yesterday but forgot to leave a tip for Micky B. He didn't hesitate to tell me she works until three today. "

"Here's your turn," Glenn said.

Annie flipped on her blinker. "We are in the middle of nowhere. Are you sure this is right?"

"It's the Eastern Shore, my dear," Glenn said. "You are always in the middle of nowhere." He looked down at his phone. "We'll be on this road for another three miles."

"So tell us more," Annie said. "Why is her car important?"

"We've had a breakthrough. Deputy Jason is being forthcoming. He doesn't want Donny Jones to go to prison, either. And Jason said when he investigated the crime scene, he found two sets of tire tracks just before the collision site. And they couldn't have been Jonesy because his skid marks were erratic and farther up the road. According to Jason, both sets of these tracks looked as if the vehicles were parked intentionally."

"Wait a minute, Mom, are you saying *two* people killed Bill Rutherford?"

"I believe the killer had an accomplice. A lookout of some sort so the killer would know exactly when Bill would be riding by. It's hard to shoot a moving target like that, especially in the dark. You'd have to be poised and ready."

"That gives me chills." Annie scrunched up her shoulders.

"Me, as well," Glenn said. "But wait a minute, are you saying Micky B. is the accomplice or the murderer?"

"My guess is accomplice. But if we can prove she was there, she might be encouraged to throw the other person under the bus to save herself, cop a plea, or something like that." I leaned back in the seat and rubbed my neck. "I haven't told anyone this, but when she saw me at Janice's party, she slid a finger across her neck before she walked away."

"She's worried, Rosalie. And you should be, too."

"Oh, you mean because Gunther Langford was outside the café yesterday staring in the window with a rifle in his gun rack and a dead doe in the bed of his pickup?"

"Mom! That's so scary!"

"Agreed."

"Here we go," Glenn said as we approached a wooden sign with an arrow that read, Bayside Bar and Grille .2 miles.

Chapter Eighty-Seven

We parked in the back of the lot, the car facing the door to the restaurant. Annie suggested we keep the Volvo running to stay warm, but the rattle of her diesel engine could draw attention. She reluctantly turned it off.

The restaurant was a red-painted shanty of sorts and looked as if it had seen better days. Most of the docks were empty, and a few hosted shrink-wrapped power boats on lifts. A pavilion, picnic tables, and a closed-up bar indicated summer was their busiest time of year. The wide expanse of the Chesapeake Bay twinkled in the afternoon sunlight, the Bay Bridge a looming shadow in the distance.

"It's two-thirty. I hope she didn't get to go home early," I said. "And I have hot chocolate and popcorn." I unscrewed the top of my thermos and began to fill the cups. As I passed them to the front of the car I said, "You each get your own individual bags of popcorn."

"I've been hoping ever since I caught the smell of butter that this would be for us." Annie took a sip of chocolate."

"Let's play who can guess the car," Glenn said. "Winner gets a free drink at the Tavern, Rosalie's buying."

"Oh," I said. "Fun game, there, Mr. Breckinridge."

"I like it," Annie said. "I say it's that blue mini Cooper with the white stripe on the hood."

"That was my guess," I said. "Okay, she's an aggressive person, so I pick that black Mustang over on the left. I could see her in a muscle car."

"Both good guesses," Glenn said. "But I'm going to have to go with that

Audi sedan, the A4, over in the corner. I think she likes to flaunt her money."

"I say you both will be buying me a beer." Annie giggled and stuffed a handful of popcorn in her mouth.

"Annie," Glenn said. "Isn't this your senior year?"

"Mm-hm."

"Not to pry, but do you have plans for what's to follow?"

She finished chewing. "My dad and I talked a lot about that in Dubai. I want to get my physical therapy license, but I'm also interested in health administration." She peeked back at me. "I've been excited to talk about this with you, Mom."

"I'm excited to hear it."

"I've been reading about this experimental program a group has been trying out in rural areas. They send out a healthcare team to people who are housebound or are at least limited in their mobility, usually the elderly, but it's open to anyone. Anyway, the team includes a nurse, a pharmacist, and whoever else is needed. Sometimes, a physical or occupational therapist, sometimes a nutritionist, especially for diabetics. They go to the person's home and get them organized. One of the best things is the pharmacist goes through the person's medication lists, checks to see what they're taking, not taking, what might be contraindicated. There's more to it, but if I could get on board with a program like that, help make it more widespread, I think that's something I would really enjoy doing."

"What a wonderful idea," Glenn said.

I couldn't stop smiling. "I love it, Annie. Are you thinking of graduate school?"

"Dad said he'd pay, so, wait—is that her?"

Micky B. was looking down at her phone as her sneakers crunched on the gravel parking lot. I believe the term bated breath was the best description of the three of us as we waited to see which way she went.

"Nailed it." Annie smacked the steering wheel as Michelle Belle climbed into the blue Mini Cooper.

"Next stop," Glenn said, "The Cardigan Tavern."

Chapter Eighty-Eight

That evening, I sat at the table, making a grocery list for the coming few days. Tomorrow was Christmas Eve. Oliver's arrival was imminent, and I needed this investigation to wrap up quickly so that I could have the holiday I'd been longing for all month.

I gazed out the window. The full moon was mirrored in the river below. Tyler and I called it the champagne river when the slow current glowed in the moonlight like effervescent bubbles. It was after six, and I was alone, Annie at the movies with Nathan, Tyler shopping for gifts for his sister's kids.

My meeting with Pamela nagged at me. Was I reading it all wrong? A lump formed in my stomach. What if?

I texted Jason. *Can we talk?*

My phone immediately began to vibrate.

I slid my finger over the screen and tapped the speaker icon.

"You okay?" he said quickly.

"Yes. Are you on duty?"

"Always."

"The tire tracks, could one set be from a Mini Cooper?"

"Yes."

"And the other set, you said they were from a truck. Is there any way those tracks could be from a Range Rover SUV?"

* * *

After I finished explaining my theory to Jason, I changed my clothes and sprayed on some perfume. It had been a mild day, the first one in a while, so I slipped into a sweater and skirt and headed to my car. The country club was only a few miles away. I still had my temporary membership and decided I might see someone I knew there.

Turning into the parking lot, I realized I would not be disappointed. Cars packed the spaces, including one very conspicuous Range Rover. I texted Jason: *She's here.*

I found a seat at the bar and smiled at Fi.

"Did you join yet?" she said, wiping down the bar in front of me.

"Thinking about it. I'm still on the complimentary membership."

"Well, drink up, won't be free forever."

"My intentions exactly. I'll have a glass of chardonnay, please."

I glanced around the room. Almost every seat was occupied. I spotted her in the last seat at the end of the bar. She was immaculately dressed in a sequined white sweater, those same diamonds in her ears. She clutched a martini glass with long, manicured fingers.

Fi placed my glass in front of me. "Is it really free?" I said.

"I just need your temporary number."

"1609," I said. Once she was gone, I texted Jason: *Call me in 10. I'll pretend it's spam, but don't hang up. I've done this before. It should work.* I added a 'fingers crossed' emoji.

I slipped off the bar chair and left a twenty for Fi by a jar of toothpicks. Pamela had already noticed me but stayed put.

"Can we talk?" I said. "I haven't stopped thinking about our conversation yesterday."

She lowered her eyelids. "I think I've said everything I need to say to you."

"Yes, I know. But it's my turn now. Shall we find somewhere more intimate?"

We walked to a high-top table in the corner of the room. The lights were dim, a small votive in the center of the table flickered from the ceiling fan overhead. I took a sip of wine and folded my hands together. "Your sister wasn't home?"

"I changed my plans."

"Clearly."

She held my gaze.

I jumped when my phone began to ring. "I'm so sorry," I said and slid it open. "Hello? Who's calling? No, please remove me from your list." I held my phone in my lap. "I'll turn this off," I said but tapped the speaker icon instead. "Sorry about that."

She tapped her fingernails on the base of the glass. "Well?"

"Let's get to it. Your husband didn't kill Bill Rutherford, did he?"

"Of course, he did."

"You said the gun was in his truck."

"It may still be there. What are you doing, Rosalie?"

"I'm no threat to you. The sheriff kicked me off the case. But I don't like to be manipulated. I know you killed him because there were Range Rover tracks at the scene of the crime. You said your husband was in his truck when he shot Bill. What I'm wondering is why was Micky B. part of this? I'm just curious. Once I know, I'll go back home and mind my own business. I've finally learned to respect rule number one."

"Michelle is an opportunist, always has been. She was our babysitter when Jackson was young. When I found out she wanted him dead just as much as I did, she agreed to help me."

"She was your lookout, is that correct?"

"I'm not going to say any more to you." She took a long sip of her martini. After setting the glass down for a moment, she picked it back up and finished it off. "Gunther will be arrested soon. It's all in place."

"People had it all wrong, didn't they? When they said, don't mess with a Langford, they had the wrong Langford." I held my phone screen away from her sightline and slid my purse on my shoulder. "I'm not judging you. I know your husband is a cruel man. But I won't be your pawn. So, good luck. You have the sheriff on your side, for what it's worth."

She sized me up. "You're formidable in your own cute little way. But you have no idea how insignificant you really are, do you?"

"Perhaps." I picked up my glass with my free hand and took a long sip. I set it down with a thud. "Goodbye, Pamela Langford."

As I headed for the door, Mason tapped my arm. "Have you decided to join?"

"Um, that's a no for me, but thanks for the free drinks."

Once outside, I put my phone to my ear, "Did you get it?"

"All of it. Nicely done. I'm on my way."

"What are you going to do?" I said, opening my car door.

"I have a confession. I'm going to arrest her. I can deal with the sheriff later."

"Let me know if you need anything else." I ended the call and started my car. I noticed another set of headlights as I backed out of the space. Once on the road, the headlights were behind me, but that wasn't unusual on River Road. Just to be safe, I decided to head into town and drive around a bit before I went home. The vehicle grew closer, and I knew immediately it was Pamela. A car approached from the other way. Lights on the roof. It was Jason. I laid on my horn, and he slowed. The headlights grew so close it was blinding. The bullet pierced my back window. Glass splayed through the car like a hail storm. I ducked and downshifted and gained some distance. Jason had turned on his lights and siren. I made the curve into town and skidded into the Sheriff's parking lot. I crouched in my seat until Pamela passed, Jason on her tail. I climbed out of the car and bumped into the sheriff.

"I've got an emergency, Hart."

"Jason is chasing Pamela Langford. She just shot a bullet through my window." He stared as if not understanding. "Snap out of it, Wilgus!" I screamed. "She murdered Bill Rutherford. Jason is going after her. She has a gun!"

He gave his head a small shake and ran to his SUV. He started it up with a loud rev of the engine and squealed onto the road, lights blazing.

* * *

I climbed back into my car, forehead on the steering wheel, trying to catch my breath and slow my heart rate. My hair was full of shattered glass, and I noticed a piece had wedged in my hand, a trickle of blood dripped onto my skirt. The sirens had stopped. I prayed no one was hurt.

A truck pulled up next to me. I was too terrified to move.

"Rosalie?"

I looked up. "Tyler?"

He opened the door, and I jumped into his arms. "My god, are you okay?"

"Yes, I think so."

He held me tight against him. "I was driving to your place," he said into my hair, "and I saw the cop car, and then I saw you driving like a bat out of hell."

"They should have the killer by now. I think it's over at last. Tyler? I'll stop. I promise."

"Don't make promises you can't keep."

"Okay, I'll *try* to stop. But this one is over."

I felt his tears on my shoulder. "Just in time for Christmas."

Chapter Eighty-Nine

I arrived at the sheriff's office the next morning, not sure if he would want to see me. Lila harrumphed as I passed, but remained silent. I sat across from him. Instead of a crossword or a wordle puzzle, he had a stack of papers on his desk, a pen tucked behind his ear.

"Is she alive?" I said.

"She stopped when she reached the water. Her fancy lawyer already has her out on bail. Who knows if she'll find a way out of this."

"But she confessed."

"She did."

"And you have the murder weapon, correct?"

"We do."

"And let's not forget she tried to kill me."

"Who could forget that?"

I rolled my eyes. "Okay, what about Micky B.?"

"She's on her way in. Already has her own lawyer. I think she's going to bargain and offer testimony. She's our only eye witness so I doubt she does any time."

"And Donny Jones?"

"That's up to the prosecutor, but the most they can charge him with is hit and run."

"Did Abigail Harrington ever turn up?"

"Tried to cash the check in Alabama. She's got a record a mile long, tons of aliases. Only reason she kept her real name this time was to run the gymnast angle. They haven't found her yet, but when they do, she'll be charged with breaking and entering and whatever other trail of charges she has in her wake."

"One last question. Does Jason still have a job?"

"He's one of the best deputies I've ever had."

I folded my hands in my lap. "Everyone was afraid of the wrong Langford."

"I'd say that's true. I mean it when I say she could slide out of this, but it won't end well either way. Gunther knows she was trying to pin it on him. Sweet, don't you think?"

"Oh, yes, she's a charmer for sure." I stared down at my lap, unsure what to say next.

He cleared his throat. "You okay?"

I looked up. "I will be. I still have glass in my hair."

"I can see it." He leaned in, forearms on his desk. "I just have one more question, and I think we can put this all behind us and get back to normal. Whatever that may be."

"Yes?"

"Did you really say to me, 'Snap out of it, Wilgus?"

My lips twitched into a smile. "Affirmative. And did you?"

"I don't have to answer that."

Chapter Ninety

It was after one o'clock, but I had one more stop to make before I went home to help Annie get ready for Oliver's arrival. He had texted her a grocery list that morning. Oliver was keeping the promise he made two months ago after we finished cooking school with Marco. The night before he returned to New York, he said he would be cooking Christmas dinner at Barclay Meadow. I hadn't spent Christmas Day with my brother in years.

Summer was behind the counter, seated on Doris' stool. A man who had an opened paper in front of his face sat in one of the chairs Doris kept in the store for the slim chance someone would be trying on a pair of shoes.

"Hey, Miss Rosalie," she said.

"Hi, sweetie. Just checking in."

"I have a visitor." She nodded toward the man.

I turned to see Neil Rutherford lower the paper and smile. "Glenn called me last night and told me everything."

"You're here."

He nodded. "I wanted to let you and Glenn know that I found the safety deposit box. My father actually took care of me this time." He looked over at his sister. "And I wanted to talk with Summer. We have a lot to discuss. I want to make sure she knows she has options."

"Options?" I said.

"We're taking it slow," Summer said. "But Neil has offered to be my guardian if I want to file for independence from my mother."

My heart swelled, and tears filled my eyes. "Oh, my goodness." I coughed out a sob. "I don't know where this is all coming from, but—"

"Maybe you should sit down," Summer said gently.

I sat next to Neil and heaved out another sob. "Oh, my. I'm so sorry. It's just—"

Neil patted my back. "You're cool. It's all cool. Right, sis?"

"Oh, yeah."

They sat with me while I got it all out. My face had to have been streaked with mascara, and I was in desperate need of a tissue, but once I finished, I wiped my nose with my sleeve and grinned like a kid on Christmas morning.

Chapter Ninety-One

Annie and I prepared all sorts of savory appetizers, and then we started on the iced sugar cookies. While Annie pulled the last sheet of cookies out of the oven, Tyler stomped his boots. We looked over to see a very large live Christmas tree on his shoulder.

"Ho, ho, ho," he called, and Annie squealed.

The soundtrack to *A Charlie Brown Christmas* played on the speaker, and the house was abuzz in anticipation of Oliver's arrival.

Not long after we secured the tree in the stand, and I draped the base with my grandmother's red velvet tree skirt, Oliver's car horn sounded in the drive. Annie was out the door in a flash, and Tyler and I grinned when we heard him shout, "Anna Banana!"

"Anybody home?" he called out. "You still have that open-door policy, Rosie?"

"No, but always for you."

He hugged me hard.

"Welcome, buddy," Tyler said.

"You keeping my sister out of trouble, dude?" Oliver said as they shook hands.

"Not even close."

Oliver held out a bottle of Ruinart rosé champagne and said to Annie, "You got any glasses around here, kiddo?"

She ran into the kitchen and returned with a tray of glasses just as the cork made a loud pop.

Glenn and Gretchen arrived not long after. Oliver greeted Glenn warmly and was introduced to Gretchen. Our voices grew louder, and the champagne flowed. When I went into the kitchen to fill up the cracker basket, Glenn followed.

"How are you, my dear? Good grief, is this a piece of glass in your hair?"

"I can't seem to get it all."

"How did you know it was Pamela and not Gunther?"

"She and I had a meeting Monday morning. She told me too much. I knew something wasn't right."

Glenn picked up one of the last crackers and bit into it. "Why didn't you call me? I would have come with you."

Facing him, I said, "You had already been through enough. You did your part, and I was worried about you. And I guess the other reason is I needed the investigation to be over. It was only two days until Christmas, and I just needed it to end." I gazed down at my shoes. "I know it was impulsive, but, well—" I looked up. "It worked."

"Thank the lord." Glenn studied me. "Perhaps there's a new rule in town."

"Don't mess with a Rosalie Finnegan Hart?"

"Yes, something like that."

We returned to the gathering just as Nathan stepped in the door with a large white poinsettia, the base wrapped in gold foil. He placed it in my hands and said, "Merry Christmas, boss." I took his coat and scarf, and he joined the others, immediately adding his own good energy to the mix.

Bini was the last to arrive and was understandably more reluctant to participate in the festivities. I poured her a beer, and she sat in a stiff-backed chair in the living room near the tree. Oliver greeted her warmly and managed to eke a small smile out of her.

Once Tyler brought the last of the ornaments down from the attic, we all chipped in decorating the gorgeous tree, singing along to carols and sipping champagne. I could barely hear the knock on the door through the sound of our raucous voices and the music filling the room with the Christmas spirit.

I opened the door to find a man wearing a down jacket, a ball cap backwards on his head. He was very nice-looking in an unassuming sort of way.

"Are you by any chance Lucas?"

"Is Bini here?"

"Come on in."

Lucas followed me into the living room and looked around.

"Lucas?" Bini hopped up.

"Hey, your dad said I would find you here."

"My *dad*?"

"We've been doing a lot of talking lately."

The room fell silent. I reached out for Tyler's hand.

"But how do you even know my dad?"

Lucas took a deep breath and got down on one knee. Annie gasped.

He pulled a small box from his pocket. "I was asking him for your hand, of course." Lucas shook his head. "He sure didn't make it easy."

Bini's lips trembled.

Lucas popped open the box to reveal a beautiful pear-shaped diamond ring. "Bini Jean Katz, will you marry me?"

She covered her mouth. Tears spilled from her eyes. "But I thought…I thought you—"

"I had to save up some money. But Bini, I knew I wanted to marry you from the moment I laid eyes on you. You're my soulmate. So, now," he shook his head, "can you please give a guy an answer?"

She nodded before the words came out. "Yes, oh yes, yes, yes."

He stood and slipped the ring on her finger. They embraced, and there wasn't a dry eye in the room.

Oliver popped open a fresh bottle of champagne. "To quote the wise man, Tiny Tim, God bless Us, Every One!"

Acknowledgements

To Bob Roth for your encouragement, support, edits, and awesome ideas.

To Lizzie and Maddy for brightening my days and making this world a better place through your endless love and compassion.

To Elizabeth Piotrowski of Contemporary Digital for my beautiful website and fabulous newsletter.

To Chris, Paul, Stacy, and Terry for your love, support, companionship, and zoom Yahtzee games.

To Lindsay, Kyle Marisa, and Sage for your acceptance and love.

To my fellow writers, Susan, Mary, Denny, Jon, Terese, Alice, Rick, Frances, Amethyst, Linda, Joe, Ronny, Ken, and Aggie for your input, camaraderie, laughs, and suggestions.

To my agent, Dawn Dawdle of Blue Ridge Literary, for finding a home for my series and for your steady support and guidance.

To my editor, Shawn Reilly Simmons for your support, insights, hard work, friendship, and fabulous covers.

To Bill Frazier, who was a good friend and great writer and is deeply missed.

And to all the support and kindness I've received from readers of the series.

Book lovers are the nicest people on the planet.

About the Author

Wendy Sand Eckel is the award-winning author of the Rosalie Hart Mystery Series. Holiday-themed *Killer in a Winter Wonderland,* is the fourth in the series.

Her mystery series has been awarded 'Best Cozy' by *Suspense* magazine and *Mystery at Windswept Farm,* the third book in the series, made the humorous novel bestseller list on Amazon. A trained life coach, Wendy writes the advice column for the Maryland Writers' Association newsletter and enjoys mentoring aspiring authors.

She lives in a small town on the Eastern Shore of Maryland, a unique and quirky part of the country, which is also the setting for her series. In addition to her husband, she lives with two male orange tabbies, Frodo and Sam, who her daughter rescued from a soybean field. She loves to cook and is happiest when her kitchen is filled with friends and family and the table is brimming with savory food and wine.

SOCIAL MEDIA HANDLES:

www.facebook.com/wsandeckel

www.goodreads.com/wendysandeckel

AUTHOR WEBSITE:

www.wendysandeckelauthor.com

Also by Wendy Sand Eckel

Murder at Barclay Meadow

Death at the Day Lily Café

Mystery at Windswept Farm

Printed in the USA
CPSIA information can be obtained
at www.ICGtesting.com
LVHW041212221123
764524LV00066B/2380

9 781685 125363